Italville

Italville

New Italian Writing

edited by

Lorenzo Pavolini

Toronto

Exile Editions

2005

This edition is published by Exile Editions Limited,
20 Dale Avenue, Toronto, Ontario, Canada M4W 1K4

Sales Distribution:
McArthur & Company
c/o Harper Collins
1995 Markham Road
Toronto, ON
M1B 5M8
toll free:
1 800 387 0117
(fax) 1 800 668 5788

Composition & Design by *Michael Callaghan*
Typeset at *Moons of Jupiter*
Printed and Bound at *Gauvin Imprimerie*

ISBN 1-55096-631-6

Italville

Editor: Lorenzo Pavolini

Editorial committee: Rita Filanti, Thomas Simpson
Barry Callaghan, Francesca Valente

Translators: Julia Garner, Lawrence Garner, Antonino Mazza, Antony Shugaar, Thomas Simpson, Ann Snodgrass, Paul Vangelisti

Italville was initiated by the Istituto Italiano di Cultura, Chicago, (Italian Government Cultural Institute) and has been supported by the following institutions:

Istituto Italiano di Cultura, New York (Director, Claudio Angelini)
Istituto Italiano di Cultura, Washington DC (Director, Marten Stiglio)
Istituto Italiano di Cultura, San Francisco (Director, Annamaria Lelli)
Istituto Italiano di Cultura, Los Angeles (Director, Francesca Valente)
Istituto Italiano di Cultura, Toronto (Director, Carlo Coen)
Istituto Italiano di Cultura, Vancouver (Director, Antonio Cosenza)
Istituto Italiano di Cultura, London (Director, Pierluigi Barrotta)
Istituto Italiano di Cultura, New Delhi (Director, Patrizia Raveggi)

Project Coordinator: Francesca Valente

Contents

PREFACE

LORENZO PAVOLINI

"A volume that would present an ample selection of writers who have come on the Italian literary scene in these last fifteen years, through stories, poems and narrative fragments that demonstrate a renewed capacity for confronting the landscape and events of their country. A story made up of many voices, in which the authors ideally give witness to the peninsula's jagged geography, trying to restore complexity to events that besiege the lives of their fellow citizens, and of course their own, events often indecipherable and lugubriously enigmatic. Writing, therefore, is a consciousness that seizes with an incisive glance even the more folkloristic phenomenon of our *Bel Paese* (Soccer, Crime, the South, Family, Religion, Television and Politics), returning them to a divided western context, based on precariousness (personal and otherwise), formative centers adrift (schools), urban solitude, loss of a sense of community. An 'unpublished vision' of Italy in action, with those who belong to its most immediate present and also create it."

In these few lines I tried to synthesize the idea for this book, when Francesca Valente first proposed thinking about a North American anthology of Italian writers. A few years have passed, enough for the scene straddling the old and the new millennium to have come into focus. This intervening time served Dr. Valente to develop a publication for which there are very few precedents. For me, the problem was how to resist the temptation to update continually the initial list of authors we had drafted, as though I were putting together an issue of a literary magazine on "Italy," chasing the dream of a literature that changes shape as it carries out its mission. I sought to hold firm to that first instinct, notwithstanding things which happened in the meantime (I speak both of things in the literary and everyday world), bringing little by little to its goal a gesture both arbitrary and irreversible in its nature. Meanwhile, the question at the heart of every anthology, demanding resolution in every introduction, kept peeking through: why these writers and not others? How to explain the reasons behind a choice?

First of all, we are talking about rendering possible a vision of the plurality of voices that cuts across recent Italian literature. That is, to render evident the richness of *a minor literature*, as this expression was understood by Deleuze and Guattari apropos of Kafka, a Jew from Prague writing in German: "A minor literature is not a literature of a minor language, but that which a minority constructs in a major language." Much the same with Italian writers today; they express themselves in a language that counts as one of the major literary traditions of humankind, but they speak to a minority of those who use it in everyday communication, more or less sharing, at least in this, the destiny of their colleagues in half the world.

This is not the place to join in certain classical grumblings about the role of intellectuals, the lack of cultural space, mass media, etc. In fact, in Italy writers have regained, even under the more customary forms, a great deal of that social status that had been extinct for them for more than twenty years. Cinema, newspapers, radio and women's magazines: writers have assumed once again their foundational roles (screenwriters and reporters) and in many cases taken on new ones in the proliferating cultural scene (with its bush-league glamour), performing at readings, festivals and happenings which have multiplied wildly in the last five years in every corner of Italy. The risk is of quickly squandering literature's cognitive legacy in favor of its entertainment value, and feeding a not always possible imbalance toward the performative aspects of the word, forcing upon *all* writers the need to demonstrate their talent physically and vocally. This "return of the writer" has happened in Italy precisely because of the persistent, ever-apparent eclipse of any of his public functions. The gorging of the mythical sixties gone, a young writer in the eighties who had the desire to dirty his hands found every avenue for social action closed. Paradoxically, for many, it was literature that bore the load of experimenting with forms of living, verbal forms and forms of thought able to inhabit the cataphract nature of time touched by chance: a long monsoon of transitions, estrangements, illusions during which the very notion of the writer was questioned in every new book, much like that of the individual, home, dignity, rights, etc.

One speaks of a "narcissistic" generation, when instead one ought to think of a kind of necessity. The construction of a narrative voice reaching towards the world has entirely the air of representing the world, while at the same time doggedly painting a self-portrait. The writer leaves a trail of bodily humors, his own snail's trail, as he drags himself high and low, looking for a secluded space in which to write down his own *sign*. Edoardo Albinati's work, with which we close this anthology, is an example of the *false movement* of the self towards the world and vice versa, of which I am speaking.

The restricted space in which minor literatures interact, such as contemporary Italian writing, counts on a relatively scant number of readers (with the exception of those authors who easily exceed sales of 100,000 copies per title, including established writers such as Alessandro Baricco, Susanna Tamaro, Antonio Tabucchi, Erri De Luca, Margareth Mazzantini, and more than a few young writers, such as Niccolò Ammaniti and Melania Mazzucco. Given the relative proportions of their different linguistic communities, these writers sell almost as much as Stephen King). This area of readership, a minority in any case, does not however lower the stakes. On the contrary, according again to Deleuze and Guattari, given that in this type of reduced space the boundary between individual and collective event becomes uncertain, every line written takes on political value: "whatever the writer says on his own already constitutes a communal action and whatever he says or does is necessarily political, even if others do not agree."

If it is always true that no one writer is representative of an entire national literature and no tradition finds in a single author its exclusive heir, in the case of Italy this has become an absolute rule. In the course of the second half of the twentieth century our country's cultural scene seemed to be animated by a special centrifugal force that, while it went on elaborating a certain common and national-television language, was everywhere fleeing in an infinite refraction of narrators and experiences, each autonomous and legitimate, however distant one from another. This was the result of a deep transformation: going from a literature of masters to a collective, diffused, plural literature. Precisely as we fulfill Pier Paolo Pasolini's prediction (assimilation for all), a large number of more or less effective artistic strategies are freed up. Encountering a scenario that appears firmly uniform, these new strategies take on reasons for storytelling animated by the same energy that brought to shore the dark wave of "the end of difference" or, more directly, "the end of history," a social and cultural energy which does not itself create nor destroy, but strengthens the individual's creative search just the way a finger rises when you blow into a rubber glove.

Thus we have before us a literature that defies description in terms of identity, groups, currents, masters . . . The plurality of voices running through it has been the primary concern to which I have sought to respond with my selection.

Then I used a more or less sharp generational cut, as may clearly be seen glancing through the authors' biographical notes: whether fifty or twenty-seven years old, with few exceptions, all have emerged in the last fifteen years. There are, it is true, two poets outside the norm, Valentino Zeichen and Luigi Ballerini. I wanted in this way to underline the bias of the selections made, even more so in the field of poetry, where Italy offers a multitude of significant voices. Here I could make a list of a hundred names whose work I would have liked to have had translated in its entirety, beginning with Valerio Magrelli, Patrizia Cavalli, Stefano Simoncelli, Mariangela Gualtieri, Antonio Riccardi, Mario Benedetti. One must consider, however, how indirectly poetry presents itself in tracing the actual profile of a country, which for me was the primary purpose of this collection of texts. To tell the story both of a current literature and a real country. For the poetry I have offered up a lightning bolt here and there, extracts from a vision that I hope might help to look deeper within the truth of the stories. And for this reason too I privileged the more "narrative" components, given the more prosaic and discursive vein notably present in the best contemporary Italian poetry. I sought, above all, to break down any hierarchy, without leveling the "stature" of the authors I was putting next to one another. I even toyed with the opportunity of placing a writer with only one book published, or maybe not even that, beside another who might already have ten or more, trusting in the positive effect of typographic proximity that sheds an equal light on all printed words and perhaps allows for some discovery or small surprise.

In the choice of texts I even tried to reproduce as much as possible the geographical distribution of a country such as Italy, made up of local realities very different from one another and most meaningful in their irreducible complexity. Rome is quite present, starting with the soccer obsessions narrated in the first person by Sandro Veronesi, the writer who more than anyone has known how to bring back the "true-to-life account" with his real life Italian stories appearing in newspapers and magazines, later collected in books throughout the nineties. But Rome is also the first landing place of Aurelio

Picca, who lives in a town on the outskirts of the capital, and transforms it through a small personal story in the stages of a visceral appropriation. Similarly, the Pugliese Nicola Lagioia leads us through 1992 in the guise of a university student away from home. Rome and its environs is also the territory for a couple's ramblings with their dog in Emanuele Trevi's narrative fragment. Not far from Rome are the Pasolini-like beaches of Capocotta in Elena Stancanelli's story.

Then the cities of the South, the suburbs, "the districts." Palermo is the hell of the Nigerian prostitute who has her say in Giosuè Calaciura's fleshy language. Naples is the theater of social climbing described by one of the most recent talents of Italian fiction, Valeria Parrella. Then the no man's land where night falls for Antonio Pascale's mobster, among dockyards and rake-offs, the confused fabric of city outskirts surrounding Naples and its province. Above all it is the latter, "the province," that still offers an unconventional look at the world, comic and grotesque but suffused with traces of humanity: examples of these are Francesco Piccolo's Caserta and the imaginary town in the Tuscan Maremma where Niccolò Ammaniti's characters converge. The provinces are Silvia Ballestra's Marches, "a kind of strange Texas" where they throw parties in honor of Iggy Pop who is celebrating his 40th birthday. The "American" references sprout up even in the northeast populated by television magicians, in Mauro Covacich's story. Apropos of Italy's *northeast*, which in the last decade has become a type of "observatory" for the country's woes, I have included, besides Covacich, only a brief text by Vitaliano Trevisan, though there are many other writers who deserved being included: Tiziano Scarpa, Romolo Bugaro, Roberto Ferrucci, Marco Franzoso. A category of his own for the peasant epos of the Parmesan Guido Conti, one of the few (though one ought also to remember Lucca's Vicenzo Pardini) who has been able to carry on the tradition of the pure narrative, with a pre-industrial flavor, of quasi-anthropological value. And who can possibly rival one of the most significant theatrical phenomena in Italy of recent years named Ascanio Celestini. Again the Po Valley, but in that area of Emilia that takes on features of a domestic California, one comes upon traces of the Larkin-like poetry of Andrea Gibellini, while Antonella Anedda takes us among the islands in the Maddalena archipelago, north of Sardinia. Dario Voltolini's brief texts possess the gray geometry of the destinies of factories and the outskirts of Turin; the poetic splinters of the quite young Francesca Genti put in play the most classic alienation of Italy's fashion center, Milan. The ancestral Sicily of the countryside in Nino De Vita's work appears like a mirage in his dialect as it meditates on the sense of nature and its relation to mankind.

The poetry of the youngest, Flavio Santi, Marco Mantello, Enrico Piergallini and Mario Desiati, is entrusted with the savage task of demolishing yet again that which their older brothers only scratched: family, feelings, social hypocrisy.

And finally school, which is not an Italian region but for its writers remains one of the privileged and/or obligatory workplaces. Italian writers, except for some exceptional cases, do not teach "creative writing," and are, instead, normal high-school teachers more often than not in substandard institutions. Right off the cuff, Marco Lodoli, Sandro Onofri, Romana Petri, Rocco Carbone come to mind, as well as the aforementioned Picca and Albinati. I chose a fragment from a novel by Arnaldo Colasanti that seems to me to carry all the drama, or personal tragedy, of what it means to be a teacher today. I also included at the last minute the account of a real event that took place in a classroom told by Vanessa Ambrosecchio, the umpteenth young feminine talent of an extremely vital Sicily (suffice it to think of the stage director Emma Dante and the singer-songwriter Carmen Consoli).

To conclude, a few words about the title. This collection was first born with the idea of being named *Italian Chorus*, because I was convinced that putting together in a room the very different voices of these writers would somehow result in hearing one chord, a mix of sound that resembles a deep note generated by a common concern. Then it happened that Italian publishing in the last year, along with an underground phenomenon of the rebirth of the video documentary, has seen a flowering of anthologies of Italian writers on Italy [here I cite only the three most important: *Patrie impure*, edited by B. Centovalli (Rizzoli), *La qualità dell'aria. Storie di questo tempo*, edited by N. Lagioia and C. Raimo (minimum fax) and *Viva l'Italia*, edited by O. Iarussi (Fandango)], something that had not happened in who knows how long. In particular, these writers were actually asked to make a political, militant gesture, while in the past the few projects for assembling writers were carried out in the name of journalistic appeal (with the doubtful result, for example, of imposing the label of "cannibal" on a writer like Niccolò Ammaniti, who has shown himself capable instead of recording the slightest tremors of infancy with a sensibility having little to do with "pulp"). In the meantime, the literary magazine for which I work, *Nuovi Argomenti*, was celebrating its fiftieth year of publishing, and after having honored its past directors (Alberto Moravia, Pier Paolo Pasolini, Attilio Bertolucci, Leonardo Sciascia) decided, according to its staunch tradition, to throw itself too into the enterprise: telling the story of Italy in the work of twelve young writers. We needed to find a title. We first thought of *Giro d'Italia (Italian Tour),* but, little by little, as the stories arrived at the editorial offices we became aware that a reference to the recent film by Lars von Trier often jumped out at us.

In the town of *Dogville*, notwithstanding the fact that there are very few people, there is the variety of all the worst qualities of humanity: above all, violence, but also opportunism, greed, abuse of power, betrayal, fear, ignorance elevated to the justice system, narrow-mindedness, misogyny, contempt for who is different, prejudice. But Dogville does not exist, it is nothing but a theatrical platform, where the actors in the production move according to a script in which the only living being left at the end is the dog Moses, who gives his name to the city and who throughout the film had only been a plaster silhouette. *Italville* is a representation of today's Italy, as *Dogville* is of America of the thirties, though perhaps less asphyxiated.

(Translated by Paul Vangelisti)

INTRODUCTION

LUIGI BALLERINI

The Opposite of Help!

Italville is a ville is a ville is a ville, just like Italrose, if sapiently coaxed, would be a rose and a rose and a rose. Yet, no matter how soothing the chain of affirmation, the question remains: couldn't a ville be a village, could it not be a town, a region, a state? If so, could it have its own reason, and would that Reason be a reason and a reason and a reason, or a reason "gone crazy," one that only politicians have the arrogance to invoke as the just and plausible principle underlying their self-fulfilling prophecies: a reason of ville, of village, of town, a reason of state feeding no one, save the politicians themselves and the decrepit chorus of hackers reporting on yet another age of anxiety in the dreamless language of complaint? Is a Full Measure of Linguistic Vacuities, a Measure after all? How can anybody fill with vacuity? Has oxymoron tumbled from the heights of semainein to the depressions of chat, of killing time, of killing people? Has the self-styled authority of video-gazetteers perverted language to such a degree that no "lustier blur," as Wallace Stevens would say, will ever be glowing again from it, to be experienced by those who refuse to merely rehash and repeat its implications?

In a moment of quiet and scrupulous enthusiasm the editors of *Italville* have clustered together texts that seem to point in the opposite direction: yes, there is a ville, a village, a town, a state; yes, it is ruled by reason, but its citizens are keenly aware that the notion of a primary obedience to axioms engendering consequential patterns of logical behavior fall quite short of an acceptable mark. What confers upon the logic, and thus to the reason, of Italville, a sense of plausibility and significance, is the basic realization that no happiness can be pursued without a proper assumption of responsibility, not merely for what one does, has done or will do, but, more essentially, for the causes that have made him/her what he or she is: the causes, as psychoanalyst Paola Mieli has repeatedly suggested, of which they are the effects.

It may look, at first, like a revocation of sanity, an act of disguised malevolence destined to shock, to prevent equilibrium from metastasizing. Indeed, it is a major break from the morphology of justice, as we see it carried out daily: a system of rewards ladled out to culprits portrayed as victims of past circumstances over which one has no control. (A mortified child can always be discovered in the deepest recess of a seasoned criminal's heart.) It is, furthermore, the signal difference between the morality of the conformist (to be enacted within the dictates of church, nation, family, etc.) and the independent ethics of those who rejoice in the exercise of intelligence and the application of imagination to willpower. This responsibility cannot be negotiated: it must be sought. And the justice it supports cannot be granted: it comes into being when individuals leap across the boundary separating origin from identity.

This means, first of all, that each inhabitant of Italville is open to, and practices to the full extension of his/her ability, the art of listening. They are all aware that answers falling within the perimeter provided by well-formulated questions, may indeed have a confirmatory nature, but can hardly induce the dawning of what William Carlos Williams had called the "formerly unsuspected"—which is oftentimes reachable, instead, through defeat—nor can they allow a new meaning, a new sense of belongingness, to burgeon from contradiction or aporia, from freewheeling and even discontinuous discourse, which is exactly where new meanings hide.

Those who do not listen to the instigations of the Other have responses but no curiosity. (The reason of State is the primary killer of the idea that things can always be otherwise.) Those who do listen to it, on the other hand, can identify wisdom with the chances they take: symmetry and reflection are not the names of the game. If anything, it is a series of shifts in which truth does not bury its head in pain and despair, nor does it submit to the tyranny of the materiality of language. In the poem, "Italian Requiem, or 'Is Italy the Land of the Dead?'" Edoardo Albinati writes:

To the birch trees that skirt the rivers
I don't know what to say, but that my love
is of little value. It gives no one employment
we'll discuss this again in the sawmill, in the disco
in those places where we yell a few words or none.
It's a new syntax. We have formed our ranks
we were ready to die
death arrived and it loaded us up.
Jesus had made me despair with his sermons
devoid of emphasis, my heart used to be set on fire with nothing
ten lines, twenty . . . The spoiled spectators are shouting
for more action, even if we're already winning 3 to nil
it demands the total destruction of the enemy
San Siro in flames, the Etna in perpetual eruption.

No serious and well-meaning reader can wade through the rich fabric of the echoes and innuendos that occupy this fugue-like composition without experiencing what American poet Paul Vangelisti calls the "embarrassment of survival". Here, "the new syntax" identifying places (of the mind) where few or no words are spoken (yelled), is buffooned by delving ironically into an expression borrowed from the Italian National Anthem (mid XIX century): "We have formed our ranks." A literary corpse no more dead on arrival than it was at departure, the despondent quality of the values evoked by this morsel of late late Romantic poetry, is humorously transmogrified by the "prosy" lines that follow it: "we were ready to die" (another pseudo-quotation from the Anthem) and "death arrived and it loaded us up" in which the popular tone of the enunciation greatly surpasses, in terms of relevance, that of the enunciation itself. Wait two more lines and, gentle reader, you will find yourself in a soccer stadium, as hot as perpetually erupting Etna.

That which is embarrassing in an act of survival, played out on the stage of awareness, blooms into an irresistibly transgressive force, one from which complaint and wishful thinking are equally ostracized. There is no psychological back and forth in the poetry of Italville, no desire for revenge or compensation; and there is no defensive irony either. That is, there is irony but it occupies an intermediate position between the Olympic serenity of the Ariostean hero who, on the rather scant evidence of a glitter, believes a city to have been actually built with gold (thus reversing the popular adage not all that glitters is gold) and the braggadocio of the musketeer who fights Richelieu's guards with his left hand and justifies his choice by stating that his right hand is for drinking only. Even the desire to play dumb and the honesty that must guarantee its credibility, are harmonized in a drama that transcends both the tragedy of myth and the comedy of reality. As Flavio Santi writes:

As if heard from an intercom,
the cloudbursts don't frighten
and the water drains
into metallic railings,
where it mixes

with the words—inside
the intercom—coming
from below
sounds of torn cardboard.
Like this
television comes
to Naples in 1955 in December:
the newspaper reports it,
San Giuseppe and the oxen.

In this culture where attending and intending blur their differences, the lyrical I surfaces again and recognizes itself to be not only divided and divided and divided, but merely the volatile expression of a reality speaking through its choice of rhythm, lexicon and syntax: a signifier, as it were, for another signifier. It recognizes, furthermore, that only through this formidable reduction of its imaginary role and the proper re-appropriation of its symbolic function can elegy be inventoried as museum piece, alongside other instruments of exquisite torture. No sense of awe is brought about by such a *diminutio capitis*. Quite the contrary: a sense of elation permeates these pages where the lying inherent in all linguistic expression is not at all exorcised, but rather invited to show its side of the matter.

Empires may not crumble at the sound of Italville's trumpets, yet something "frumious" is at hand in the persuasive and disenchanted peel of their laughter, and it will soon nip in the bud whatever attraction the formulas of revenge and self-pity might have been thought to possess. Is there a patron saint peculiar to Italville? I do not know. If there is one, however, I would not be surprised to learn that it is Antonio Delfini. *Poems for the End of the World* might be to Italville what the apocryphal Gospels were to early Christian Churches. This, at any rate, is what I sense in reading a poet like Marco Mantello, whose candidly shrewd performance seems to work particularly well as the provisional conclusion of these brief remarks:

And then, dear Lucia,
if tomorrow I take a gun
with me to school,
I'm afraid that the special agents
of the police
will also go to your house
looking for this poem.

So rinse out your mouth

and read me carefully
since you're the only one
able to prove
we were together that day:

I, with fingers crossed
up to the last minute—
you, with pale lips
screaming the opposite of help.

Amorgos, August 24, 2004

DECEMBER 9th

from TI PRENDO E TI PORTO VIA

Niccolò Ammaniti

It was December 9th, 6:20 in the morning, and a rainy, windy storm was lashing the countryside. A black GTI turbo Fiat Uno (a relic from an era in which, for a few liras above the price of the standard model, one could buy a coffin on wheels which drove like a Porsche, guzzled gasoline like a Cadillac, and crumpled like a can of Coca-Cola) had just taken the exit ramp that led from the Aurelia road to Ischiano Scalo. And it kept going on a two-lane road that cut through fields of mud. It went by the Sports Complex and the building of the Agro-Consortium, and then into the town.

The short main street, *corso Italia*, was covered with clods of earth the wind and the rain had swept in. The ad poster for "Ivana Zampetti's Beauty Salon" had been blown off and was now in the middle of the road.

Not a soul was around, except for a lame dog, which had more breeds in its blood than teeth in its mouth, that was rummaging around in the garbage of an overturned dumpster.

The Uno went right by him, raced past the shuttered Marconi butcher shop, the tobacco-cosmetics shop, and the Rural Credit Union, and continued on to the *piazza XXV aprile*, the town's center.

Bits of paper, plastic bags, newspapers, and rain swirled around the open space in front of the train station. The yellowed leaves of the old palm tree, in the center of the little garden, were all blown to one side. The door of the small station—a gray, square building—was closed, but the red sign of the Station Bar was lit up, an indication that it was still open.

It stopped in front of the Monument to the War Dead of Ischiano Scalo, and stayed there with the engine running. The exhaust pipe was spewing out thick black smoke. The smoked-glass windows didn't allow you to see in.

Then, at last, the door on the driver's side opened wide, making a kind of metallic groaning sound.

First, you could hear "Volare," the version by the Gypsy Kings, and then right afterwards a large, heavy-set man got out. He had a big head of long blond hair, beady little glasses, and a brown leather jacket with an Apache eagle made of beads embroidered on its back.

His name was Graziano Biglia.

The guy stretched his arms out. He yawned. He stretched his legs. He pulled out a pack of Camels and lit one.

He was back home again.

The Seagull and the Disco-dancer

To understand why Graziano Biglia decided to go back to Ischiano Scalo, his birthplace, on that December 9th, after having been away for two years, we have to go back a little in time.

Not a lot. Seven months earlier. And we have to jump over to the other side of Italy, to the east coast—more precisely, to that area known as the *riviera romagnola*.

Summer has begun.

It's Friday evening and we're at the Marina Starfish (also known as Mario's Stinkfish on account of the stink produced by the cook from Caserta), a little, inexpensive restaurant on the beach just a few kilometers from Riccione, specializing in seafood and gastroenteritis.

December 9th

It's hot, but there's a light wind coming off the sea which makes everything more bearable.

The place is jammed. Mostly foreigners, German and Dutch couples, northern European types.

And here's Graziano Biglia. Leaning on the bar, he's downing his third Margarita.

Pablo Gutierrez, a dark-complexioned kid with bangs and a carp tattooed on his back, enters the place and goes up to him.

"Ya want to start?" the Spaniard asks him.

"Let's do it." With a knowing look from Graziano, the barman crouches behind the bar, pulls out a guitar, and hands it over to him.

This evening, for the first time in a while, he feels again like playing. He feels inspired.

Maybe it's the two Margaritas he just knocked back, maybe it's the soft breeze, maybe it's the friendly, intimate atmosphere of that rotunda on the sea—who knows?

He sits down on a stool in the center of the small dance floor lit up with hot red lights. He opens the leather case and takes out his guitar, the same way a samurai would unsheathe his *katana.*

It's a Spanish guitar made just for Graziano by Xavier Martinez, the famous Barcelona guitar maker. He tunes it, and it seems to him as though there's a magical flow between his instrument and himself, making them partners capable of producing fantastic chords together. Then he looks at Pablo. He's standing up, behind a couple of congas.

A spark lights up their eyes.

And without wasting any more time, they start off with a piece by Paco de Lucia, followed by one by Santana, a couple of pieces by John McLaughlin, and finish up with the ever-popular Gypsy Kings.

Graziano's hands scurry over the fingerboard of his guitar as if he were possessed by the spirit of the great Andrés Segovia.

The audience loves it. Applause. Shouting and whistling their approval.

He has them in the palm of his hand. Especially the female contingent. He can sense them turned on like rabbits in heat.

Some of it's because of the magic of Spanish music, but most of it's on account of the way he looks.

It's difficult not to go crazy for someone like Graziano.

The head of blond hair, like a lion's mane, that goes all the way to his shoulders. The huge chest, covered with a soft, light-brown carpet. His Arab eyes, like Omar Sharif's. The faded blue jeans torn at the knees. The necklace with turquoise stones. The tribal tattoos on his bulging biceps. The naked feet. All of it part of a scheme to melt the hearts of his female listeners.

When the concert is over, after yet another encore of "Samba pa ti," after yet another kiss to the sunburnt German girl, Graziano gestures to Pablo and goes off to the toilet to take a leak and to get recharged by puffing on some Bolivian pick-me-up.

He's about to exit when an oversized brunette, sun-tanned like a chocolate cookie and getting up there in age, but with two tits that look like aerostatic soccer balls, comes into the bathroom.

"It's the Men's Room," Graziano lets her know, pointing at the door.

The woman puts up her hand to stop him. "I'd like to give you a blowjob, do you mind?"

Ever since the world has existed, every man has known better than to ever turn down a blowjob.

"Be my guest," Graziano tells her, pointing towards the stall.

"First, though, I want to show you something," says the brunette. "Look over there, in the middle of the place. You see that guy in the Hawaiian shirt? He's my husband. We're here from Milan . . ."

The husband is a thin dude, his hair slicked down with brilliantine. He's gulping down peppered mussels.

"Say hi to him."

Graziano gestures with his hand. The dude raises his cup of champagne and then gives Graziano a round of applause.

"He thinks you're great. He says you play like a god, that you've got a gift."

The woman pushes him towards the stall. She closes the door. She sits on the toilet seat. She unbuttons his jeans and says: "But now we're gonna put some horns on him."

Graziano leans on the wall and closes his eyes.

And time just fades.

This was the life Graziano Biglia led in those days.

A life lived to the max, like the title to a film. A life made up of chance encounters, of lucky unforeseen events, of energy and flow, all in a positive direction. A life lived to the tune of a merengue.

What could be more beautiful than the bitter taste of a drug that numbs your mouth and, like a gust of wind, sets in motion a billion little molecules in your brain, but doesn't do you any harm? Or a stranger's tongue caressing your dick?

Tell me, what?

The brunette invites him to join them for dinner.

Champagne. Fried calamari. Mussels.

The husband has an animal-feed factory in Cinisello Balsamo and a Testarossa Ferrari in the restaurant's parking lot.

I wonder if they do drugs? Graziano asks himself.

If he could manage to peddle a gram or two and pick up a few extra liras, the evening would be classified not just as "good" but "magical."

"You must have a fantastic life, nothing but sex, drugs and rock 'n' roll, right?" the brunette asks him, as her teeth bite into a lobster claw.

Graziano gets depressed when people talk to him that way.

Why do people have to open their mouth and spit out words, senseless *palabras*?

Sex, drugs, and rock 'n' roll . . . The same old story.

But during the dinner he keeps on thinking about it.

Actually, there's some truth in it.

His life is sex, drugs and — no, not rock 'n' roll, really . . . and flamenco.

What's wrong with that?

Of course, a lot of people would say a life like mine sucks. No anchors. Without any foundation. But it's fine with me, and I could care less what other people think.

One time a Belgian, who was sitting in meditation on a flight of stairs in Benares, had remarked to him, "I feel like a seagull carried on the currents . . . by positive currents that I control with just a slight flap of my wings."

Graziano also felt like a seagull.

A seagull with one great commitment in life: to do no harm to others or to himself.

For some, dealing drugs is evil.

For Graziano, it all depends on how you do it.

If you do it just to get by and not to get rich, then it's okay. If you sell to friends, that's okay. If you sell quality stuff and not crap, then it's okay.

If he could make a living just playing music, he'd stop dealing in a second.

For some, taking drugs is bad for you. For Graziano, it all depends on how you do it. If you go overboard, if you let drugs fuck you over, it's no good. He doesn't need any doctor or priest to explain to him that coke has unpleasant side effects. If you get wasted every now and then, there's absolutely nothing the matter with that.

And sex?

Sex? It's true, I get a lot of it. But what can I do if I happen to like women and women like me? (Let's be clear, though, sex with men is a turnoff.) It takes two to have sex. Sex is the most beautiful thing in the world if it's done right, without too many handjobs. (Graziano has never thought much about how obvious that statement is.)

And what else did Graziano like?

Latin music, playing the guitar in bars and clubs (*when they pay me!*), catch some rays on the beach, dick around with friends while a huge orange sun slips into the sea and . . .

. . . and that's enough of that.

You can't believe people who tell you that, if you want to enjoy the good things in life, you have to bust your ass. It's not true. They want to fuck you over. Pleasure is a religion and the body is its temple.

And Graziano had organized himself just for that.

He lived in a studio apartment in the center of Riccione from June to August. In September he moved to Ibiza, and in November he went off to Jamaica for the winter.

At forty-four and then some, Graziano Biglia called himself a professional gypsy, a dharma bum, a wandering soul in search of his karma.

That's what he used to say, at least until that evening, that damned evening in June when his existence crossed paths with Erica Trettel, the disco cube-girl.

And so, here we have the professional gypsy about two hours after gorging himself at the Marina Starfish.

He's now in the upstairs section of Club Hangover, slumped over a cocktail table as if someone had mugged his spinal column. His eyes reduced to little slits. His mouth half-open. In his hand a Cuba Libre that he's unable to drink.

"Jesus, I'm really wasted," he keeps saying to himself.

The mix of coke, ecstasy, wine and deep-fried fish nuggets has destroyed him.

The producer of animal feed and his wife are seated next to him.

The disco is jammed worse than a free-samples stand at a supermarket.

He feels as though he's on a cruise ship because the disco is swaying left and right. The place where they're sitting sucks, even if some people say it's a VIP section. A huge speaker, hanging over his head, is shattering his nervous system. But he'd sooner have his right foot amputated than get up and go look for another place to sit.

The producer of animal feed keeps on screaming things in his ear. Things that Graziano doesn't understand.

He looks down.

The dance floor looks like a fuckin' anthill.

All that's left in his head are a few simple truths.

It's crazy down there. It's Friday. And Fridays are always crazy.

He turns his head slowly, like a Swiss Holstein at pasture.

And he sees her.

She's dancing.

She's dancing naked on a cube in the middle of the anthill.

He knows the moves of all the cube girls at the Hangover. But this one he's never seen before.

She's gotta be a new one. She's a helluva piece of ass. And the way she dances . . .

The loudspeakers pump out a heavy backbeat on a carpet of bodies and heads, sweat and arms, and she's up there, all alone and inaccessible like the goddess Kali.

The strobe lights catch her in an infinite sequence of sensual and plastic poses.

He looks at her with that gaze so typical of drug users.

She's the hottest chick he's ever seen.

Man, would that be somethin' to have her as his girlfriend! . . . To have one like that next to you. Just think how everybody would be jealous of you! But who is she?

He'd like to ask someone. Maybe the dude at the bar. But he can't manage to get up. His legs are paralyzed. And, besides, he can't take his eyes off of her.

She has to be really amazing, because Graziano usually isn't much interested in young heifers (that's what he calls them).

It's a problem of communication.

His hunting grounds are, shall we say, more *âgé*. He prefers more mature, generous women, who can appreciate a sunset, a moonlit serenade, who don't give you a lot of headaches like a twenty-year-old, and who are up for a good screw without expectations or paranoid baggage.

But in this case, every category, every classification has gone down the toilet.

Someone like her could turn a gay man straight.

Man, what a lay she'd be.

A faded image of intercourse on a white atoll beach flashes before his mind. And as if by magic, his dick begins to get hard.

But who is she? Who is she? Where'd she come from?

God, Buddha, Krishna, the Foundation of All That Is, whoever You may be, You made her materialize right on that cube in order to give me a sign of Your existence.

She's perfect.

Not that the other cube girls dancing on the sides of the dance floor aren't perfect. All of them have a firm ass and legs that'll take your breath away, ample round tits and a belly that's flat and muscular. But nobody's like her, there's something special about her, something that Graziano can't quite define in his own words, something animal, something that he'd only caught a glimpse of before with the black women of Cuba.

This girl's body doesn't respond to the music, it is music. The physical expression of music. Her movements are slow and precise like those of a master of Tai-Chi. She manages to stay in place on one foot while her pelvis undulates and her arms move sinuously through the air. The others are spastic by comparison.

Amazing.

And what's incredible is that no one in the disco seems to be aware of her. All those troglodytes keep on gyrating and jabbering when, right in front of them, something miraculous is taking place.

Suddenly, as if Graziano had sent off to her a volley of telepathic rays, the girl stops and turns towards him. Graziano is convinced that she's looking at him. She's motionless, there on the cube, and she's looking right at him—at him in the middle of all that chaos, at him in the middle of those delirious people, at him and at no one else.

At last he manages to see her face. With that short hair, that mouth, those green eyes (he even manages to see the color of her eyes!), and that perfect oval face, she looks just like an actress . . . an actress that Graziano has on the tip of his tongue . . . .

What's her name? The one who did Ghost*?*

He'd love it if only someone would tell him: Demi Moore.

But Graziano can't ask anyone, he's under a spell like a cobra before a snake charmer. He extends his fingers towards her and ten little orange-colored beams of light spring from his finger tips. The beams come together and continue snaking their way like an electrical charge through the discotheque, above the oblivious crowd. They finally make it to her, in the middle of the floor, enter her navel and make her sparkle and shine like a Byzantine Madonna.

Graziano begins to shake.

They are united by an electric arc which melts away their individual personae, transforming them into imperfect halves of a complete being. Only together can they be happy, like angels with a single wing: their embrace will allow them to fly and to reach paradise.

Graziano is on the point of bursting into tears.

He's overwhelmed by a limitless love, something he's never experienced before—a love that's not vulgar debauchery, but a perfectly pure feeling, a feeling that feeds the desire to reproduce, to defend one's own woman from all peril, to build a cottage and raise a bunch of little kids.

He extends his hand, trying to make imaginary contact with the girl.

The two Milanese look at him nonplused.

But Graziano can't see them.

The discotheque doesn't exist anymore. The voices, the music, the wild scene, they are all swallowed up by a mist.

And then slowly the gray haze lifts and a jeans store appears.

Yes, a jeans store.

Not a crappy jeans store like the ones in Riccione, but one that resembles, in every detail, the stores he'd seen in Vermont: there are neatly ordered stacks of Norwegian fisherman sweaters, rows of heavy-duty Virginia miner boots, bundles of socks handmade by the old women of Lipari, jars of Welsh marmalade, and fancy Rapala lures. And there he is with his disco-dancer girl, by now his wife, clearly in a family way, and they're standing behind the counter, which isn't really a counter but a surfboard. And this jeans store is in Ischiano Scalo, in the same place his mother's little dry-goods store used to be. And everyone who passes by, stops, comes in, and sees his wife, and they're jealous of him and they buy penny loafers and Gortex windbreakers.

"The jeans store," Graziano whispers enthusiastically with his eyes closed.

That's what in store for him in the future!

He has seen it.

A jeans store.

That woman.

A family.

Basta with this stray-dog life, with all this freak shit, *basta* with sex without love, *basta* with drugs.

Salvation.

Now he has a mission in life: to meet that girl and take her home with him because he loves her. And she loves him.

"Lu-u-u-v," Graziano sighs, and he gets up from his chair and leans over the railing with his arms stretched out to reach her. Good thing the woman from Milan is there to grab him by the shirt and keep him from falling over and breaking his neck.

"Have you lost your mind?" the woman asks him.

"He likes the little hussy there in the middle." The producer of animal feed bursts out laughing. "He wanted to commit suicide on account of her. Don't you get it? Don't you get it?"

Graziano is on his feet. His mouth is wide-open. He's speechless.

Who are these two monsters? And how dare they? More to the point, what are they laughing at? Why are they pissing on a pure and fragile love which has sprouted despite all the ugliness and garbage in this rotten society?

The man from Milan looks as if he's about to explode with laughter from one minute to the next.

This motherfucker is gonna die right now. Graziano grabs him by the collar of his Hawaiian shirt and the dude stops laughing right away and puts on a smile with all his gums showing. "I'm sorry, forgive me, . . . I'm truly sorry. I didn't mean to . . ."

Graziano is about to smash his nose in, but then he decides to drop it—because this is the night of his salvation, there's no room for violence and Graziano Biglia is a new man.

A man in love.

"What could you possibly understand . . . you heartless people," he says *sotto voce*, and he goes staggering off towards his beloved.

The love story with Erica Trettel, the cube girl at the Hangover, was to prove to be one of the most disastrous episodes in the life of Graziano Biglia. Probably that mix of cocaine, ecstasy, deep-fried fish nuggets and the Lancers Rosé that he'd downed at the Marina Starfish were the immediate cause of the lightning bolt that had short-circuited Biglia's mind—but his penchant for excess and his congenital blindness were really the underlying causes.

Normally, when one comes to after a night of heavy drinking and the ingestion of psychedelic substances, one can barely remember one's name. And, in point of fact, Graziano had erased from his memory his success at the Starfish, the producers of animal feed, and . . .

No!

The girl who was dancing on the cube.

No, he hadn't forgotten her.

When Graziano opened his eyes again the next day, the image of him and his love in the jeans store had clamped onto his brain neurons like an octopus, and it ruled his body and mind for the whole summer.

Yes, because that damned summer Graziano was blind and deaf—he didn't want to see or hear that Erica wasn't right for him. He didn't want to understand that his obsession was irrational and a harbinger of pain and unhappiness.

Erica Trettel was twenty-one years old and breathtakingly beautiful.

She came from Castello Tesino, a little town near Trent. She had won a beauty contest sponsored by a sausage manufacturer and she'd skipped out of town together with one of the members of the jury. She had worked at Bologna's "Motor Show" as an Opel girl. There was a photo or two of her modeling bathing suits for the catalogue of a company in Castellammare di Stabia, and she had also taken a class in belly-dancing.

When she danced on the cube at the Hangover she managed to stay focused, to do her very best, to become one with the music, because positive images would keep flashing in her mind like the lights on a Christmas tree: she saw herself as one of the dancers on *Domenica In*, her picture appearing in *Novella 2000* as she leaves a restaurant on the arm of someone like Matt Weyland, a quiz show contestant, and on television demonstrating how to use an electric Moulinex grater.

Television!

That's where her future lay.

Erica Trettel had very simple, concrete desires.

And when she met Graziano Biglia, she tried to explain that to him.

She explained to him that these desires didn't include marrying some old hippie freak obsessed with the Gypsy Kings and who looked like Sandy Marton after the Paris-Dakar Rally—nor did she have any interest in ruining the best years of her life by giving birth to a bunch of whining brats, and even less interest in opening up a jeans store in Ischiano Scalo.

But Graziano would have none of it and he explained to her, the way a teacher might explain something to a pigheaded student, that television is the worst mafia of all. He was all too well aware of it. He'd played a couple of times on *Planet Bar*. He told her that success on TV doesn't last.

"Erica, you have to grow up, you have to understand that human beings are not made to be put on display, but to find a space where they can live in harmony with heaven and earth."

And that space was Ischiano Scalo.

He even had a recipe for getting *Domenica In* out of her head: leave for Jamaica. He claimed that a vacation in the Caribbean would do her a lot of good, that that was a place where people know how to have a good time and relax, where all the bullshit of this fucked-up society counts for zip, where friendship is everything and you can just lie on the beach and chill.

He was going to teach her everything there was to know about life.

Maybe this gibberish might have made some headway with a fan of Bob Marley's and a supporter of the legalization of light drugs, but not with Erica Trettel.

Those two had about as much in common as a pair of ski boots and a Greek island.

Why, then, did Erica lead him on?

This snippet of conversation between Erica Trettel and Mariapia Mancuso, another of the cube girls at the Hangover, while they were getting ready in the dressing room, may help us to understand.

"Is there any truth to the stupid rumor you're going with Graziano?" Mariapia asks, as she plucks with a pair of tweezers a superfluous hair from the areola of her right nipple.

"Who told you that?" Erica is stretching in the middle of the dressing room.

"Everybody says so."

"Oh, that's what everybody says?"

Mariapia looks herself over in the mirror, checking the right eyebrow before attacking it with the tweezers. "Is it true?"

"What?"

"That you're going with him."

"A little bit . . . let's just say that we get along together."

"In what sense?"

Erica grunts irritably. "What a pain you are! Graziano loves me. Really truly. Not like that asshole Tony."

Tony Dawson, the English DJ at the Anthrax, had had a brief fling with Erica, and then he'd left her for the singer with Funeral Strike, a death-metal band from the Marche.

"And do you love him?"

"Of course I love him. He doesn't try to rip you off. He's an okay person."

"That's true," concurs Mariapia.

"Did you know that he gave me a little puppy? He's so cute. A Brazilian Fila."

"What's that?"

"A very rare dog. A special breed. They used it in Brazil to hunt down slaves who'd escaped from the plantations. He keeps him, though. I don't want to have him around. I called him 'Antoine.'"

"After the hairdresser?"

"Right."

"And what about the story going around that you're gonna get married and go live in his little town and open up a clothing store?"

"Are you outta your mind!? What happened was that the other night we were on the beach and he begins with this story about his home and this jeans store with Norwegian sweaters and his mother's little sewing store, and that he wants to have kids and marry me, that he loves me . . . I told him that the idea was nice . . ."

"Nice?!"

"Just wait. You know how it is when you're talking just to talk. At the time it seemed like a nice idea. But he can't get it out of his head. I'll have to tell him, though, that he can't go around telling this story to everybody. I'll look like an idiot. He's gonna really make me angry if he keeps on doing that."

"Tell him so."

"You bet I'm gonna tell him."

Mariapia moves on to the next eyebrow. "But are you really in love with him?"

"I can't say . . . I told you, he's kind. He's just the sweetest guy. A thousand times better than that sonuvabitch Tony. But he's too superficial. And, besides, there's this whole business of the jeans store . . . If I'm not working at Christmas, he said he's gonna take me to Jamaica. It'd be a blast, don't ya think?"

"And . . . do you give it up to him?"

Erica stands up and stretches. "What kinda crazy question is that? No. Usually not. But he keeps up the pressure, and so every once in a while, I end up . . . giving it up to him with . . . ? What's the word?"

"What'd you mean?"

"When you give someone something, but not all that much—ya know, you give it up but you're not really into it?"

"How should I know? . . . Apathy?"

"Whadda ya talkin' about? Apathy!? C'mon, what's the word? With . . . ?"

"Frugality?"

"Nooo!"

"Restraint?"

"That's it! Restraint. I give it up with restraint."

In his efforts to hang on to Erica, Graziano humiliated himself as he'd never done before. He looked like a total jerk, waiting hours on end for her when everybody knew that she wasn't coming; he lived on the telephone, trying to track her down all over Riccione and the surrounding area; he was misled by Mariapia, who covered for her friend when she went out with that sonuvabitch DJ; and he got up to his neck in debt in order to give her a Brazilian Fila puppy, a super-light canoe, an American passive exercise machine, a tattoo on her butt, a rubber dinghy with a 25 hp outboard motor, a Bang & Olufsen stereo, a bunch of designer clothing, and a pair of shoes with 20 cm high heels, and a countless number of CDs.

Anyone who cared at all for Graziano told him to drop her, that he looked pathetic, that that girl would end up destroying him.

But Graziano wouldn't listen. He stopped hitting on older women and playing music; and he continued stubbornly to believe in the jeans store (though he didn't talk anymore about it with Erica because it made her nervous), and that sooner or later he'd change her, ridding her mind of that bad weed that was television. He wasn't the one who had decided all this, it was destiny—it was destiny that had wanted it and had set her, that night, on a cube in the Hangover.

And there was a moment in which all of this, as if by magic, appeared to be coming true.

In October they were in Rome.

They lived in a rented studio apartment in Rocca Verde. A little hole in the wall on the eighth floor of a big apartment building squeezed between the east bypass and the belt road.

Erica managed to convince Graziano to come with her to Rome. Without him she feels lost in the big city. He has to help her find work.

There's a ton of things to do: look for a good photographer for her headshot; a sharp agent with the right contacts; a diction coach who'll help her to get rid of her ugly Trentino accent and an acting coach to get her to relax.

And then there's the auditions.

They leave early in the morning, spend the whole day going around to the studios of Cinecittà, the casting offices, film production companies, and go back home in the evening, completely burnt out.

Sometimes, when Erica is at her lessons, Graziano puts Antoine in the car and he goes off to Villa Borghese. He strolls through the deer park, continues on to *piazza* Siena, and then goes down to the Pincio. He walks quickly. He likes to go for walks where there's greenery.

Antoine keeps pulling him backwards. With his big paws he has trouble keeping up. Graziano pulls on him with the leash. "C'mon, get a move on, you lazybones. Let's go." Nothing doing. So he sits on a bench and he smokes a cigarette and Antoine begins biting at his shoes.

Graziano no longer bears any resemblance to the "Latin lover" of the Marina Starfish. The guy who used to make German babes swoon.

He looks ten years older. He's pale, with bags under his eyes, his black hair growing out, a warm-up suit, his face unshaven with white stubble, and he is unhappy.

Unhappy beyond words.

Everything is fucked up.

Erica doesn't love him.

She stays with him only because he pays for her lessons, the rent, her clothing, the photographer, everything. Because he's her driver. Because evenings he goes out to buy rotisserie chicken.

Erica doesn't love him and she will never love him.

She doesn't give a damn about him, let's be honest.

But what am I doing here? I hate this city. I hate this traffic. I hate Erica. I have to get out of here. I have to get out of here. It's a kind of mantra that he repeats obsessively.

And why doesn't he do it?

In the final analysis, it's easy enough to do, just get on a plane. And . . . sayonara.

If he could only pull it off.

There's a problem: If he's away from Erica for even half a day, he feels ill. His stomach hurts. He can't breath. He begins to belch.

It would be wonderful if only he could just press a button and clear out his brain. Get out of his head those soft lips, those slim ankles, those deceitful and bewitching eyes. A really good brainwashing. If Erica were only in his brain.

But she's not there.

She's implanted herself like a shard of glass in his stomach.

He's in love with a spoiled child.

An idiot. A bitch. As good as she is at dancing, that's how bad she is at acting and standing in front of a TV camera. She gets all flustered. The words become mush in her mouth.

But Graziano loves her even if she's useless. Even if she's the worst actress in the world.

Damn it . . .

And the worst thing about it is that the more of a bitch she is, the more he loves her.

When there aren't any auditions coming up, Erica spends her day in front of the television eating frozen pizza and ice cream out of the carton. She never wants to do anything. She doesn't want to go out. She doesn't want to see anyone. She's too depressed, she says, to go out.

The house is a shithole.

Piles of dirty clothes thrown in a corner. Garbage. Stacks of plates with sauce caked on them. Antoine, who pisses and craps on the carpet. Erica seems to be comfortable there, in all the shit. Not Graziano, who gets pissed, screams that he's fed up with living like a bum, shouts enough is enough, that he's going to Jamaica, and then ends up taking the dog out for a walk in the park.

How does he manage to stay by her side? Not even a Zen monk could take her. She cries at the drop of a hat. And she gets mad. And when she gets mad horrible things come out of her mouth. Bullets that sink deep into Graziano's heart like butter. She's full of venom, and as soon as she gets a chance she spews it out.

You're a piece of shit! You disgust me! I don't love you, can't you understand that? Do you want to know why I stay with you? Do you really want to know? Because I pity you. That's why. I hate you. And do you know why I hate you? Because you only hope that things won't go my way.

It's true.

Every time an audition fails to work out, Graziano is exultant deep down inside. It's one more small step towards Ischiano. But then later he feels guilty.

They don't make love.

He calls it to her attention. And then she opens her legs and arms wide and says, "Go to it. If you feel like it, just fuck me like this." And a couple of times, in his desperation, he even did it—and it was like doing it with a corpse. A warm corpse that, every once in a while, when the ads come on, grabs the remote and changes the station.

That's the way things went on until December 8th .

December 8th is the day Antoine dies.

Erica is in a cosmetics store with Antoine. The salesgirl says to her that dogs aren't allowed. Erica leaves him outside; she has to buy some lipstick, it'll only be a minute. But a minute is enough for Antoine to see a German Shepherd on the other side of the street, to go into the street, and in that same minute he is to be run over by a car.

Erica goes back home crying. She says to Graziano that she wasn't strong enough to go and see the dog. The dog is still there. Graziano runs out the door.

He finds him on the side of the road. In a pool of blood. He's barely breathing. Black blood is streaming out of his nostrils and mouth. He takes him to the vet, who finishes him off with an injection.

Graziano returns home.

He doesn't feel like talking. He really liked that dog. He was funny. And he was good company.

Erica starts to say that it wasn't her fault. That she'd only taken a minute to buy the lipstick. And the idiot who was driving the car didn't try to brake.

Graziano leaves the house again. He gets in the Uno and, to calm down, goes for a spin on the belt road at 110 mph.

It was a mistake for him to come to Rome.

It's all been a mistake.

He's made a colossal blunder. In reality, that woman isn't really a woman at all, but a chastisement sent by God to wreck his life.

Over the past month they've argued almost every day.

Graziano can't believe some of the things she says to him. She lashes out with insults to the very core of his being. And there are times she attacks with such violence that he's not even able to defend himself. The kind of attacks that make him want to give it right back, to tell her that she's completely incompetent.

For example, the other day she accused him of giving her bad luck—that Madonna would have stayed Louise Veronica Ciccone if she'd had someone like him at her side. And she threw in that everyone in Riccione said he was a lousy guitar player, only good for selling stale tabs. And then, just to put frosting on the cake, she finished up by saying that the Gypsy Kings are a band of fags.

Basta! I'm leaving her.

He has to do it.

He won't die. He'll survive. Even the addicts manage to survive without stuff. You go cold turkey, suffer unbelievably, you think you'll never be able to do it, but then in the end you get through it and you come out clean.

The death of Antoine, at least, has helped him to come to his senses.

He has to leave her. And the best way is with a cool, dispassionate talk, without getting pissed. The kind of talk you'd expect from a strong man whose heart is broken. Like Robert De Niro in *Stanley & Iris* when he drops Jane Fonda.

Right, enough is enough.

He goes back home. Erica is watching *Lupin III*, a Japanese action cartoon, and eating a cheese sandwich.

"Can you turn off the TV for a minute?"

Erica turns off the television.

Graziano sits down, clears his throat and gets down to it: "There's something I want to tell you. I think the time's come to call it quits. You know it and I know it. Let's be honest with each other."

Erica looks at him.

Graziano continues: "I give up on this whole thing. I really believed in it. Honestly. But now, it's over. I don't have any more lire. We argue all the time. And besides, I can't live in Rome anymore. It's disgusting, it makes me depressed. I'm like the seagulls—if they don't migrate, they die. I just can't . . ."

"You know, seagulls don't migrate."

"Good for you. Like the damned swallows, does that make you happier? Right now I should be in Jamaica. Tomorrow I'm leaving for Ischiano. I'll pick up a little money and then I'll leave. And we won't ever see each other again. I'm sorry things. . . " His little De Niro talk dies away.

Erica remains quiet.

She's never heard Graziano talk like this before.

He has a strange tone to his voice. Usually he makes a scene, screams and gets all pissed. But not now, he's calm and resigned. He seems like an American actor. Antoine's death must have really shaken him up.

Suddenly she realizes that he's not doing his usual pathetic bit. This time he's really serious.

If he leaves, what will happen?

It'll be a real nightmare.

Erica can only see dark clouds before her. She can't even imagine a future without him. Her life is the pits, but without Graziano it would be hell. Who would pay the rent? Who would go out to buy the rotisserie chicken? Who would pay the installment due on her acting class?

And besides, she's not so sure anymore that she's going to make it. Everything seems to say to her that she has no possibilities. Since she got to Rome, she's auditioned a ton of times, and not a single audition went her way. Maybe Graziano is right. Television isn't for her. She's just can't do it.

A sob begins to creep into her throat.

Without even a lira to her name, she'd have to go back to Castello Tesino. But before she'd go back to that frigid place with those two parents of hers, she'd hit the streets as a hooker.

She tries to swallow a bit of her sandwich. But it just stays in her mouth, as bitter as bile. "Are you really serious?"

"Yes."

"You really want to leave?"

"And what am I gonna do?"

"I don't know what to tell you."

Silence.

"You've really made up your mind?"

"Yes."

"Really truly?"

"Yes."

Erica begins to cry. Very quietly. Her teeth sunk into the sandwich. The tears make her makeup run.

Graziano plays around with his cigarette lighter. He lights it and then puts it out.

"I'm sorry, but it's much better this way. At least we'll have a beautiful mem . . ."

"I . . . I . . . wa . . . want to come with you," Erica sobs.

"What?"

"I . . . I want to come with you."

"Where?"

"To Ischiano."

"And what would you do there? Didn't you say that the place disgusts you?"

"I want to meet your mom."

"You want to meet my mother?" Graziano repeats parrot-style.

"Yes, I want to meet Gina. But later we'll go to Jamaica for a vacation."

Graziano doesn't say a word.

"You don't want me to come?"

"No. It's better if you don't."

"Graziano, don't leave me. Please." She grabs his hand.

"It's better this way . . . You know so yourself . . . It's too late . . ."

"You can't leave me in Rome, Grazi."

Graziano can feel that his insides are churning up. *What does she want?*

She can't do this. It's not right. Now she wants to go with him.

"Graziano, come here," Erica says with her ever-so sad quiet voice.

Graziano gets up. He sits next to her. She kisses his hands and hugs him tight. She lays her head on his chest. And she begins to cry.

Graziano can now feel it in his gut, a boa has awakened from its slumber. He suddenly feels his windpipe unplug. He can breathe in and out.

He hugs her in his arms.

She shakes as she sobs: "I . . . I'm sor . . . ry . . . I . . . I'm sor . . . ry."

She is so tiny. Defenseless. She's a child. A child who needs him. The most beautiful child in all the world. His child. "Okay. Alright. Let's get out of this goddamned city. I won't leave you. Don't worry. You're coming with me."

"Ye . . . es, Graziano . . . take me with you."

They kiss. Saliva and tears. He cleans off the smeared mascara with his T-shirt.

"Yes, tomorrow morning let's leave. But I have to call my mother, so she'll get the room ready for us."

Erica smiles. "Okay." Then it clouds over again. "Yes, let's leave . . . It's just that the day after tomorrow, damn it, I've gotta do something."

Graziano is immediately suspicious. "What?"

"An audition."

"Erica, you're the same old . . ."

"Wait! Just listen. I promised the agent that I'd go. He needs girls from his agency just to pretend they're auditioning. The director has already decided who he wants, someone with connections, but the thing has to look real. It's the same old crap."

"Don't go. Tell him to get lost, the asshole."

"I really have to go. I promised him. After everything he's done for me."

"But what did he ever do for you? Nothing. All he ever did was squeeze money out of us. Tell him to get lost. We have to leave."

Erica takes his hands. "Listen, let's do this. You leave tomorrow. I'll go to the audition, close up the house, pack our bags, and the day after I'll catch up with you."

"You don't want me to wait for you?"

"No, you go. Rome has stressed you out. I'll take the train. That way, when I get there, you'll have everything ready. Buy a lot of fish. I really like fish."

"Of course I'll buy fish. Do you like monkfish tail?"

"I don't know. Is it good?"

"It's great. And what about clams, should I buy some?"

"Clams, Grazi. Pasta with clams, excellent." Erica comes up with a smile that lights up the whole house.

"Nobody makes pasta with clams like my mother. You'll see. We'll be all right."

Erica throws herself into his arms.

That night they make love.

And for the first time since they've been together, Erica goes down on him.

Graziano is stretched out on that messy bed all covered with sweaters, stinking T-shirts, CD cases and bread crumbs, and he looks at Erica there, in between his legs, sucking his dick.

Why did she decide to give him a blowjob?

She's always said that giving a blowjob was something disgusting.

What is she trying to get him to understand?

It's simple. That she loves you.

Graziano is carried away with emotion and comes.

Erica falls asleep naked in his arms. Graziano stays still so as not to awaken her, holding on to her tight. He can't believe that this beautiful girl is his woman.

His eyes never tire of looking at her, his hands of caressing her, his nose of smelling her.

How many times has he asked himself how a creature as perfect as she could have been born in such a Godforsaken little burg. It's a miracle of Nature.

And that miracle is his. Despite all the misunderstandings, despite Erica's personality, despite their different ways of looking at the world, despite all of Graziano's shortcomings.

Now they are united. United by a bond that will never be broken.

It's true that he's made mistakes: he was weak, indecisive, cowardly, giving into every one of Erica's whims and letting the situation deteriorate to the point that things had become unlivable. But that one last move that he made turned out to be heaven-sent. It freed both of them from the cobwebs that were suffocating them.

Erica had felt that she might lose him forever, that he wasn't playing games anymore. And she didn't let him leave.

Graziano's heart is overflowing with love. He kisses her on the neck.

Erica mutters: "Graziano, can you bring me a glass of water?"

He brings her the water. She sits down and, with her eyes closed and holding the glass with two hands, gulps the water down, dribbling some of it on her chin.

"Erica, you have to tell me something: Do you truly love me?" he asks her as he lies back down on the bed.

"Yes," she replies, and she curls up next to him.

"Really truly?"

"Really truly."

"And . . . and do you want to marry me?" he hears himself saying. As if some evil spirit had put those terrible words in his mouth. A spirit that wants to fuck everything up.

Erica snuggles up even more, pulls the quilt over her, and says, "Yes."

"*Yes!?*"

For a moment Graziano is speechless, overwhelmed. He puts a hand over his mouth and closes his eyes.

What did she say? Did she say she wanted to marry him?

"Really truly?"

"Yes," Erica murmurs, half-asleep.

"And when?"

"In Jamaica."

"Right. In Jamaica. On the beach. We'll get married on the rocks off Edward Beach. It's a fabulous place."

This is why Graziano Biglia left Rome at five in the morning on December 9th, despite the raging storm, in order to go to Ischiano Scalo.

He'd taken along all of his worldly possessions and some good news to report to mom.

(Translated by Lawrence Garner)

GUAPPETELLA
(STRAIGHT IN THE EYES)

VALERIA PARRELLA

I had always sort of liked the Gimp. He called me Guappetella because I played the tough girl with him. When I finally decided to be his girlfriend, I made him keep begging for awhile, so he wouldn't think he could just strap on the feedbag.

His wife treated me with respect, and I showed her the same. All she really wanted was his monthly paycheck from the railroad, and that he should sleep at home.

That was it. She didn't care about anything else. The Gimp ate his meals at my house, and I washed his work clothes. After handing over his salary to the wife and kids, the Gimp would spend the rest of his money on me.

And we had lots of fun. The Gimp would pull in as much as three grand a day when he got word of a choice piece of cargo, or maybe a Rolex, or a stereo. He never came back empty-handed. We would go to Pozzuoli and eat seafood till we burst.

The Gimp and Guappetella.

"*Essa è cchiù bellella*" . . . But I really liked the Gimp.

I remember, on my way to school in the morning, I'd take the long way around so that I could say hi to my mother, who would be standing around with other women, warming her hands over a fire in a steel drum, waiting for contraband. I would hang around till I saw him emerge from the alley. He would limp on down the hill, dragging his right leg behind him.

I was doing my third year of infant care. Once I got my certificate, that was it for school. I was sixteen years old, and I had a body that made even priests stop in the street and stare.

There were teachers who flirted with me, but it wasn't men I was interested in. I was busy observing women. We shared the same building with other high-school institutes. I would inspect the high- school girls specializing in classical studies, and the girls studying languages. They were willowy, slender, and small-breasted. They wore helmets when they rode their mopeds. They would dutifully punch their tickets when they got on the bus.

When parent-teacher meetings were scheduled, the aunt of one of my schoolmates would come in from the neighborhood and take notes for all the girls. The teacher took all this agreeably in stride: any one of us girls had a good forty pounds on her.

Meanwhile, I studied the mothers of the other girls. Fine ladies, accompanied by their husbands, wearing low-heeled shoes and almost no makeup. The teachers and the principal took turns gushing compliments.

"She's got money," my aunt would say.

Sure, she definitely had money, but so did we. In the neighborhood, there was plenty of money, but nobody ever murmured "*signora*" to us like that, enunciating each syllable.

We left school with our third-year certificates, because the neighborhood was pitiless, and especially because it was changing fast, and you could barely make money before you needed more. The mediaeval loggias were sprouting satellite dishes. Under the Supportico Lopez, where nothing had changed since it was built during the reign of the Spanish Viceroy, there was a tanning parlor, L'Inferno Giallo.

I never went to tanning parlors. The ladies I hoped to become had golden skin, and when they went to the beach they used sunscreen. Not like us: we weren't happy until we were red as lobsters, so badly sunburnt we couldn't stand to wear a bra.

When I was seventeen, one of my classmates had a baby girl at the Ruesh Clinic. If you were going to have a baby, it couldn't be anywhere but there. You just couldn't receive visitors from the neighborhood unless the room cost at least 300 dollars a night. The baby girl weighed eight and a half pounds. The labor and birth had ripped my girlfriend's insides to shreds. She was lying there, fifteen stitches, nursing her baby girl. The newborn was clutching my friend's breast and biting at her. My friend burst into tears.

"She's mean!"

"No," said the doctor, "she's not mean. Life will do anything to survive."

That evening I went back to the neighborhood, and I started going steady with the Gimp.

I really did like him, but I took more than I gave. Well, what else can a man expect when his girlfriend is seventeen and he's thirty-five? I had no father, and the neighborhood by and large couldn't care less about that sort of thing. The Gimp's wife lived at the far uphill end of our street and you never saw her walking around. I was very well known and always on the move, and everyone called me Guappetella, just like he did.

If I'd been the daughter I wish I'd been, the daughter of the lady that I wanted to become, then my mother would have reported the Gimp to the police. She would have sent me out of the country to study. Instead, my mother said:

"Get him to put a house in your name."

I had already thought of that myself: the Gimp put an apartment in my name when I turned eighteen.

"Let's get some blacks in there, that'd be a nice piece of monthly income."

Everybody was getting black tenants.

"No, I want to get coeds. They'll keep it cleaner, and they pay a lot better."

In 700 square feet, you could get quite a few coeds living off-campus.

In the summer, the Gimp would give me fifty bucks every day, so that I could go to the beach at Baia with my sisters. He would punch the time clock at the railroad and then catch up with us at the beach.

Then, one day, a neighborhood boy drove up on his moped.

"The Gimp wants you to come. He's been shot in the chest."

The bullet was lodged just an inch or so from his lung.

A neighborhood retailer, *Il Principe*, had taken him to a doctor he trusted: a doctor who had a little studio down the street from the old Polyclinic, where he kept a few instruments and a little medicine, and no one ever came around asking questions.

"He's out of danger, but down here, without an operating room, I can't take out the bullet. It'll have to stay in."

The Gimp was a tough customer, and *Il Principe* didn't want problems:

"The bullet stays."

He was going to keep the bullet there, in his chest. I gave him a kiss, and then I told the boy: "Go tell his wife."

When I thanked *Il Principe* he half-turned on his heels:

"Guappetè, you know I did it only for you."

I looked him hard in the eyes. Then I turned and left.

In the courtyard of the Polyclinic, I recognized the husband of one of those ladies that I wanted to become. He was walking alongside a doctor, calling him professor, and asking him how the birth had gone.

So, I discovered: the ladies that I wanted to become didn't give birth in a clinic, but in a hospital.

I could sense that there had been some confusion about how to use all this money, but I wasn't quite sure where.

The Gimp convalesced at home with his wife. When word got out around the neighborhood about the bullet in his chest, he got a new nickname—Highlander. I went to see him every single day. I bought him a Game Boy because he wasn't comfortable staying in bed, doing nothing.

He went back to work at the beginning of the winter and gave me a Roberto Cavalli overcoat for a gift. He did our styling: his clothing was expensive, it was advertised everywhere, and it all featured the same tiger stripes and leopard spots and zebra stripes that the neighborhood had always considered the hallmark of elegance.

But I didn't think of myself as intriguing or taboo-shattering in those clothes. I felt like a slut. The ladies that I wanted to become wore cream-colored outfits by Marella.

The time had come to dump Highlander. I did it as soon as he wound up in jail.

"I'm breaking up with your husband. Give me your identity card: I've got to go tell him to his face."

On my way to get a fake identity card made, I stopped at the cafe and sent an espresso over to *Il Principe* with my compliments.

Il Principe. He had been a shopkeeper like any other, until he opened a boutique that sold formal wear. Then he opened a second one near the National Museum, and then a third shop, almost directly across from the cathedral.

"In all of Naples, only Barbaro has an operation that compares with mine."

I never thought of him as having real power, but in his avid pursuit of money he had really made a bundle. He was highly respected.

His favorite shop was the one across from the cathedral. I went by to thank him personally for the roses. He was at the door of the shop, chatting with a bishop.

"*Principessa*," he greeted me. "May I offer you an aperitivo?"

He turned and hurried into the shop.

"I'll just put on a jacket."

"No, *Principe*, let's not get fancy."

But when he stepped out the door he was wearing a blazer. He really was a fine-looking gentleman. Right away, I felt comfortable walking around town by his side. I was practically the same height, and when I turned to look at him, I saw his copper-colored goatee tucked behind the ample white collar of his dress shirt.

Il Principe was pushing forty and he had a daughter who was almost my age. He was hardly a self-made man, and now he was mainly interested in enjoying life. I was ready to enjoy life too, but I was going to make sure I made no wrong moves.

He was deeply and truly moved when the time came to show me his prize possession: a yellow BMW Z3. It was a beautiful machine, but if he thought an expensive car was all he needed, he had miscounted his aces. "That's a beautiful shade of yellow!" I told him.

He redoubled his efforts. He would murmur sweet nothings to me, at first trying to use proper Italian, until he became tongue-tied and continued in Neapolitan dialect.

I had him wrapped around my finger. It was clear to everyone, including his wife. She was used to his cheating, but no one had ever been *principessa*, not even her.

One day she pulled up next to me and leaned out the window of her car, a very nice automobile.

"Listen, you, what are you trying to do to me? I'm old enough to be your mother."

"So what's the problem? There's plenty for both of us."

"But I love him, I really love him."

"Well, you may love him but you don't know how to hold him. You think I'm the first one?"

"Now he's talking about divorce."

I looked her straight in the eyes without blinking. It did me no good for him to leave his wife. I didn't want to change his life, at least not permanently.

But he had bought a little vacation apartment for the two of us in Posillipo, and I was planning to cook him breakfast there for at least a couple of years.

I was about to tell her not to worry, but I was distracted by the sight of a lady walking into the Marella boutique. She had just gotten out of a taxi.

"That's not my fucking problem," I said, and that was the last I saw of her.

With *Il Principe* everything was on a much higher level. The other tenants were quiet, impeccably behaved. Some of them were like us, and you could tell by the gold, the way they chewed gum open-mouthed, or with their mouths exaggeratedly closed. When people like us were in Posillipo, we went out of our way to behave properly.

Then there were people like the accountant who had sold us the apartment: radiologists, pharmacists, financial advisers. Their money was worth more than our money, even if we had twice as much. Behind the smiles we exchanged, there were private clubs that had stopped accepting new members.

One night, we were watching a show on TV when I realized that all the women were just like the ladies that I hoped to be. I don't know if the real women copied the characters on TV, or the other way around, but the ladies in my apartment building were just like those in the movie. So I forgot about the plot and started studying them with care.

"This one, what's she got that's different from me?"

"You are prettier than she is, *principessa*."

"Come on: *looks aside*, what does she have that's better than me?"

"Cell phone: I'll buy you one tomorrow."

From that evening on, we were watching two different movies, and from then on, as long as we were together, that was how it went. The actress would walk into a room, and a cocaine deal was going on. *Il Principe* would lose patience. "I wouldn't give a gram to a girl with a face like that: the minute she walks out the door looking like that, the cops'll search her."

That's when it hit me: they were speaking proper Italian, not dialect. From the opening credits to the last scene, every character in the movie spoke nothing but Italian. They didn't use big words; they spoke naturally and easily, so that I understood everything they said without even realizing it. If there was a line in dialect, it came from a waiter or a mechanic, and it would make the ladies laugh.

The next day I went to see my student tenants. I was only a few years older than them, but I was like their mother. I sat down with the one who had been there longest, the one I still charged only 125 dollars a month for a bed, as if she were under rent control.

This is what we arranged. I enrolled in a private school. In two years, I could finish my courses and get a proper diploma. The student stopped paying rent, and she gave me lessons instead. I was twenty-three, and I was still young enough to fix the way I spoke.

The girls told me I had to read a lot. One student loaned me a few bestsellers, and the first one was that book by someone called Tamaro.

It seemed like a ridiculous book. If I had "followed my heart," I would have been knocked up at age thirteen in the delivery truck of Totonno the Ragman.

"*Principessa, si je capess' addò vvuò arrivà', je t'aiutass.*"

"Speak Italian."

"If I understood what you're trying to do, I could help you . . ."

"One of us is going one way, and the other is going the other, and that's how things get complicated."

"I've always said that you were born to be a princess, so now that you're getting your diploma, I'll put a shop in your name. You want a shop?"

"Sure, but nothing illegal."

"We'll call it 'Princess of Naples.'"

"I want a Marella franchise and I want to run it myself, no interference. I'll deal with the suppliers, I'll deal with the accounting, everything."

"But if it's a franchise then we can't put your name on it."

I opened the shop in a strategic location, on the edge of the neighborhood, but on the other side. I was on the corner of the official shopping street. There were two display windows at street level and a window on the second floor. And behind that window was me.

They came down from Milan with logos and merchandise. I welcomed them cordially with a smile that flashed no teeth; I let them select the salesgirls. The only thing I demanded was that they not be girls from my neighborhood.

Signing a fake pay stub was unnecessarily risky. In Milan under-the-counter labor is called on-the-job training. Everything was perfectly legit.

The only sizes we carried were 4 to 12. If some extra-large woman stepped into the shop, it was to keep an eye on how I was set up. In the neighborhood, they turned the nickname game upside down and dubbed me Marella. I was almost invisible: I was rarely seen on the street, or in the shop. I had two small video cameras, and I watched everything that happened on my monitors.

Whenever *Il Principe* came into the store, it made me nervous. To keep things calm, I would immediately invite him upstairs.

It was around then that I began to spend time with some ladies I'd met at the gym: I was wearing myself out with aerobics trying to slim down my woman-warrior physique. They spent all their time doing Hatha Yoga and having massages. In the afternoon, we would go out and drink tea together; sometimes they showed up with Singhalese babysitters and perfect little brats who addressed me as "ma'am."

"No, sweetheart, Marella is mommy's friend; you don't have to call her ma'am."

Whenever I heard the word friend, a deep-seated instinct made me plunge my hand into my purse, where I would finger the switch-blade knife that the Gimp had given me.

I did my best to restrict my socializing in their homes to a minimum: once you got past the living room, astonishing dramas played out.

"Mommy, you are a turd and a whore," the little ones would scream, with perfect diction.

The older snot-noses would shut themselves up in their bedrooms, holding the telephone hostage.

One day, a little girl who'd eaten nothing but crackers for weeks asked me if I was her daddy's new girlfriend. I gave her a backhanded smack that knocked her down flat on the hardwood floor. From that day on I was her confidante. For months the only way her mother could communicate with her was through me.

Anyway, I decided that none of that was my concern. The lady that I was going to become existed only at Gambrinus, with a glass of *prosecco* in one hand.

One morning the Senator's wife came into the shop. She wanted a new overcoat.

I had known the woman nearly all my life; I remembered her campaign visits to our neighborhood. Her name was Anna, just like my mother. For as long as I could remember, every July 26th, Saint Anne's Day, my mother would send her a gift pack of Flor-do-cafè.

"You look different," she said.

I smiled at her. "Would you like an espresso?"

But she wanted to hear me talk.

"Are you still dating *Il Principe*?" It was an odd question, because the Senator's wife, and the Senator, and the Senator's lowest-ranking secretary, and every last cobblestone in our neighborhood, all knew that we had broken up.

"No, but he sends me a bouquet of roses every week." And everybody knew that, too.

She picked out an overcoat and asked to have it delivered to her home. Then she stroked my cheek.

"Say hello to your mother for me."

I hated the Senator's wife for four days. Then the Senator came to see me.

He came in just as the shop was closing, with a good-looking man, younger than him.

I came down the steps, saying goodnight to the salesgirls, and then halted on the third step from the bottom, just to establish who was boss.

"Good evening," he said, and leaned over to kiss my hand. I pulled it back, sharply.

"Hand-kissing is for priests and *mafiosi*. Which are you looking for?"

"Hand-kissing is for ladies as well."

"I'm not a lady."

I didn't like not knowing what was going on.

Moreover, I was defenseless: I had established my distance from *Il Principe* and his boys, while the Gimp's switchblade knife was nothing more than a key chain. I had long since abandoned the leather of high boots and the scratch of long fingernails. The spit of my dialect.

"I came to introduce you to my close friend, the lawyer."

I held out my hand, I looked hard into his eyes. I had no other defense.

"I dare only shake your hand, though it would deserve so much more."

"Please, make yourselves comfortable."

"The Senator and I have come to ask for your advice and, if possible, your help."

They wanted a favor, because I knew nothing about politics. I had always voted for the amnesties and referendums I had been told to vote for.

"The elections are coming up in April."

"Senator, you have always won elections."

"True, but things are looking different now. Not so much the political elections, but the administrative ones. It's a mess: the city coalition government has managed to hold together for eight years now."

I took half an hour of my valuable time to evict the coeds personally.

"Without notice?"

"What did you want, a telegram?"

"Couldn't you just wait till after Christmas?"

I thought it over: I needed the office for the campaign committee immediately, but the new floor tiles wouldn't be installed until January, at the earliest. I was about to wish her a happy Christmas season and leave, when the little shit overdid it:

"I loaned you all those books . . ."

I saw myself in my mind's eye, intimidated, with a pile of glossy books in one hand.

"Get out!" I screamed, and overturned a dresser full of panties. "Scram!"

The lawyer was a councilman whose term was almost up, the designated successor to the Senator, and he took great pains to keep his hands clean: when he defended a boss in court, he made sure that it was as a public defender. Together we selected the furnishings for a small smoking room where the men could withdraw to discuss the more delicate matters. It was here that *Il Principe* sifted out his own contribution to the cause, gram by precious gram.

At this point, I could have shot off fireworks every evening of the week. I could play the prima donna: they were all guests of mine. They were all, theoretically, my lovers.

But I decided to hold out for the culminating Roman candle.

I invited the lawyer out for dinner, and I handed him the keys to the apartment: "I think you can handle this as well as anybody."

"I didn't know you were so tractable."

"You don't know me at all. But you can make up for lost time."

"Tonight?"

"When the Party can spare you. I am a patient woman."

I made myself scarce at the campaign committee, I would head home no later than eleven, in a taxi. I wore pale colors, I wore my hair in a knot for the whole month of January, and I would take so much time to put on my makeup that by the time I was done, it looked like soap and water. The Senator would observe me. Once I met his glance, and he had the look of someone who understood and approved. In his way, he was wearing his hair in a knot.

The lawyer tried to take me to bed three times. Obviously, I couldn't pretend I was a saint. I could just let him glimpse that somehow for me this was unusual.

"I'm sorry," I would say. "This is different."

The fourth time, I let it happen, after dinner at my apartment: I gave him the blowjob of a lifetime.

We decided to get married after the elections. Then I'd hire someone to run the boutique, I'd rent out all the apartments, and I would retire to be his wife: his career called for travel, regular trips to the capital, and I needed to be free to go when needed.

There was a little celebration at the campaign committee, with enough toasts that we were tipsy.

But I was afraid I might have miscalculated. Accustomed as I was to acting in a hurry, I had assumed that all that was needed to get married was a man and a woman determined to take the plunge. I hadn't taken into account that I would first need to marry his friends, his name, his mother. His family was determined not to meet me: they had gathered information, and my past, which had been my only reason for living, had also become my sole obstacle. He was truly in love, and it seemed to embarrass him. He never wanted to discuss it: if I tried to bring it up, he would say: "That's all right. It doesn't matter."

But could I trust a thirty-five-year-old cokehead who still lived with his mother?

In the meanwhile, the elections were drawing closer, and soon they would be over. If it all went well, they would bring a breath of fresh air into his life, a new source of confidence. And when men are strong and confident they feel that they can do without anyone.

If I had been the girl I used to be, I would have sniffed the scent of danger like an animal. I would have tensed my muscles and hurled myself into the only action available, either victory or retreat.

But now I was pondering the variables. I was interested in just how the problem was going to be solved. I sensed something new, something crucial developing for the woman that I would become.

I could take sugar pills instead of contraceptives, and lay a trap.

Instead, I took a seat and decided to wait.

Just seventy-two hours before the end of the campaign, I put on a pair of leather pants and dark glasses. I called the Senator on his cell phone and told him to meet me at the edge of the neighborhood.

"Get in." I opened the car door from inside. "Let's talk."

I drove up Stella, Santa Maria Antesaecula, Salita Capodimonte, and I parked in the shadow of the observatory. These were streets he had never seen. These were people he had never even dreamed of meeting.

"Get out of the car, Senator."

We walked about fifty yards into the bushes. Beneath our feet, plastic bags, bottles, needles. Then the city. All of it, reaching to the sea. I thought of Totonno the Ragman.

"Senator, listen to me. Votes that cost fifty dollars apiece. Local mafia bosses standing in front of the polling places. Checking the stamps on the ballot. That's what I know about politics; that's what you have shown me for thirty years. Right? But maybe this time there will be no need. And why?" He looked out at Capri. "Not because we have changed, Senator: because we have created a genuine consensus."

The day before the elections, the Senator sent a car to pick up my mother.

"Dress in black," I had told her, "you're a widow. And keep your mouth shut."

From the depth of her sixty years my mother felt neither old nor like a widow, but she was intelligent and she understood that she had better play the part. An old widow could not help but remark: "*C'e mettimm'int'o sacchino*."

I looked at her, severely: this notion of slipping them into our pockets sounded to me like an operation that I was not willing to name.

We arrived at the house of my future in-laws in succession: the Senator and my mother, me and the Senator's wife, the expensive pastry arrangement from Scaturchio. My fiancé was overjoyed, my mother made a gesture of benediction, as if to say, "My new son," and then for the rest of the evening, the Senator's wife held my mother's hands in her hands.

The Senator held court for all the time that my mother-in-law needed to study me, then he raised his glass and proposed a toast.

He would take care of everything. We could take our vows between the first and second ballots. The Senator would stand up for me, and so the lawyer had better get busy finding a best man.

That evening, the lawyer took me home and we did it in the car. The next day was a day of victories: the Senator sailed off to Rome and my fiancé was elevated to the city council on the first ballot. When we went to city hall to say our vows, a city policeman practically genuflected when he saw us. Then there was a big party to prepare, because the prime minister was expected in town, where he would be campaigning for our candidate on the second ballot. But we didn't care much about that, by now. Walking out of city hall onto the Piazza Municipio, I saw before me a cluster of pine trees, and amidst the pine trees, the Marine Terminal, and behind that, Mount Vesuvius.

That was when my father-in-law offered me his arm and murmured to me: "*Signora.*"

(Translated by Antony Shugaar)

BELOVED ROME, I WILL NEVER DIE

AURELIO PICCA

I was so much *my own*, in 1960, so innocent. One, two, three: and I was three when I first saw Rome.

I was with Annunziata, her cheeks soft as a Shar-Pei; her diamond earrings that looked like slices of lemon; her black dress that had not yet been wrinkled by death. I clasped her hand. And I was all my own in my little checkered overcoat, as the bus roared into motion down the Via Appia, as empty as a Sunday.

The ruins of the aqueduct, on our left, were an architectural model built for lizards. And the tunnel on the Via del Quadraro held us close, me and Annunziata, wrapped in a smell, the scent of Rome.

In the apartment blocks of the Don Bosco quarter, the washing hung out to dry seemed like the last flags of the war. And the clouds were whiter, more filigreed, than the clouds of today.

The rooms I walked into were filled with the air of springtime. And *that* young girl smiled. I looked at the ground, my dolly in my hands. I was shy, and so bitterly disappointed when the little lady grabbed my toy.

All the while, I could feel her moving through the house. I wanted to look at her so much it made me tremble, while Rome, emptied out, was filling up every inch of the day.

If I think back more carefully, if I glean my harvest of memories, then I remember that I had been in Rome once before, and not before my birth, but a few months before my trip with Annunziata.

I hadn't seen Rome at all. I'd spewed a mouthful of blood over it, then I left.

This memory takes me back to a series of fragments dated about two and a half years.

I am inside a huge, dimly lit room. Running along the walls are an unbroken line of chairs—wooden chairs, made of varnished beechwood. A gentleman (later I would find out that he is a doctor), dressed in an ample white lab coat (half cape, half toga), with a tranquil demeanor and an exaggeratedly ponderous gait, walks toward me from the chair opposite my own, from the far wall of the vast room. The gentleman comes closer, skillfully adjusting a tiny video camera that is mounted in the middle of his forehead.

When he reaches me, I realize that on his head, in the middle of a white band, what is observing me is not a video camera, nor is it the eye of a samurai. Mounted in the middle of his hair is a round mirror. But with astonishing timing, even before I can mirror myself in it, the gentleman slips a steel squid into my mouth.

The scene changes.

I am sitting on some sort of high chair. Or is it an aluminum seahorse? I am wearing a horrible smock.

The scene changes.

I am lying on my back on a little cot, with a sheet pulled up to my chin. I am silent. I have never uttered a word in my life. All around me is a flight of cherubs, their little weewees covered with hoods. On my left, where I now turn my head and my eyes, there is a large glass window. Outside is a garden filled with palm trees and a turn-of-the-century apartment building. This is Rome.

When I was four, I did not yet know that one day Rome would be dead. I did not even know that one day I, too, would be dead. I knew only that I was happy to be riding in a train. Towards Rome.

My brother Marco was in the Ospedale del Bambin Gesù (Hospital of Baby Jesus). I didn't know that my brother was dying: I was just happy to be riding in a train, to be going to Rome. I didn't understand anything else. It was as if someone had told me: "Come on, let's go to the beach." And momma was waiting for me. I hadn't been to the beach with momma in such a long time!

Marco had a big square head and a little arm strapped down to a panel. There was a needle bandaged to his vein. His little cot had netting on each of the four sides, and the shadows of sunset were stretching over him: the golden shadows of the Janiculum Hill, sifting down from the tall windows.

Then momma handed me to a lady, and she walked me up to the plaza, to watch the marionette show. Rome, beneath us, was motionless as a postcard.

Rome is a city of pink shadows, corners dripping with piss, a sky that belongs elsewhere, and streets for beggars. It's not a rich city, in fact it's poor; it is the only city that lets its mother be raped so that it can go the beach at Castelporziano, or so that it can take the thug girl of the week out to dinner at the Due Ladroni.

In 1966, the Upim department store, across from Santa Maria Maggiore, had a neon light that drowned out even the Basilica's coffered, gilded ceiling (covered with gold from the first cargo sent back from the New World, thanks to Pope Alexander VI Borgia's devotion to the Madonna).

I was in Rome with my grandfather and grandmother. We were there to pick up three colts that the lady who rented rooms in the Via Giolitti hadn't paid us for. The lady in question, however, no longer had the horses, or the money, or even promissory notes to sign. She didn't even have two beds for us to sleep in. She was so lazy that she didn't have the energy to take off her boots when she went to bed at night. Luckily, she had a husband who helped tuck her in, with both her boots still on her feet.

In the morning, we went to the wedding of the son of the lady who rented rooms in the Via Giolitti. We woke up early. And when the bridegroom drove off in a Ford that was bright red and miles long, I noticed that he wore shoes with heels and that his hair fell over his eyes just like Bobby Solo's. And I remember that we went to eat in Testaccio. And then I don't remember a thing.

In 1968, in the Via Palestro, there was a pizza man whose collar-length hair was full of tight, oily little curls, and who had a silvery semi-automatic pistol.

Back then, I wasn't racist yet, but the pizza man was. And back then there were maybe a few dozen blacks in Rome, and they all tended to hang out around the Termini train station.

"These niggers, I'm going to shoot them in the head," the pizza man said, intently cutting pizza with one hand while he waved the pistol around with his other hand, a pistol that seemed fake but which was very real indeed. The pizza man's neck was bursting with veins, and he wore a gold bracelet and a gold cross. He would cut the pizza and wave the pistol, loose-wristed, giving it a spin before slipping it into his black coconut-fiber belt.

Early one morning, when the streetsweepers were still out with their brooms, and the roustabouts were coming in and out of the storehouse, carrying sawhorses and stalls on their shoulders, Francesco the fish vendor noticed that the pizzeria's steel shutter had been ripped open. And so they stepped cautiously in. They found the silver pistol lying drenched in the bowl of peeled tomatoes.

A few days after that, I happened to pass by one morning, and I crossed the street holding Ida Di Benedetto's hand. Ida was young and beautiful, and she wore a foulard.

In 1969, in the Via Teulada, my aunt had a cat in her apartment. That part of Rome never really looked like Rome to me. The palazzi were surrounded here and there by a little of the greenery of Monte Mario, but for the most part they had fallen prisoner to the transmitter towers of the Rai.

The cat was very old. Everyone, slavishly, would bow to it, petting it and treating it like a pasha, which is exactly what the cat thought it was. I was the only one who failed to pay the cat obeisance. So, one day, when I was sitting in the breakfast nook reading *Il Messaggero*, the pasha snatched at the newspaper with a pawful of claws, tearing it from my hands. But the real battle was waged that night.

I was sleeping in the guest room. The room that the cat occupied during the day. The door was shut. But the cat wasn't in the room, it was outside, while I was inside the room, not outside in the cat's place. And so, the exiled monarch began to scratch the wooden door frame, and tried to break the frosted glass panes. It desperately wanted in, the spoiled creature; it wanted to reclaim its kingdom. Everyone woke up. No one could tame it. The mangy old cat had turned into a ravening tiger.

The night passed like a nightmare. Luckily, the door that protected me remained shut.

The next day was Sunday. I went with my girl cousins to a party at the Piper Club. It was that afternoon that I first met the kids from the Parioli district, the Pariolini. They wore high-waisted trousers. Some of them had butterfly-shaped laces at the small of their back. Their shirts were open on their chests. And their shoes had pointed toes and two little bells on the sole. Outside, lots of boys were standing around their Mini Coopers and their GTs, listening to the soccer championship games on their radios, while others leaned against cars and motorcycles, with smiles on their lips.

Inside the Piper, my cousins and I were completely unaware that back at my aunt's house, they were still waging war with the cat. He (or she?) just wouldn't calm down. Even my uncle, who was very fond of the cat, was unable to reason with him. Apparently, the pasha finally leapt at my uncle's throat. At that point, my uncle tried to defend himself with a knife, and he plunged it into the cat's chest. The veterinarian diagnosed feline insanity.

We drove around Rome with the Pariolini. From the Via Cipro to the Piazza Augusto Imperatore, all the way up to the observatory on Monte Mario. In the Piazza Euclide, there were twice as many Pariolini. Rome seemed as dead as the day they assassinated Caesar. Julius Caesar, who conquered Cisalpine and Transalpine Gaul, and tried to cancel the memory of Marius and Sulla.

In 1970 Armando Petrosilli killed himself. He jumped out a seventh-story window, at the Alberone. He had married at the age of forty, and I don't know whether at the time it was for love, but in any case, he was ready and eager to cater to his Annetta's every whim. When I was little, my nanny (who was Annetta's mother), took me to see them, when they still lived in Campobasso, where he was serving as an officer in the Guardia Forestale. And now that I am standing in the morgue of the Verano cemetery, looking at his body with a plastic ear and a nose that doesn't look like his, I am reminded of the summer that we went to see them in Termoli. On the beach. On that wild beach. Etched in my memory by a photograph.

This much I know for certain: he had been in love with Annetta, at least I don't think they could have faked it to that degree. I was able to observe it myself when my nanny took me to their house at the Alberone. He was big and heavy-set, and he fluttered around her. He did the fluttering in her place, though she was the real bird. In fact, he called her "my little birdy."

Annetta had a relationship that had been going on for more than three decades with her uncle, who had wrested her from the claws of the nuns, where my nanny had been forced to leave her because her husband (Annetta's father) had been killed.

The forest ranger, unfailingly kind and thoughtful, from the day of his wedding, when he posed with Annetta for the photograph, their arms twisted together holding crystal glasses brimming over with spumante, one day learned the horrible truth. From then on, his hands lost their strength. The wedding pastry, water, and wine of the Castelli, and the bread of Genzano fell to the ground, while his legs began to tremble, and so did his head.

From that day on, the forest ranger began spending every blessed day in slippers and a short dressing gown, sitting by an open window overlooking the transmitter towers of the Via Appia Nuova, across from a high school, the Liceo Augusto. As time passed, he got even worse until one day, he climbed up onto the window sill, and sailed out into the void.

When he hit the ground, he looked like a crushed tin can.

Sometimes, Rome disappears. In its place, there remains the name of a street or a square, or the name of a person who reminds you of Rome. And so Rome disappears only because just then it has a different name.

The names of the Via Sommacampagna, *Sor* Andrea, and the Via dei Volsci all come to mind. Or else: the Piazza Vescovio. I was madly, deliriously in love with that square. On sunny afternoons especially, it seemed like a reliquary. A reliquary inhabited by cats. And by the three old ladies who fed them.

In 1973, '74, and '75, the Palaeur arena was a flying saucer. And the EUR quarter would turn into an immense emporium of spacecraft.

One night, during a Carlos Santana concert, the flying saucers caught fire, while earth automobiles were pelted with rocks and pounded with sticks by kids, both revolutionary and non-revolutionary. The Palaeur was in flames; it was spouting tear gas.

Pier Paolo Pasolini lived in the EUR. And that sky of a new, western Aventine, the Friuli-born poet distilled it all into *Petrolio*: a novel about cocks and skies. Certainly, the skies were not merely maritime and western, but in more general terms, Latial. And cocks, on the other hand, were units of measurement to touch variable heights of mood.

And it was in Rome that they first called me *signorino.*

I had developed a habit of going for a walk, after lunch, among the headstones of the Verano cemetery. It was just one of my usual cemetery strolls—ever since I was a child! Well, before I could go through the gate of the dead, I had to walk by a double line of flower ladies who tried to rope me in, with their carnations and lilies in hand: "*Signorino*, *signorino,* come over here to us. Take these flowers, *signorino*, you'll see, your dear departed ones will be happy."

I liked Piazza Bologna. While the last shots of the revolution were dying down and many of my future young literary friends believed that in order to become refined literati, it was necessary to take airplanes, do a translation or two, and hang out with the new small, medium and large publishers, I was going to Piazza Bologna, spending the night at Maybe and at Blue Music. And when I wasn't there, I would be getting my body into shape in the American bars of Gaeta, and then in Naples, on Sundays, I would fence, to improve my style. The only writing I knew by heart, though, was d'Annunzio and Machiavelli.

At Maybe you could find the blackest black women of all Africa. And they wouldn't do anything but give blowjobs. At Blue Music, on the other hand, you would find the most abject Roman serving girls. Or the hat-check girls who would have made Guido Gozzano's mouth water at his horniest.

As I emerged from those caverns at three in the morning, the Piazza Bologna was a huge room made of travertine. It was blank desperation. And I would write poetry.

In the eighties, I began sleeping in the street, while the others would go have fun on Saturday night. I would spend time in the shop of Pino Vinci, at the Piazza del Popolo. And in 1984 I bought a *Neapolitan Madonna*.

In 1985, I would go eat vegetable soup prepared by a woman with beauty marks. And in the Via Tiburtina there were the Leopard-women. Mario Cecchi Gori asked me to write for him. Clearly, I am a great actor. The only great Christian and animal actor.

In the nineties, Rome (the little fool) began training for immortality. The city injected its bones with calcium, to keep from dying. Doing all it can to stay alive.

O Rome, my Rome, how "unusual" you are (Amelia Rosselli), how ridiculous in your Ciociaria heaven. Bumpkin! And the cock of the gladiators? Not even up Cinecittà's asshole. But do you know, at least, what is Gioacchino Belli's most shameless con job?

(Translated by Antony Shugaar)

EPISTLE TO THE COLOSSIANS

MARIO DESIATI

1

I wait each day
in the blue night of the streetlamp
sleepless the whole time that passes
in other people's dreams.
When Wednesday comes,
market day, along the Boario Forum
right there they tell me that time
is precious, the oranges are reasonably priced
the lemons are Calabrian, the potatoes from Bologna.

I walk with the anxiety of the sick
those for whom there is no cure, those who require psychoanalysis
that is not covered. Those who pass the time in an easy chair,
stepping out for a bit, to hear the prices of the oranges,
where the lemons come from, the cabbages.

"What, you're here?" the women, the old men, call out
in surprise and it's all a rustling of bags
an intermittent noise of tumbling fruit.
I walk with this anxiety of the sick
with swollen ankles, cold hands
a burning forehead, a parched throat
I hear each day the questions hard as fruit in winter

that knocks around in shopping baskets
like a rattling cough.

When I sit, I wonder
and think, waste my time, but think
I await my last Passion, among the smell
of incense: the little sticks
those you find at village fairs
among the alternative vendors
in some hostile stall. Disjunction.
Consumption. I observe the ashes, I spread them
along the furrows of my hand. I breathe in the odor
sweet enough to burn my lungs,
I'm waiting for a phone to ring, a color to paint with.

And the hours of glass pass
I have troublesome ailments, always getting worse
in time it'll get better, they say—they warn.
At any rate tomorrow I'll have the strength to write to you.
That is enough for me, as I wait.
I turn on the radio. The music makes me happy
like potassium, chocolate and wine.
They say they are bad for me, so I wait
every day I wait, that's how I'll get better.
My mood is out of sync, the vocal chords drugged
worn out from waiting, a novel touches me.
I don't want to mislead you. I need it.
I want to be happy.

I go to bed late, better this way
I sleep less, wake up at ten
the sheets wet with sweat and nightmares

rough seas: the invasion of Albania, Luciana
colonialism in the Dodecanese islands.
The buzz of the alarm clock. Dampness.
The radio brings news that there is a new government.
Are these dreams? I sleep little
too little to have common dreams.

At the post office the lineup is amusing
when people quarrel, there is a fragrance
in the presence of attractive mothers who still possess the feeling
of being women, of being loved.
At the post office I wait one hour, perhaps two
then those mothers with the knee-length skirts
the black stockings, the high heels, the vulnerable eyes
go away, and I feel ill
I smell the awful odors, the fire burns inside
my temples a river of slime.

I don't know which road to take
the old mule-track goes straight
to town
the highway makes a big,
stupid detour, surrounds the countryside
the commuter parking lots
you can see the Ilva range,
the craters of enormous caves, then
finally, you get to the town.
When we take the old mule-track
I gather old newspapers, all kinds
tomato sauce stained dailies
tabloids dirtied with sperm, a book.
The poems of Giuseppe Giusti.

2

Now they are knocking, they probe the territory
they know about the godlessness
a censer, the aspergillum and lots of cold
water sprinkled along the walls.
The neurotic step echoes
under the icy vault of the church
through the hurried murmuring of the rosary
in the benedictions of the host and on the chalice held tightly

and then this clinking of the vessels
right behind the sacristan's back
in the rotten odor of the refectory
and the residual water of baptisms
with the mice that run over architraves
and the blackened organ pipes
mice with monkey-like faces, furtive
awaiting the word of the Lord.

And minutes would pass in waiting
oppressive silences broken by knocked-over benches
and a cry like a blackbird's
announced Christmas, Easter
religious feasts, storms
                                        and how
similar that leaden sky was
to an aristocratic overture of an end foretold.

3

The Dead

The dead come back to us unexpected
half-hidden in unknown faces
they turn on the intermittence of leave-taking
break the fragile thread of forgetfulness.

These far away faces come back
in the gazes of the new neighbor
of the landlord, that old schoolmate
or even in the movement of clothes hanging on a line
in the black garbage bags full of wind
tumbling over the countryside
as the tractor rolls by, in the smell
of spring.
For a sudden brief flash
the plastic gleams golden
by grassy old stones and empty snow-caves
you meet departed friends, stunned old women
whom you hadn't seen in years.

The dead come back to us unexpected
at our arrival at the station, among the traveling salesmen
washed-out knick-knack merchants
long-faced Algerian peddlers
the Indians of the Termini station, pockmarked drug addicts.
Those great big flocks in Piazza Cinquecento
on their way east to avoid the smoke

of the espressos and the engines
they are garnet autumn leaves.
They make you wish you were old.

(Translated by Antonino Mazza)

SAURO NEVER GETS ANGRY

ELENA STANCANELLI

You just can't go to the Capocotta beach on Saturdays or Sundays. It's too crazy, the road is all backed up. Cars are double-parked on the right-hand side, their engines running because they can't find a spot, and mopeds are chained, one after the other up against the dunes. You have to walk barefoot in the middle of the street, weaving your way through the brutal traffic, with your magazines slipping out from under your sweaty armpits. And the lines to buy sandwiches, the screams, the beach paddles, the parachute surfing, the suntan lotions, the sand shaken from the towels, the helicopters . . .

That's what people say on Saturdays and Sundays, even as they are sprawled out on Capocotta beach getting a tan. Then, every once in a while, they get up and take a dip, and when they come back, they say you can't go swimming at Capocotta because the water's too dirty. Meanwhile, they clutch their towels to their chests and shake the water from their wet hair all over the backs of their sleeping friends. I walk along and for me it's all the same. I do have to be a little more careful so that I don't trip over the women's pantyless butts that meld into a single mattress of flesh on Saturdays and Sundays; or accidentally stare at the throng of naked men swinging their "thing" around with ease. Everything else is the same, neither better nor worse.

On the beach I never take off my gym shoes, long pants, T-shirt, red Ferrari baseball cap on backwards, or my leather shoulder bag. I sell music-CDs. When someone calls me over I walk up to them and hand them an entire stack of CDs. Each person leafs through them and if he can't find what he wants, I hand him the others, pulling them out of my bag. I keep I Nomadi, Queen, the Cure, David Bowie, and Blink 182 in the bag, but I hold onto Laura Pausini, Saranno Famosi, Tiziano Ferro, Buddha Bar, and Moby. Some of the naked men, usually the ones that are alone and who strut back and forth along the shoreline before jumping in the water, ask me for different things: Patty Pravo, Mina, the *Moulin Rouge* soundtrack, Madonna. It's a kind of password, always followed by a smile. I don't go behind the dunes. Not even if there's a fair amount of money at stake. I'm from Senegal and I'm Catholic. When I can't sleep I think about it over and over. Especially the nights that I sleep on the floor. There are nights when I sleep on the floor and nights when I get to sleep on the bed, taking turns with the other guy. But in the end I always come to the same realization: that in my opinion men should act as men and women as women. But that's just what I think. Other people can do as they please.

Sauro sleeps behind the dunes, concealed by a kind of hutch made from sheet metal and covered with branches. In the evening, after sunset, he swims in the sea—like me, when the beach has emptied out. We swim side by side, and his wetsuit glitters in the wake of the sun. I'm faster but I wait for him because the way he does the breaststroke makes me laugh. He says he doesn't put his head under because he doesn't want to hear the sound of the sand scraping against the rocks.

When we're further out I pretend to drown him. Sauro never gets angry, even if he's only fourteen and, despite being Italian, has to sleep in his hutch amidst the dunes.

"What about your parents?"

His wetsuit has short sleeves. It's big on him, and he has this habit of sticking his hands inside the opening for his skinny little arms, wriggling around until he gets them to pop out at the neck. It's like one of those jokes where you pretend to strangle yourself. Sauro never replies. I've never seen anyone like him. He's different, unique.

He's blond, but never combs his hair, so it's down to his shoulders and tangled. The wetsuit, which he never takes off, covers his legs and most of his body. You can only see his feet, which are very small. When it rains, he stays closed up in his hutch and paints his nails red with polish he found on the beach. He's good at finding things and he also digs through the bar's garbage for food. Among the things that he's found is a pocket mirror. Ever since then, whenever he wants to be silly, he calls me Sauro, like him. I turn around and he starts laughing, with that little girl's mouth of his.

I gave him my CD player. The one that I played the CDs on at the beach before selling them. Now the customers have to trust me, which is actually better. I sell more. They look me in the face and then decide, he's honest; it's something about my eyes, forget about fingerprints. And I only sell the good CDs. I choose them in the evening, listening to them on the CD player which belongs to the guy who sleeps in my bed. The ones that sound only so-so, I give to Sauro.

In return, he shaves my head. He has a real gift for it, a light touch. He lathers me up with shaving cream, taking care not to let it drip into my eyes, and then he shaves my head, from my forehead to the nape of my neck, from one ear to the other, over the bony bumps. He leaves my scalp so smooth, like a statue, and then he tightens my baseball cap. When my head's been freshly shaved and I go swimming, I can feel the water breaking, its coolness falling over me like snails around my head. Then I get out and I shake my head as if I have hair, and Sauro laughs. Sometimes he isn't there. So I go look for him, slipping my clothes over my soaking skin, and we have a cigarette together in front of his hutch while I wait for the bus.

Sauro has a beautiful voice. It's strange to think of it as his voice. It's truly moving. It seems like a little bird's, soft and high-pitched, or like that of a little girl. But it's also strong and confident. He sings in English; he learns all the songs from the CDs that I give him and he doesn't understand a word. Yet, he echoes them perfectly. When I don't find him at the hutch, I look for him by following his voice. Even when he is off in the distance, in some out-of-the-way place, his voice reaches me like an arrow.

That was the only time I ever saw him without his wetsuit. In fact, it was actually the wetsuit that I saw first, tossed on the sand as though it were Sauro lying there dead. I stopped dead in my tracks, my heart pounding. Ridiculous really, because meanwhile I could hear him singing, so he couldn't be dead. How stupid of me. When I tell Sauro about this, we'll have a good laugh. And as I climbed up the dune I could hear him singing "Your Song" by Elton John, like in *Moulin Rouge*. It was almost dark because it was late and big clouds loomed above. It was one of those torrid days and I was sweating like a leaking gutter.

The naked man couldn't see me because he had his eyes closed. He was sitting with his back against a rock. Sauro was nestled in between his legs and he was singing. His tangled hair was somewhat buried in the sand. Both of them were bathed in sweat, I don't know how they couldn't be cold. Even in the heat, my teeth chattered on that horrible night, with all those clouds, the wind, and the sand blowing in my eyes. I would have liked at least to have turned around my cap to shield myself with the visor, but I was worried they might notice me. I didn't want to make my presence known. I remained motionless in front of the two of them. They looked like a tree, like the twisted trunk of an olive tree.

Sauro's skin was as I had imagined: white as snow, thin, pure. His back, twisted and thin in that embrace, looked like a wrinkled gauze curtain. But it was crossed lengthwise by folds, a kind of embroidery of scars, blows, whip lashes—I don't know. It was both a beautiful and monstrous sight to behold. And that naked man listened with a blissful smile to the song of his little battered bird.

At sunset, the people on the beach usually begin to leave. A lot of people say that twilight is the most beautiful time of day because it isn't hot and the hustle and bustle has died down, but as they say this they're departing together with everyone else. Except Saturdays and Sundays, when they sit at the bar and have an aperitif. Someone might take a stroll or a last dip in the water. The beach doesn't really clear out on Saturdays and Sundays until nine or ten, when it's already dark.

Taking small steps, Sauro covers the distance between the dunes and sea. The people who have stayed on the beach turn to look at him. He seems like one of those young kids that travel the world surfing, one of those types, covered with tattoos and piercings, that bring their dogs to the beach and never wear swimsuits. But he is much skinnier and walks in a funny way, as though he were afraid of the sand, feeling it burning under his feet. He starts to run and it's as if he has little wooden sticks for legs, like little birds before they have learned how to fly.

As soon as he arrives, I jump in the water and wait for him. I have left my bag, cap, and clothes at the water's edge.

Sauro's wetsuit glistens like silver in the light of sunset. His back moves up and down on the water's surface, and I think of what lies underneath, of those rope-like lines etched in his white flesh. I think to myself that perhaps by dint of swimming they could dissolve, that one day I might see them emerge from under the wetsuit, slither out from the ankle openings like worms and slide past my well-shaven head. I swim behind him even though I could go much faster. We go out a great distance from the shore and as we swim, someone is stealing my bag of CDs back on shore. We don't know where to go, there are no buoys to reach, no boats to cling to. We swim, nothing more. I do the crawl, and he the breaststroke. Every once in a while we stop and I pretend to drown him. Sauro never gets angry.

(Translated by Lawrence Garner and Julia Garner)

BIRTHDAY OF THE IGUANA

SILVIA BALLESTRA

Around four in the afternoon he showed up at the Medusa, a ratty, rundown beach club of sorts. Pale Girl was watching the attacking hook shots that Ziocane was launching against the defending figures manned by his friend Francia. With each furious shot, the foosball table moved an inch or two across the floor, tipped up on one set of legs, while the spare balls in the side compartment rattled furiously against the wooden frame.

Somebody told him once that he looked like John Lydon, but he could care less. He had dyed his hair fuchsia the last time he was in Hamburg. Fuchsia hair, like an authentic two-bit drug dealer.

He sniffed loudly, tucked a cigarette behind his ear, and looked around. "Fucking hot," he said, staring vaguely at tourist couples outside the glass. He pulled away from the line of plate-glass windows that ran along the wall overlooking the water, and moved over to the perch around the soccer table. "Were you waiting for me?" he asked, flatly.

"As if," replied Pale Girl. She thought to herself that for the past forty-five minutes she had been keeping an eye on the front gate, the hedges of Japanese mock orange plants, the emptiness all around her. She had been keeping an eye on emptiness: a front gate leading to emptiness, mock orange bushes enclosing emptiness.

He said, "I went everywhere, looked in every corner of Porto San Giorgio. Nothing going on in that morgue. I even went over to the Rotonda, but there was no sign of Betto. I'll bet that idiot's still asleep." He waved a hand at Francia and Ziocane without looking over at them, and stood there looking at Pale Girl's profile. He shrugged. "You don't give a shit, do you?" he said. "I do, though. I give a shit, and my veins give a shit. Let me tell you."

He ran in place, cartoonishly, lifting his knees exaggeratedly: Sylvester the cat on the run. He laughed. "Come on, let's beat it. Want to go?" he asked her.

He walked off, paying no attention to whether Pale Girl was following him. He strode purposefully over to the water fountain beneath the shed-roof of the beach club, pulled the insulin out of its transparent case, and turned on the faucet. The stream of water filled the little plastic bag. He clamped the top shut with two fingers, turned toward Pale Girl, and held out his arm. The plastic sac, swollen with water, wobbled slightly. He gave her a look of ironic camaraderie, and said, "You mind lifting your feet?" He handed her the precious little plastic bag, as if he were a young carny running a booth in a sideshow. "No goldfish, this time. Sorry."

"What kind of prize is this, then?" asked Pale Girl.

"Dead, the goldfish is dead. It must have drowned." He walked back to the beach club. "Wait there for a second, please," he added. He disappeared behind the hedge of mock orange, leaving her standing like a fool, holding her booby prize.

Pale Girl folded her arms and tried to hide the plastic bag as best she could. She just didn't want to look like a fucking fifteen-year-old girl who was into enabling addicts. She leaned back against the white cement wall that separated the sidewalk from the beach. She looked down the line of alternating palm trees and oleander bushes that stretched out along the beachfront, the sequence of parallel beach umbrellas behind it. This was some sort of strange central Italian Texas, right here.

He re-emerged from the mock orange hedge with a can of Coke and half a lemon, wrapped in a paper napkin, in one hand. He was hurrying along, overwhelmed by a stickler's attention to the details of the ritual.

He seized Pale Girl by the wrist. "I need to talk to you," he said. "It's important."

"Where are we going?" asked Pale Girl. She jerked her wrist away. "Look, I have an appointment at the dermatologist at five o'clock," she said.

"At the dermatologist," he repeated, sarcastically. He shifted his weight from one foot to the other. "What the fuck are you going to see a dermatologist for?" he asked. He snickered to himself. "I got it. You have some damn STD, don't you?"

"No, it's not an STD," replied Pale Girl. "Maybe I just need a doctor to help me get rid of creeps like you."

He shook his head, tugged her along by the sleeve without saying another word.

Together they crossed the road, the two yards of short grass that covered the median strip, until they reached the little white Fiat 127 parked diagonally against the sidewalk. He got in on the driver's side, stretched his arms out on the steering wheel, and looked around anxiously. He said, "Well, what the hell are you waiting for?" He adjusted the inside rearview mirror, rolled down the window on the passenger's side, and leaned out. "Oh, you asshole," he hissed. He got out, walked quickly around the car, just inches from the line of the hood, and jerked her door open, with plenty of unnecessary roughness. He said, "Okay. Get in."

"Okay," she said, "I'll get in. But you have to swear we'll be back in town by five."

"I swear," he said. He took the plastic bag full of water from her hand. "Now get in." He went back around to the driver's side, laid the open end of the bag between the door frame and the door, and left it there, abandoned on the floor like a soft pear. He started the engine.

He had said that he needed to talk to her about something important, but now he was close-mouthed. He drove the 127 as if he were riding a motorcycle. As if the car occupied less road space, as if it could zip away with the acceleration of a two-cycle engine.

They drove past faces displaying the typical local physiognomy, broad as tambourines, with eyes the size of saucers, icons of Our Lady of the Ambro dangling from the interior rearview mirrors, crappy souvenir decals of the Monti Sibillini.

"You're so quiet," the guy said, every so often. "So far away, little sister."

Pale Girl said nothing.

They pulled up behind a Jaguar, British racing green, license plate TE 197235. If it had ended in an even number, she felt certain that he would have stopped his bitching. She liked playing secret little games with license plate numbers.

He said, "If you loved me, you'd try to make me quit. You really ought to, you know? I mean, for the good of yours truly. But, obviously, you don't care about my health. You're just a selfish kid, that's all. A little bitch who wants to have some experience with outsiders like us. You think it's exciting that I shoot up, don't you? You think it's exciting for some poor idiot to shoot shit into his veins. It really makes your motor rev, doesn't it?"

"You're just a filthy pig. You talk like a filthy pig," Pale Girl replied.

"I'm a filthy pig, huh? Well, let me tell you something, little sister. There are people who make their living off of filthy pigs like me. Filthy pigs like us come in very handy to plenty of the shitheads out there. And you know what I think? I think that you don't get it, you don't understand a thing, you don't know what it means to be a fucking sacrificial lamb in this goddamned sewer!"

"Oh, Jesus," she said. "You sound like a broken record, friend. Really. You just whine and whine, friend." She slid her back down on the car seat, lifted her legs up, and planted her feet against the dashboard. She hummed the final riff of "Jimmy Jazz" by the Clash, while he whizzed through a tight curve, the steering wheel spinning rapidly under his fingers.

"Of course," he told her. "What else could you possibly say? Well, thanks, thanks a lot," he added, slowing down as they came up to the intersection with the state highway. "Nice fucking girlfriend you turn out to be. What a shitty friend, Jesus H. Christ."

"You don't have a friend," answered Pale Girl. She got the dashboard dirty with her shoes, then she pulled her packet of Marlboros from her shirt pocket. She said, pronouncing the words carefully: "You know what you really want right now? You want to shoot up. You just want to shoot your veins full of beautiful smack. That's all you can think about, isn't it?" She watched him shivering in withdrawal, his eyelids quivering, beads of flopsweat along his forehead and neck. She did not feel pity for him, not even a little, with all his warning signs of a young desperate animal. She said, "Then why don't you get high, just this once. If you do, we'll all feel better."

"Sure," he said. "We'll all feel better. Me and my arms, we'll all feel better." He bit his lip. She glimpsed a flash of white teeth.

He gave an angry smack to the bunch of keys that dangled from the car's ignition. He said, "Do you have any idea that all my friends in the street are warning me to stay away from you? They're all telling me that you fifteen-year-old girls could fuck me up. You're dangerous, because it's easy for you to find someone to fuck you, that's why." Then he proffered a squishy smile, a lover's smile, and added in a whimper: "You could really make me suffer, if you keep acting like this."

"Horseshit," said Pale Girl. "Truth is, guys who are twenty-three who go around with a spare spike in the glove box, looking for girls who are fifteen who want to have their cherries popped, their armcherry after their main cherry . . . those guys are really dangerous, when they tell their friends, 'That bitch doesn't want to shoot up!' God! they're dangerous, and God! they're filthy pigs."

He shrugged, snickering to himself. "You're crazy," he said, sarcastically. "I'm not sure what kind of crazy, but according to yours truly, your brain isn't hitting on all four." He shook his head. "Who the fuck understands you, you psycho," he said.

They pulled up onto the cliff over the cemetery, at the end of a completely empty country lane. He stopped the 127 at the edge of the little lane. It was a fairly clean spot, compared with other junkie hangouts.

He pulled the aluminum-foil packet of smack from the interior compartment of his plastic ID holder, and clamped it between his lips. He pulled a cigarette out of Pale Girl's packet, ripped apart the cellulose fibers, and slipped the filter between his lips, too. He popped open the can of Coca-Cola. "Want some?" he asked.

Pale Girl shook her head, and looked down at the open space down below.

The guy poured the soda out the car window. He rummaged under the dashboard, and said "Do you mind very much moving your legs out of my way?" He found an Exacto knife at the far end of the little shelf, cut the opening of the soda can, and then started rummaging under the dashboard again. "Move! What the fuck are you making that face for, you arrogant little bitch?" he said. He tugged a Kleenex from its packet, and dried the bottom of the soda can. He buffed and polished his little oven.

He performed each step of the ritual with evident satisfaction, looking over at her after each one to see if she was duly impressed.

"Tonight, everyone from the street is going to the Oceanic," he told her. "There's a party in honor of Iggy Pop. It's the Iguana's birthday. Just think, Iggy Pop is turning forty. I could pick you up around ten and go by, take a look. Cesaretto's going," he said. "So's Mimmo, so's Fabio."

"I've got to stay in tonight," Pale Girl said. "My old man is on the warpath, he's plenty pissed at yours truly. Plus, the crowd from the street turn my stomach. Even if they're having a party for Iggy Pop. They just make me puke."

He said nothing. He just shook his head and continued with his work.

Pale Girl knew the liturgy in detail; by now she knew it as well as he did. In the few months she'd been hanging out with him, she had seen him in action loads of times. Still, she did her best to watch every single step, not to miss a thing. It was exactly like going by a place where there's just been a crash, and everything's still fresh, with shattered bits of orange reflective plastic and puddles of battery acid on the asphalt.

He reached back and grabbed his canvas jacket from the rear seat, pulled his spike out of the right pocket, and opened the driver's side door, taking care not to spill water out of the priceless plastic bag.

He slid the needle into the plastic film. He was light years away from everything, now, nicely catapulted out of the car interior.

He performed the rest of his checklist carefully, then held out his spike, erect, in his right hand. He showed off his relay-race baton from the junkie Olympics, and muttered, "Christ on a crutch, this is my last fix." He looked at Pale Girl, sunk in his silence, intent as any bomb squad technician as he fingered the flesh of his neck. When he tipped his head back, she saw his slender throat, the throat of a boy.

He craned to line up the field of view of the inside rearview mirror. He tilted the mirror slightly downward. "I'm going to shoot a lot, Jesus fucking Christ," he said. He plunged the needle into his neck. He slowly pushed down on the plunger. He was gentle now, so careful and delicate in every motion, the way he never was when he was between her legs, penetrating her. He let the plunger sink down the graduated cylinder of the syringe, but stopped before it reached the bottom. He turned to look at Pale Girl. "There's three lines left, little sister," he said. "You want me to leave some for you?"

She kept a lookout outside the car. "Listen, don't get swept away with your generosity," she answered. She looked out over the deathly composition of the funerary vaults down below, climbing up the cliff side, the prow of the cemetery jutting out over the sea with the huge angel, visible from afar, that cared for the souls of the dead. She heard his voice, crumpling, as he said, "Good girl, I'm glad to see you're stronger than that, you know?"

He thought he could indulge in certain sermons from his needle-ridden pulpit.

Then he said to her, "There'll be hell to pay if I ever find out that you're messing with this shit." Once the white shit started flowing through his veins, his usual traits of a wasted father-figure bobbed to the surface. "I'll beat you black and blue if I find out that you're shooting up," he said. "Because you understand that I'm just putting you to the test, right?" He booted, pulling a plume of vermilion blood back into the graduated cylinder of the syringe. "I'm proud of my tough little girl," he said, glassily.

His head slumped back on the car seat, the pallor of an anemic vegetable welling up in his face, the relaxed deterioration of a comatose junkie. He scratched his nose.

Pale Girl looked at his half-closed, wrinkled eyelids, the all-mighty syringe dangling from his neck.

He was panting now, flopped over on the car seat.

"Hey, what the hell's wrong with you? Are you okay?" she said to him. She reached out for one of his hands, but it was completely limp. She pulled the spike out of his neck, tried to clean away the bit of blood around the puncture, wiping with a Kleenex. "Hello?" she said, but he said nothing. He was slumped awkwardly against the car door, his forehead pressed onto the glass. He went down in slow motion, like a duffel bag full of rags. She took him by the shoulder and shook him, but it was no good. She couldn't wake him up from that astonishing sleep.

There were a couple of Flying Dutchman class sailboats pitching and yawing just offshore, the triangles of their sails perfectly distinct against the horizon. It was a strange thing. The sailboats were skimming swiftly along on the surface of the water, but way up here, instead, the air was perfectly still.

Pale Girl was sitting on the ground, leaning back against the front bumper of the 127. For sure she would completely miss her appointment with the dermatologist now.

"I'm fifteen years old, and I am completely immersed in fiction," she said to herself. "And him, back there, he's twenty-three, and he is immersed with smack up to his neck."

She thought to herself how much she cared about him, jerk that he was, just because he had been her first one. With his officially accepted girlfriend, who lived at Torre di Palme, a more-or-less secret boyfriend, and the rest of the fine company of hopheads that he would hang out with whenever withdrawal would force him to get off his ass, she felt like getting into the car and shaking him awake, slapping him silly, force him to get dressed and drive that junkheap out of there. Tell him that no one could stand to talk with this welling pool of tears always in his pocket and all these melodramatic junkie morality plays, like all the druggies that seemed to sprout up around there.

A little later, the guy started calling her. He wanted her to help him get out of the car because he was fine, just fine, but he felt a little weak, that was all.

"Hey, little sister," he was saying. "Right here, little sister!"

(Translated by Antony Shugaar)

TWO POEMS

MARCO MANTELLO

Rocco '78

Dear Lucia,
I'm afraid that special agents
of the police
will knock at the door one fine day
and take me away.

I'm afraid "the best years
of my life"
will be a discotheque sign;
I'm afraid to go down the street
with the letter A for anarchy
and such a mid-eastern profile
that I can't gaze for long at others
standing still, resounding.

I'm afraid of rhymes with rose.

Dear Lucia,
I'm afraid of your "How come"
and of immigration centers;
I'm afraid of tobacconists,
of razors and gyms;
I'm afraid of those

who never do without and then
start talking about "we."

I'm afraid of my grandmother
and of the blood she says she sees
on the bronze face
of the Madonna;

I'm afraid of light, certain evenings.

Dear Lucia,
I'm afraid of open windows
and the height of Italians;
I'm afraid the new broomflowers
won't grow well in the city;
I'm afraid that wherever I go
I'll end at the sea—here it is now!
I'm afraid all the traffic laws
will force us to die peacefully in bed.
I'm afraid of the "Please don't"
of the "Observe the"
printed on a black panel
from Monday to Friday
and never claimed.

I'm afraid of the crosses of crusaders
of round communion wafers
and of what they put inside.
I'm afraid our love
is a moderate one

Then, dear Lucia,
if tomorrow I take a gun
with me to school,
I'm afraid that the special agents
of the police
will also go to your house
looking for this poem.

So rinse out your mouth

and read me carefully
since you're the only one
able to prove
we were together that day:

I, with fingers crossed
up to the last minute—
you, with pale lips
screaming the opposite of help.

Tears of the Punkabbestia[1]

From when I picked up the vice
of breathing
from when the razor I keep in my pocket
cut up my hands,

I have always loved the same person—
maybe because
I could see in her eyes
my own bell ringing

I buried my dog in Freiburg
under the grass of a field
where the Germans once
broke crystal
that no one has changed

On the brass tombstone
filled with stars of David
and arabesques,
it took two days to engrave her name
and then I added: "your master"

with a crest red enough
to be envied by the reddest
imaginable sunset,
by the still bright light of the boulevards

---

[1] *Punkabbestia* is the name given since the 90s to people who live in the streets, often in groups and always with lots of dogs, who dress punk style. In Rome they usually gather in Trastevere and Campo de' Fiori (editor's note).

in the passersby with shopping bags
in their damned glasses
without any color.

If that night I even vomited
my heart,
it was the only way there was
to keep both eyes dry
and leave spoiled food
on the ground, at least for the pigeons.

(Translated by Ann Snodgrass)

THE SHIP

Giosuè Calaciura

I was already a Nigerian *buttana*[1] and didn't know it as I crossed the swamp barefoot to fill up the goatskin bag. I was afraid of the swamp. Its mists had swallowed up all of the village's missing. And to build up my courage I would sing the song of the anteater who eats ants and of the hyena who eats the anteater—and all the animals of creation would devour one another over the course of my singsong rhyme. An endless chain of animals, but it wasn't enough to stifle my fears. Even those fears, though, became part of the game: I felt lost in the fog, and I pretended that there was no one left in the world but me, leaving imprints of my bare feet, making the sounds of splashing water, master of all the animals, queen of the swamp. And that lasted until I got to the last few pools of water just beyond the mist, where I could glimpse the silhouettes of women and hear them talking, though they couldn't see me. But by then I'd filled the goatskin bag and wasn't afraid anymore, because I was on my way back.

My mother used to send me to fetch the water because I was the oldest. I had strong, round arms, presaging an adolescence filled with dreams, and tiny, brittle ankles for playing in the schoolyard of the mission, where they taught me God in the afternoon. Maybe it was there that I became a *buttana*, because I fantasized about the priest's member brushing against my soul, I imagined the evening shadows,

---

[1] The author uses the Sicilian word for "whore," buttana, with slightly euphemistic connotations (translator's note).

his hands, the white, immaculate skin of his buttocks. I can't remember having fantasized about anything else.

I became a *buttana* when the ship was out to sea. It was a ship all rusted out and it didn't even have its navigational lights on. They had us board the ship at night, but we didn't depart right away. They were waiting for favorable winds and a pause in the patrols which monitored the entrance to the port. We stayed in the ship's stronghold that entire night and the next day. It was hot, and we had to keep quiet or they threatened to put us ashore. We marveled at the miracle of the floating ship, and in the twilight we followed the sea's reflection in shimmering waves, which made sounds like moths.

We left at night, and it was pitch black. In the hold there were no more reflections of shimmering light—there was only blackness, repeated a thousand times over, countless times; and a thousand times over the sound of suffocating gasps, the salvation novena, the prayer of the tormented. And everybody repeating ad infinitum the little story they'd memorized on departure in order to fool the coast guard, the port authorities, the border guards, the customs officials— first names, last names, lies, countries of uncertain idiom: "I come from the Tukul," "from the other side of the Atlas mountains," "from beyond Lake Victoria." And each one without a face—only short breaths in the darkness, performing the shaman's rites against the evil eye or invoking his formulae for good luck, repeated over and over again and driving you crazy. It gets all confused and jumbled up in your mind, because later, when they asked me where I was from, I answered, "I know how to cook, I know how to cook, I know how to cook." And when they asked me what my legal status was, I answered, "My name is Shobba, but you can call me Dalia, Ophelia, or Felicity, and if you give me papers you can fuck me, and if you don't tell anyone you've seen me, you can bugger me."

And in the hold, the darkness of my own skin blurred into and joined with the darkness of the skin of others, trembling with fear no matter the little tricks we used to try to lessen it. The only smells I could recognize were sweat and the acrid odor of fermented excrement—they wouldn't allow us into other bowels of the ship. And when they opened the skylights to pass down the potato rations, sailors wearing shoes were shocked by the stench, and they cursed, and they left some places open for air to get in. Others appeared over the opening where a crack of light came in, and we could see a human silhouette counting us, looking at us, listening to us. They would stay there for a long time, observing us, studying us. Then they would close the hatch, like a submarine, and we would drown in our oxygenless night, in our own breath—talking to one another only with our breathing, because we hadn't found words for our new condition as seafarers. There were only the remains of little singsong rhymes from the swamp, songs from the rainy season, prayers to placate the hungry lions. I prayed, my cheeks stinging with the chill of the bulkhead, and in that darkness I didn't want to see, I didn't want to imagine the other faces—because they were the same as mine.

I became a *buttana* because he penetrated me, taking me with my back turned, and he moved with the certitude of the ship's engine, and I loved him because he was not part of that wave of gasping. He pinned my back down with his elbow and put a hand to my mouth. As he took my virginity, my cheeks were pressed against the steel, swelling up as they hit against the wall. And my ear could hear the straining metal of the connecting rods turning in the engine's cylinders. Along with the coded sound of the engine I could hear the water splashing up against the hull and the cries of the whales as they made way for the surging prow of the ship. And I implored them, "Sink it with your mighty tails, wipe it out with one great swirling surge." And I could hear the call of the dolphins, gathering together to leap over the waves with an instinctive, aimless joy. And I could sense the creatures of the deep observing from the ocean floor the outline of the enormous, black ship as it passed on, leaving in its wake a trail of swill. I felt the trembling of the starfish and the octopus tightening its grip on its rock, the shark gone mad and the flying manta ray torn asunder, the schools of silvery fish which had lost their path. It seemed to me as though all the flesh of the sea—in reality so indifferent and distant—were shuddering on account of my pain. And through the fingers of his hand I let out a moan—and he gave me a pitying caress by lessening the pressure of his elbow. Pleading with him, I called him mother. But I wasn't crying out for my mother. I cursed him with a gesture of my hand, and I sunk my nails into his forehead because there was nothing closer to me in all the world. And again, the pressure of the elbow, enough to break my bones, and I loved him, crying out to him not to abandon me to the thud of the engine, to the dizzying swirl of the sea, on this first night of my many nights of cocks and loneliness.

When streaks of morning light lit up all the faces, I went searching, and one by one I looked into the whites of their eyes. With each stirring of a blanket they turned their gaze upwards, and in all of them I could only find astonishment that we were afloat. And no one carried on his forehead the mark of my curse. I alone could see: he had opened the eye of my belly while I was half-asleep in my inner oceans, now dried up into crusts of blood on my thighs.

And they want to turn back. But neither the God of men, nor the God of water, nor the God of snakes ever showed me another path.

We would go down to the waterfront in groups from our rooms just off alleyways. The rooms had a single window looking out over an eternally unchanging wall just opposite. And I traveled all my days along those four walls: all the cracks, the mold, every bit of salt caked on them, the clumps of paint. It was a perimeter without surprises, which varied only when it rained. The colors and hues became even gloomier. That universe had a single vantage point: from the bed. But I never slept in that room—only poorly paid fucks after a round of blowjobs to the rhythms of music coming from the other side of the alley. Of my take, I had to give so much to the landlord, so much to the laundry woman who did the sheets, so much for electricity and water, so much to my boss, and what was left I got. But even this left-over went back to the boss. After all, he paid for the condoms, and my whole life, even the sheets and the laundry, belonged to him. He got the wallets of the customers, those who were down and out or so exhausted they fell asleep, he got the IOUs from the deadbeats, the reduced rates of the dissatisfied, the silence of the impotent guys, the grocer's vegetables, the baker's cannoli and all the other payments in kind and merchandise, the made-up stories of the loafers, the threats of the thugs. And I was rewarded with words of encouragement and "good work"—except for the times he slapped me and split my lip, and then another slap would come my way because now there was a reason: "You asked me why I did it." Then came a third slap because I didn't say anything, a fourth one because I failed to amuse him, and a fifth one just to be playful and comfort me before fucking me.

An hour after sunset a pack of us would go down to the water-front. Halfway down we would discover a reflection of ourselves in the store windows, a bewildered band of four dressed-up hookers. Along the road they picked us out one by one, and they had us get into their cars and took us away, but not far. And we would look at ourselves laughing in the reflection, one next to the other, our faces all pale on account of the powder that had whitened them, changing our color and erasing all expression from our faces. That pallor made us all look the same, with our stained leggings, the scuffed-up shoes with stiletto heels, worn down and splintered, our smiling gums as red as blood. And we would do little dance steps to see them reflected in the windows, and, as we clutched one another and laughed, we would make our way towards the waterfront. And with us, little Indian children would go down to the waterfront in two's with roses they'd stolen from funeral wreaths, and they'd try to sell them in restaurants.

They'd look at us, hiding their eyes behind the petals, and they'd work up their courage to ask me, "Are you a 'ho?" "I'm like your mother, a hooker with black skin, foreign pussy, a dark hole where the lion who eats you gasps his last breath." And they would run off laughing, telling each other the illusion of another fairy tale.

We would go down towards the waterfront and occupy strategic corners, and we would gesture "come, come," and with the thumb and index finger of the left hand forming a circle we would push the index finger of the right hand through the circle: fuck, fuck. Special fuck.

"All the girls fuck. All I have to do is go around this corner and I can find a hundred 'special' fucks. What do you do that's so special?"

A blowjob. I'll put your balls in my mouth too.

"A blowjob is nothing special. Do me with your asshole."

My asshole goes for a hundred thousand lire.

"Jesus, do ya shit gold or somethin'? Nothing but shit comes outta your asshole too, ya know."

An ass like mine, you've never seen before. Look at how high and firm it is.

"Gimme a touch."

You want to touch, you have to pay.

"If ya want a hundred thousand, ya have to let me touch it first."

I walk around him and look at him. Then I turn my back to him and stroke my ass in his face.

"I want to feel your ass with my own hands."

I walk around him a second time, and, with my back turned to him, raise my skirt.

Only the ass!

"And the hundred thousand includes pussy too."

First give me the hundred thousand.

"And the pussy alone, how much is it?"

Forty-five thousand.

"Forty thousand, an even amount."

The five thousand are for the ass touching.

"I'll give you thirty-five, but first you have to wash your pussy."

Washed, it costs a lot more.

"How much more?"

A lot more, because it makes me feel cold, and you've got to pay extra for the chill it gives me.

And we would go down to the sea, where there's a convent and the night, the sound of the outgoing tide like breathing, the labored gasping of the asthmatics, the verses of the inspired, the angry cursing of those who have come for the first time and are repulsed at discovering the sewer stench of the sea, the desolation of the metal junk left to rust, the washing machines gutted to serve as love stations. And we recognize one another because our powdered faces shine and beckon to one another. And all of us are there, glimmers of black hookers ready to cleanse ourselves in the sea. I had never seen it before, even though it had carried me there. Now I look at it for a long time, the way I look at a lover who has thrown me on the trunk of a car and I have to pretend to like it—and in the blackness of the sea a navigational light is passing, suspended in mid-air like the moon. It's the ship of my redemption, and I am on it, and I can see myself, as it carries me in the pure blackness of my beginnings somewhere else, following the other path of my destiny, guided by the cardinal point of another compass. I'm the one there on the deck, and I wave my hand to myself, and I wave back, together with all the animals of the singsong rhymes from the swamp that had come on board Noah's Ark without purpose, and now are saved.

(Translated by Lawrence Garner)

SIX POEMS

FRANCESCA GENTI

My Constructive Side

it's my grandfather
he's a surveyor
and in his hand is a blueprint

here he sets some trees
here a field of poppies
here three large pots
farther off the sea

he spreads gravel along the walkway

here he sets a house
inside, charcoal for Christmas

to the right a wood oven for the grilled meats
two benches for laughter
farther away other trees
then more poppies.

farther still a cemetery

he takes the glue
he takes the ladder
climbs up to the sky
attaches the sun

climbs down the ladder
comes in from the balcony
over the bed
he attaches love.

(in the kitchen
the cardboard cartons of stars
wait for him

each one smiles

inside its carton
they can't wait
to be eaten).

My Destructive Side

it's my grandmother
she goes to parties
and shatters her hands

she likes to gaze at
very strange landscapes
from desolate bridges.

she is very beautiful,
and at important parties
great men
look at her admiringly.

she sits alone
and in the setting sun
repeats obsessively
"it's not the fairies' fault

if summer ends
with malicious fires
if stinging loves
reveal themselves to be roses."

(with a few thorns
of an artificial color
with no plausible reason
to really hurt you).

To the Organic Supermarket of Love

i buy an ice-cream
depicting the sun.

(the real sun
is less colorful
true love
has no hazelnut).

In the Mental Hospital of Spring

there is a haberdasher's

it sells three colored ribbons

the red one
to tightly
bind
blood to heart

the blue one
to stick
on top of thoughtless
gifts

the yellow one
to join:
hands and wrists
your love letters
childhood postcards
forgotten polaroids.

documents of Destiny
with authenticated signatures.

(that save your life
when you enter without a name
into the sunless courtyard
of the summer hospice).

Dry Biscuit in the Shape of an Animal

made with farmed eggs
made with tasteless yolks
with preserved milk.

stamped in the shape of a lion

of cat lynx zebra and dog
and panda bear cow alligator.

mute

without blood or color
movement
or sensation of pain.

without sugar
changes of mood
without
brown marrow.

(but i like
what you are made of
the idea
that you will never be slaughtered
as i dunk you
i am able to think
that you don't suffer
while you are being eaten.)

My Collective Unconscious

with the doctors with glasses
with scalpels and white gowns
that sprout a pair of wings

with the cooks in clean gowns
who dirty their faces and hands
tasting of our local specialties
and sharpening military knives.

(with the snow the lakes and the mountains
the oceans and the polluted desert
where waves the white flag that belongs
to the soldier inside the armored tank.)

with the cakes of whipped cream
decorated with artificial colors
prepared by lying chefs
and given to the doctors with wings

who wash their snow-white hands
while they cut slices of cakes
to be served with lemon sorbet
before going to bed, after having eaten:

with the golden pill of death.

(Translated by Antonino Mazza)

HARD LOVE
from L'AMORE CONTRO

MAURO COVACICH

"So they're telling me that we have three minutes until the end of the broadcast. After that, my friends, we'll make a date for Tuesday, same time—the wee hours are magical, don't you think?—and same station. Let me remind you again that if you want a private consultation, and I guarantee you I will be as discreet as your best friend, you need only call the number that you see on your screen and you will speak with a very nice secretary who will arrange the meeting. If you wish to write to me, mail your letters to P.O. Box 2025, Padova, and I will personally reply. Let me also remind you that the beautiful silver talismans behind me cost only thirty thousand lire and protect against all forms of evil. And also, look, they go around your neck. They're marvelous for both little boys and girls. Now let's take the last call.

"Hello?"

"Yes, hello, I'm Patty. I'd like to know about love."

"Where are you calling us from, honey?"

"From Campo San Piero. I'd like to know about love."

"Yes, I got that, sweetheart. Where do you stand? Are you looking for it or are you afraid of losing it?"

"I'm looking for it."

"Let's see here . . . But the cards tell me that there shouldn't be obstacles, that you're the problem. You see, I say it all the time, before you look outside yourself you have to search within. Then he will show up on his own. Do you follow me?"

"Yeah, pretty much."

"Let's set aside the cards now. I always tell you, I'm neither a magician nor a fortuneteller. I'm just someone who wants to help people. The cards give me inspiration, but it's my experience and intuition that guide me. Because I've seen just about all there is to see in this world. And I've suffered just as you are suffering when you call me, even more. I've suffered for love. And I've suffered for my sister, because you all know, I always tell you that she was born unlucky. She ran away from home but I tied a thread of love to her without her noticing, that way even if I don't know where she is now or what she's doing, I feel her close to me. I pull on the thread and feel her close, do you understand? That's how sensitive I am. I'm aware of it because I look within myself. That's why I tell you to do the same. Search inside yourself, honey, and you'll see that you'll discover things.

"O.K. Time's up. Nothing left but to say goodbye to each and every one of you. Remember that these calls serve simply to break the ice, but if you want complete results you must come visit me. Call this number. We'll meet in one of my suites. Once again I remind those of you who want to write to me, it's P.O. Box 2025, Padova. I'd like to thank TeleSanto for hosting us and always being so kind to us. I'm sending a kiss, as always, to my only sister, my little sister, hoping perhaps that on some occasion she might see me. Friends, your Vangelya bids you farewell."

My father wanted me to become a TV talk-show host. "You've got the build for it and you know how to speak well," he'd say. And it was true; sixty or seventy kilos ago, I had the physique of Pippo Baudo, and even today I'm still pretty good with words, unless I get jittery, but that only happens when I'm embarrassed. "Study to become a talk-show host," he'd say. "Ask if they will take you on at

TeleFriuli." I never understood why he had me study accounting. Maybe because he thought the closest things to TV were money and wealth, so naturally accounting would've been essential. It was when he figured out that I could care less about TV, along with everything else, that he started to oppose every action of mine, quoting the proverb that says that to build something you must lay one brick on top of the other, one at a time. "You don't have any plans, you lack ambition," he'd say. And it was true; I've never been able to picture myself involved in anything lasting. I've never found anything that was more worthwhile than anything else. I just don't know how people can make plans for the future or how they always come up with some great reason to get out of bed in the morning. The very expression "realize your potential" makes me feel sick to my stomach. How do you go about it and what's the point? In life aren't we already too damned real? So, when I came home with my first job, my father, without taking his eyes off the TV, said, "With a degree in accounting you're an orderly who cleans up cadavers at the hospital? Great, now find yourself a house too."

Finally I'd found a reason to openly hate my father. In any case, I wouldn't have stayed another minute in that place, though it was my place. For years I'd done my homework on that table in the living room where my father now parks his legs and stores up more and more bile, going over in his mind all the broadcasts in which they had to find a substitute for me. It was my table, the table on which the future of our family would've depended. It had never once entered the mind of my mother or father that I might not give a shit about my own future, let alone ours as a family. When they realized how I felt, the very least they were going do was kick me out of the house, as indeed they did, giving me the opportunity to sincerely hate them. Now I go visit them two, maybe three times a year, and I don't pretend to love them. I bring my mom a box of Mon Cherry and a carton of MS cigarettes for my father. They ask me if I need anything, if I've gained some more weight, but the whole time they continue to stare at the TV. I can see the TV's images reflected in their faces, and I don't say a word. For about half an hour I stare at that light blue veil that slides in all directions across the motionless faces of my parents, then I say goodbye and leave.

At least three months have gone by since my last visit. It was during Easter. My mother actually asked me if I wanted to come back for lunch on Monday of the Angel. I said yes, but of course I didn't go. I'm going to have to make up my mind to go see them. The last few times even my father was different. I think that he has resigned himself to the fact that I don't have the right physique for it anymore, that no one would hire an obese talk-show host. And my getting fired from the hospital must have done something to him. Of course, it's strange because being a septic-tank pumper is not much better than being an orderly at a morgue. And yet this change has had an effect on him. I think he particularly detested my first job for reasons of modesty. With time I convinced myself that he was afraid that after his death I would be the very one to wash his body. Someone else might've been pleased not to be handled by a stranger when you can't control what's done to you anymore. Not my father. On the contrary, I think it was precisely the powerlessness of a dead body that made him fear my presence. He couldn't stand the idea that this jerk, who had torn apart piece by piece his blueprint for happiness, his blueprint for "realizing one's potential," the one stupid dream of an entire family, would not only be able to see him die, but even to wash his dick, sprinkle it with talc and stick cotton wads up his ass.

The same doesn't go for my mother. For her the problem isn't me, neither as an orderly who washes cadavers nor as a septic-tank pumper, but rather my father. My mother has never existed except as a stand-in for my father. Her hatred of me is a carry-over of his, just as mine for her is a reflex. I deliberately express myself in this way because I want it to be known that I really could've been a talk-show host. I have to make up my mind to go see them.

In addition to our hatred for one another, the thing that unites us is TV. I also don't do anything besides watch TV. As soon as I get home from work I turn it on. And I turn it off at four or five in the morning, when the static slowly penetrates my sleep and wakes me up. The TV is my companion; it would be better to say that it watches me.

It's the TV that looks after me while I wash or make myself something to eat. The TV is the lady of the house. I reciprocate the favor when I settle down on the couch with my toilet paper in hand and wait for the right moment to clean my pipes.

I only watch private stations, the local ones where you see faces with heavy makeup and you hear real voices distorted by the shoddy microphones, voices that reach my ears as though they were hidden behind the TV set, in the corner among the electrical outlets. Telemarketers, magicians, ballroom singers—it's as though they're all by my side. If I wanted to, instead of changing channels, I could tell them to shut up. I often have the sensation that I could interrupt them and join their program. If I don't do it, it's only because I'm scared that it could really happen.

I'm not interested in hot-lines. All those lathered-up girls on the video that take turns rubbing their vaginas with the telephone receiver or licking their nipples make me sad. They're thrown at you with their tits of rubber—how sad!—with their fake jungle-bunny get-ups. An abyss separates them from the women seen around Udine or the rest of the planet. Kilos and kilos of sadness that accumulate in your belly and would humiliate any erection. So I prefer to quickly skip over them and get to the local TV broadcasts. The women who call the magicians, their voices, their hesitation, excite me the most. The very fact that they're alone, with the telephone in hand and the TV in their eyes, and that they're asking questions about themselves to a stranger—that's enough to please me. I hear her name, I imagine her with her house frock, her greasy hair and something broken inside her, too beautiful for me. And she too is curled up on the couch. No, she's so agitated she's sitting on the edge of it. I see her waiting in silence and I can't hold back. I've usually finished before the answer arrives. Then I use two pieces of toilet paper, set the roll on the floor and get comfortable.

Yesterday, I thought that instead of coming by myself in front of the TV I could have gone to check if the chick from Friday morning had been pulling my leg. But in the end I couldn't find the courage to do it. The stupid idea that she was my girlfriend stopped me. I don't know where I got this idea. And yet as soon as the thought occurred to me, I could clearly see her house with the two of us inside. I saw the bathroom where I could've taken a shower. There were two toothbrushes in the cup on the sink. I recognized mine. On the vanity, next to a woman's comb, was my hairbrush. Underwear and T-shirts—mine—were set out on top of the washing machine. She was seated on top of the toilet lid, watching me as I washed myself. Yeah, so everything was as if it were our house and she were my girlfriend. I couldn't have thought of anything more absurd, I know. I can imagine the next encounter with my parents. "Hi, I brought you the Mon Cherry. Here, take your cigarettes." "No, I don't need anything." "Yes, I've gained weight." "Did you hear the news?" Silence. "I'm dating a prostitute." Laughable, right?

"Remember—Paris, Vienna, London, Venice, Vicenza, Verona, Padova, Treviso, Rovigo—Amelior has his own spiritual centers in all these places. So remember that in Paris, Vienna, London, Venice, Vicenza, Verona, Padova, Treviso, Rovigo there are Amelior spiritual centers, where you can go by appointment. Also remember never to accept an appointment in a hotel. Stay away from those people because they are not esoteric guides. I'll say it clearly, they aren't the real thing because the people who receive you in a hotel are not esoteric guides. Don't even go if it's Claudia Schiffer. So, when they invite you to a hotel remember that you won't get anything out of those people. You'll waste your money, that's for sure, and you won't get anything in return. But what's worse is that you will discredit magic, which is real, which exists, and which is as ancient as the world is old. Because, as I told you earlier, through dualism, a philosophical conception which entails conceiving reality as dependent upon two contrasting principles, good and evil . . . Magic exists because life exists, magic exists because much of it is taken from the Bible, and the Bible is that sacred text which all of us should own. Everyone should have at least one at home. Amelior has several because he has studied several, but everyone should have at least one. Because the Bible is related to tarot cards. It's enough to see that among the major arcana are Force, Justice, Temperance, which are virtues of the Church. That's why the tarot with their arcana descend from the great Tree of Life. The Chariot is Charlemagne's, then there's Death with 13 and the Fool with 0, because each of the arcana has a number which goes back to the unity of divine primordial essence. The Tower is the Tower of Babel, the Hermit is Diogenes. Here are the images of the Kabbalistic alphabet, each one has a number. The Magician has 1, the Female Pope has 2. The arcana have a Path, a Letter—obviously a Hebrew one—and a symbolism. There are thirty-two Ways of Wisdom, formed by the ten numbers and the twenty-two letters of the Hebrew alphabet. And Amelior knows all these things, because he has a university degree and has analytically studied every individual arcana. Every man is inscribed in a pentagram, there are four limbs and one head, in fact arcana number 5 is the Pope, who is halfway between Man and God. And therefore, to be true guides of the occult it is necessary to study chiromancy and oriental philosophy . . . as Amelior has done. Only after years of meditation can one attain a mysteriological condition.

"And so now you know what you can expect from the tarot and the major arcana, because magic—I've told you this so many times—is only for those who possess the necessary cultural foundation, as did Nostradamus, Papus, Cardanus. I've already shown you this article in the Gazzettino, but I never run out of steam. Look, as you can see, Nostradamus had a medical degree. Cardanus had a university degree, so did Papus, they all did . . . So now you've understood that to face the intricacies of the occult, to be a master of esoterica, you have to be a university graduate, and then, after a long period of practice in the subject, and years of study and meditation, you arrive at that special level of awareness which few have attained . . . Nobody can endow himself with the title of spiritual guide or of cartomancer if he hasn't earned a degree, if he hasn't got the cultural foundation, because if this person comes to me and we speak of magic, you'll see that if someone hasn't met these basic requirements they will never be able to speak of it at all, because to understand magic you have to have knowledge. What is it that must be understood? The Bible; it's the key to everything. Because you know . . . well, what do you really know? You know the arcanas, and then there's the path, the arcana, the letter, the Hebrew one of course, the symbol, the tarot. The tarot—I've told you this many times—is a reference to the Tree of Life. But few observe the Tree of Life, and this is an example of what I'm talking about. If you look at the Tree of Life, you see that everything is represented within it. Now you know who Amelior is.

"You're still here, live with Amelior, as you can see. Amelior is here and is still responding to people's questions. Amelior . . . and if you can't get through to him tonight, call tomorrow morning, tomorrow afternoon, during the day tomorrow, and always the number that you see on your screen and you will receive a personal response at no charge. I repeat, if you can't get through to him tonight, call tomorrow morning, tomorrow afternoon, during the day tomorrow, and always the number that you see on your screen and you will receive a personal response at no charge. In other words, you are not paying Amelior anything! You don't have to send a telegram or a postal money order—it's entirely free! So tomorrow morning, tomorrow afternoon, tomorrow during the day, call the number that you see on your screen and you will receive a free answer. I repeat. At no charge, you will get a personal response and be able to express yourself freely."

Amelior always talks about himself as if he were another person. He doesn't say, "I have healed thousands of people of the most varied illnesses," but rather, "Amelior, your Supreme Guide, has healed thousands of people of the most varied illnesses, and he will cure you too." He never shows his face, but always appears in such a way that only his hands are in the frame. They are hairy hands, the fingers covered with rings, and with long fingernails, and they're always turning over cards or drumming agitatedly on a background dancing with stars and planets. Magician's hands, distorted by the fluorescent light. What I like about Amelior is his arrogance and sadism. I like it when he shows off his degrees in magic and his consulting offices scattered across half of Europe, when he mistreats women on the phone, when he forces his most faithful customers to give long testimonials to his powers, without even allowing them to remain anonymous. His trump card is certainly his mean-spiritedness and obnoxiousness. That way of stringing together scores of important-sounding words in long incomprehensible trains, then twisting them, mumbling over and over again in hypnotic cycles. That way of absolving and condemning. That way of humiliating whoever takes the hook in the mouth like the dumbest fish. Yeah, those are the things that keep me glued to Amelior's broadcasts. It's the hate I feel for him that keeps me bound to him.

On the other hand, I really couldn't say why anytime I get the chance, I watch Floriano Cagnazzo. Maybe because he's the only one who talks about séances, and he does it as if he were speaking about a staff meeting at work. Serious, exhausting, transparent. Maybe I'm attracted by his guilty air, like that of a teacher's pet, the sleaziness of his little tricks, in which it seems to me there's a sort of excuse-me-for-being-so-clever attitude. I don't know why, but I never miss a Floriano Cagnazzo show. On the screen: up high, his name; immediately below it, his profession: MEDIUM. On the right-hand side, the list of cities that receive the broadcast: Montebelluna, Verona, Padova, Vicenza, Udine, Trieste. Down below, the call-in number and the number for making an appointment. The background is black. More or less at the height of Cagnazzo's shoulders there's an oval frame containing a photograph of his grandmother. It's a homey photograph; the grandmother is wearing an old-lady dress and has newly permed hair. Cagnazzo portrays himself as humble and modest. He never stops saying that he simply wants to help people. He's more or less my age, 35 max. He wears a gray sharkskin jacket and a pink shirt. He insists that he owes all of his immense paranormal powers to his grandmother. It was she who launched him in the techniques of the occult from an early age, and it is she—now that she's dead—who makes it possible for him to conduct an exclusive dialog with the beyond. I've never understood why Cagnazzo, while he explains how he dispatches his business with the dead, always has "Merry Christmas" playing in the background. I believe that like me, the women who call him are attracted by the disorientation they experience under his liquid gaze.

Just as I don't get Cagnazzo's soundtrack, I don't get Vangelya's name. Why the allusion to religion? You can see from a mile off that she doesn't have the look of a nun. Vangelya could be a bargirl or a salesgirl in a department store, nothing more mystical than that. Yet she has given herself that name and even spelled it with a Y.

But she doesn't promise cures, she is not magnetic, she doesn't speak with the dead. She relies on a smattering of tarot which she enriches with constant references to her own life experience. In fact, she is convinced that all other lives can be explained by using her own as the handbook. Trial and error, all archived, lesson upon lesson, for the common good. Despite people's efforts to be original, she always discovers that the elements making them similar to others are more numerous than the ones making them different from others. That's why I like her: the idea that my story is the same as others, that I can see it flowing beyond myself together with a river of other stories, that my story can be interchanged with others, have pieces of it substituted, that it can be solved like a geometry problem. Vangelya has dug up a lot of theorems from her own experience. During her broadcasts she just indicates in a simple way how they can be applied to an individual problem. All the rest is staging, including her card reading.

I imagine her checking the signs of the zodiac each time before she starts. And there's got to be some text on the teleprompter about the talismans that are on sale, because whenever she talks about them she fixes her eyes to the right of the TV camera. But who the hell cares, because Vangelya knows about life. No one can top her there. She can't be older than forty, but she seems to have soaked every year, one by one, in the dirty water of feelings. She wrings them out in my face with every piece of advice, years of feelings pulled out of the dirty water that I can smell and slosh around in my mouth. Yes, I smell them and slosh them around in my mouth until I have to get up from the couch, direct the stream at the TV, and empty the seminal ducts.

The last time, however, after I looked at the splotches on the screen, I realized I could never again make love with Vangelya. In fact, only in that moment did I realize how much she looked like the chick of that famous Friday morning. I'm not saying "like the whore of Pontebbana," because, whether I'm awake or dreaming, that image keeps coming back to me of the two of us together in the house, her bathroom with my hairbrush, etc., and me sitting on the toilet seat as she gently dries off my back. This image, which I don't seek out but also do not avoid, keeps me from masturbating while thinking of her; and now it's preventing me from doing the same thing in front of Vangelya, given the extraordinary resemblance between the two women. I emphasize extraordinary, and don't rule out the possibility that it is fear—a vague and unmotivated fear—that blocks me in this way.

(Translated by Lawrence Garner and Julia Garner)

from THE DOGS OF NOTHING

EMANUELE TREVI

When we go out the street door, it's almost midnight. If I let her decide, once we get to the street Gina always yanks the leash to the right. Unless I have some particular need, I never resist. This is something to be done without discussion: the nocturnal walk. A habit, an unfailing certainty in the labyrinth of doubt. Whatever might have happened during the day, or rather, the more frequent case, whatever might *not* have happened. There is no need to interact much with the animal. At two ends of the leash, we are a form of bicephalous life, unified and split at the same time—a new step on the evolutionary scale. Near the streetlamps, our shadows blend, then separate again.

Gina sniffs every centimeter of street. But she will choose quickly: her bladder is full at this hour. And in fact, after a few steps, here she is hunched over with her rear paws splayed, in a position that might vaguely recall a frog. If she decides to do it on a piece of terrain with no incline, this position reveals itself to be entirely infelicitous. The little pond spreads out like an oil slick, encircling her on all sides and Gina rises out of her own piss, like Venus from the froth of the sea. *Venus Urinaria*.

We direct ourselves toward a building with a yellowish tint, of anonymous appearance, silent, poorly maintained. There inside, on the second floor, I believe, there was an apartment used by the SS or the Gestapo, I'm not sure which, to torture prisoners during the war. Now it's a museum and in the morning they take schoolchildren there. On the second floor of the building across the street, there is a bald gentleman leaning out the window. It is rare not to find him there. He smokes his cigarettes, stubs them out on the windowsill, and lets the butts fall onto the sidewalk. He surveys the street with his shiny elbows sticking out. He never seems to look at anything with particular interest or concern. I imagine his house, behind him, as a completely empty room: a mere pretext for the window.

He's not alone this evening. Right below his window the Old Woman is passing, the sad Unadorned One. She is wearing the usual shapeless overcoat and the usual headscarf. She holds a worn-out plastic bag in her hand. She proceeds with unreal slowness toward the end of the street, which is dominated by an immense Roman ruin, the arch of an aqueduct in reddish brick. She stops in front of all the garbage dumpsters. She opens them and picks through the trash with consummate attention, like a housewife, as if the dumpsters were chests in a bedroom. She observes the refuse, she holds up a piece in front of her eyes, shaking it or turning it around, but then she puts everything back in its place. Rather than seeking something useful from the garbage, you'd say she was checking to make sure everything was in order, that the stuff inside really does have that damp, filthy, decomposing appearance one would imagine. It's a sort of meticulous verification, a maniacal inspection, a last touch-up in preparation of a long-awaited ceremony. And just as the Old Woman shuffles toward the last dumpster on the street, and the Bald Man at the window stubs another cigarette out on the sill—the Fast Man turns the corner, with perfect intuition of the necessary dramatic tempo. The cast, now, can be considered complete. The Fast Man lives in our building. About him, we know that he is affected with some kind of grave motor neurosis. He walks all the time, and his pace is always clipped, fast. He spends his life walking, night and day. Sometimes he comes home, closes the door, and after a few moments, he's out again, out the street door. Apparently, he even walks at home. Whereas the Bald Man and the Old Woman are completely mute, the Fast Man is quite loquacious, of a decidedly friendly character. He greets you and always asks for a cigarette. If someone makes to pull out their pack, he begins to move in a circle around him, so as not to interrupt his long march, the harsh task he has imposed on himself. Then he heads off rapidly. He calls all men "Francesco" and all women "Ludovica"—a simplification not without a certain practical intelligence, all things considered.

The building of the SS, or the Gestapo, seems, at this hour of night, to shine with its own light. Or rather, it radiates its own cautious but obstinate phosphorescence—a rag of flesh of an immense jellyfish floating in the sea of night.

The bell of a nearby convent strikes midnight at the exact instant when the Fast Man and the Old Woman cross paths, proceeding from opposite directions below the window of the Bald Man, who lights a new cigarette. Without even a look, without needing to send one another even a minimal sign of shared intent, the three carry out their dance with an infallible sense of symmetry. They are initiates, the thought arises, and they are enacting a secret. They possess an alphabet, a key of access to some obscure truth. The force of their silent eloquence invades the street—deserted, except for Gina and me in enchanted contemplation. Even Gina, in fact, surrenders to the mystery of that authoritative, implacable staging. She stares fixedly first at one, then at another member of that unapproachable Trinity. While it is impossible to cross the gaze of the Bald Man, or to direct speech at him, the Old Woman and the Fast Man give no sign of being aware of us—they don't even see us, so intent are they on performing their parts. Leaving out the Bald Man, who with his crossed arms and perfect immobility must be in some way the director, the choreographer, the *soloist* of the spectacle, the Old Woman and the Fast Man are perfectly armored against the surrounding world. They spin around the window of the Bald Man as though around a pivot. Their strength, the absurd beauty that pervades and sustains them, comes precisely from their capacity to ignore others.

The first is still, in a sleeveless T-shirt. He smokes.

The other hobbles with impassive slowness toward the end of the street, moving from dumpster to dumpster.

The third has come to the opposite end, and turns the corner.

Gina poops.

I stop at the entrance of the yellow building. After an attack, the landlord installed a closed-circuit camera over the doorway. I look straight into the lens. Somewhere, on a monitor inside the yellow building, or on a tape in a cassette that night after night winds and rewinds, the camera is capturing the images of our street. A man and a dog standing still, in the heart of the night, in front of a public building, an advance post of the Law but on an insignificant corner, neither new nor old, of a big city. They have them everywhere in the world; in function, most of them, or transformed into museums, like this one. Vigilant German and Italian functionaries, *guardians of order*, united in the certainty of their mission by a special degree of fantasy, by obedience to clearly formulated orders from above, tore out fingernails and teeth, dealt burns and electric shocks, massacred with blows and kicks. Their hymn, the melody of certainty and belonging that resonated in their hearts, consisted precisely in this: in the hard daily work, in the awareness of a job well done.

Men with photos of their wives and their children in their wallets. Sons who became fathers—in the furrow of tradition, of faith, of legitimate desires. Foot soldiers in the war of possession, exchange, and profit. Shepherds of shepherds, guardians of guardians. Guardians of the Mystery.

When we get back home, the house is almost dark. Martina has gone to sleep. Under the plaid cover over the cage, the birds are sleeping too, balanced on their perch, with their necks turned around and their beaks resting on their backs. In the hallway, weak lights are blinking blue yellow and green, left over from the holidays. Down at the end, in the kitchen, a tepid, weak light is still on—it must be the one in the hood over the stove.

Here we are, then, we're all inside, the hour has come to draw the chain across the door. This, at least this, then, seems evident, seems true, indubitable: another day has passed, we're safe, we've stuck another finger up the asshole of death and desperation, a useless gesture of defiance, certainly, that resolves nothing, that is purely *dilatory*, let's admit it—but the fact remains that now it's time to go to sleep . . .

One morning like any other among the other mornings of our life, last winter, a Saturday morning, we went to visit the Etruscan necropolis at Cerveteri. You take the Via Aurelia and head north, with the sea always on your left, traveling almost parallel to the train tracks and the sandy coastline, beaten by a low, never-changing tide. On the right, gas stations, giant supermarkets, little burgs, a few traces of old farms. The least interesting landscape in the world, maybe, along the infinite road that leads to Tuscany, to Genoa, to who knows where. After a few kilometers, the road splits to the right and cuts across the countryside until it reaches an asphalt plaza. That's the parking lot and ticket office for the necropolis. There were no other cars that morning. The guards, seeing as we were the only visitors, allowed us to bring Gina along, who at first we thought would have to stay in the car. And so having paid the fare, we headed off, all three of us, through the streets of the city of the dead. That's right, because that place has not the slightest character of a cemetery. At first sight, in fact, you'd never even think it. There are streets and rows of doors that face onto the streets, crossroads, and plazas. There are zones that seem like exclusive neighborhoods, with their *residential* air, and others that seem decidedly more common. The real difference is understood only when entering one of the doors. Just beyond the threshold, narrow stone stairs lead down. At the bottom are the rooms, carved out of the earth. Usually, a rectangular space with a stone bench along the walls, and two doors that lead into two smaller rooms.

The nightlight over the stove is tenuous and it has always had a flickering amber tone. Despite its dimness, all the objects absorb that little bit of light and make it vibrate delicately across their surfaces—the glasses and silverware on the dishpan, the trash already knotted and forgotten there in a corner, the glass jars of rice, salt, and teabags. Somewhere, someone is moaning in their sleep at mostly regular intervals. On the refrigerator door, held up by a pineapple-shaped magnet, there is a white piece of paper, well bent and creased by now, with D'Annunzio's poem about dogs. On an edge of the sheet, slightly curved outward, you can make out the lines—

. . . the bones gnaw their bones,
they never stop gnawing their bones . . .

We had never seen Gina as happy as that January morning, as the wind swept away the clouds to replace them continuously with new ones, coming from the sea, filling us with salt air, over the low round knolls beyond the road, many of which are surely Etruscan burial mounds, which are covered in summertime with ripe oats and clusters of broomflower, while in winter they are a silent, bleak terrain, barely grooved by a path here and there and shadowed by a rare oak. Never, I mean, had we seen Gina so grateful for life and so light, so sure of herself—with the air of returning from a long exile, of coming home. She went in every door, scrambled down the steep stone steps, and sat in the center of the underground rooms, waiting for us to catch up. She seemed, what's the word, *proud* of that place. She wanted us to follow her everywhere, from hypogeum to hypogeum, burial mound to burial mound. It was a long trip, but guided by her, we had to take a look at every single thing, at least a glance . . .

At this hour, perhaps the Bald Man, the Old Woman, and the Fast Man are sleeping too. Perhaps they are joined even in sleep—and in sleep they exchange roles in their dance. The Bald Man runs around the block. The Old Woman lights a smoke at the window, while the Fast Man picks through a dumpster. The same pineapple-shaped magnet, other than the poem about dogs, also holds up a color photo cut out of a newspaper. There's a young man stretched out on the ground, an anonymous segment of asphalt in an anonymous place in the world. Even lying on his back, with his arms slightly away from his chest, you can tell that his physique is agile and slim. He's wearing a white sleeveless T-shirt, and between his elbow and forearm he's wearing something that, at first, could be some strange barbaric amulet, a heavy bracelet, the ring of a chain. Actually, it's a roll of packing tape, the beige kind. As he fell to the ground, a Bic lighter must have slid out of his pocket and stopped a few centimeters from his legs. The face of the youth is covered by an adherent balaclava of dark material. In the moment when the photo is taken, his life is abandoning him. From an opening in the balaclava, perhaps from the arch of his eyebrows, a jet of dark blood spurts out and describes an arc of about twenty centimeters before curving back to earth, onto the asphalt, into a puddle that grows ever wider. There is another youth, bent over him, who is trying to help. He puts a hand on the prone boy's chest, at the level of the heart. Probably, precisely at that moment, the moment when the photograph is snapped, that heart is ceasing to beat, has already stopped. There is always, in a photograph, something that you can understand with certainty beyond the limits of the frame, beyond the limits of what we are actually seeing. These two youths, the one spilling his last blood and the one kneeling, who would like to help but can only place his hand over the other's heart, are suspended in the middle of a battle: one because hit, the other because moved by an elemental instinct of pity. Their companions are already fleeing—in the photo, you can make out other legs, the shoes of people running. Their enemies are ferocious, they are advancing implacably. Soon, in just a few seconds, the kneeling boy will have to draw his hand away from the chest of the one on the ground, cut the cord. And every time, opening the refrigerator, I look at that photo, I surprise myself by urging him, in my thoughts—get up, I say, get out of there, they're coming, there's nothing you can do anymore.

There, in the grand and solitary necropolis at Cerveteri, that January morning, going in and coming out of the houses of the dead, from the houses of the wise and ironic dead Etruscans, infected by Gina, we also fantasized homecomings. Spurred by the wind, we enjoyed a bizarre sense of *certainty*, of being rooted in who knows what, who knows where. The trees rustled. At the northern border of the necropolis, a net of barbed wire separated us from a small group of boys playing hooky. They had arranged their mopeds in a circle, they were passing a joint, and every so often the sweet and pungent odor of grass would spread into the morning breeze. They were laughing loudly. Young Etruscans going about their eternal business, that of their fathers and their fathers' fathers, on up through the chain of time—enjoying the passing days, between the long sandy beach and the hills of oat and broomflower, the little stands of oak.

I had come to the limit of the fence, but they hadn't noticed me, they were talking intensely, between one burst of laughter and another, with an air of knowing the subject well and returning to it gladly. The subject was a woman, a girl, a certain Lidia, Livia, or Linda, who worked in a bar at Campo di Mare, a place nearby. When I see those tits, a small blond kid was saying, I forget what I want to order. And another, tall and scrawny with curly hair, cupping the joint in his palm to protect it from the wind, with a suddenly more serious, more convinced tone, added immediately after: *I would like to lick her all over*, enunciating each word one by one, as though his desire rendered them more true and more full, rich with meanings never taken into consideration before, capable of imposing silence around them.

In this kitchen, this May night, in the stove's weak light, time seems to flow away like a liquid, more than anything as though the level were going down, like water in a bathtub when you pull the plug—somewhere, in a zone of darkness, a little whirlpool . . .

I am here, immobile in this half light that doesn't conceal the dark, the work of the dark . . . I look at the photo of the boy on the ground, the white sheet with the poem about dogs—they vibrate lightly together with the refrigerator, the fact that another day is passing, another day that will never return, all its water already swirling, its last millwheel turn around the hole. This event does not bring with it any progress, something understood once and for all, a small increase in consciousness . . .

I WOULD LICK HER ALL OVER.

Unseen, I walked away from the Etruscan boys, who were laughing and smoking, talking about the tits of the girl who works in the bar at Campo di Mare—in the smoke, in the circle of mopeds, they made a figure appear, the outline of a distant, powerful beauty, the spark of a desire no less happy, no less profound, no less fatal for being hopeless.

I turned back on my steps, then followed a path through the necropolis, and after a while, having passed several burial mounds, I saw them, Martina and Gina, in a grassy spot a few dozen meters away—a woman and a dog, two females tending to the warmth of life in the weak sun of January. They were playing without thinking, so they looked to me, running in circles, in the changing light of a winter morning. *I'm going to catch you, I'm going to catch you*, Martina was saying, and Gina, mad with love, wheeled around her, slipped from her grasp, changed direction, but kept close at the same time, quick and ungraspable, the way, it seems, the gods would do in these parts when they showed themselves to men. As she ran, with her tongue hanging out, she never stopped watching her even for a second.

. . . the bones gnaw their bones,
they never stop gnawing their bones . . .

This is the moral, I think. To piss and light up your last smoke and tumble into sleep. The more arcane and beautiful, the more inexplicable things are, the simpler they are, they don't really mean anything, they don't seem even to want to make the effort . . .

Here, still standing in the kitchen, still undecided, as though I'd lost my way right in the middle of my own house, at this late hour of night, here, now, in this moment, I think of those past things. I think with regret and desperation, true regret and true desperation, at their having passed. And all this thinking, with this desperation and this regret, is useless, it doesn't change things at all, it doesn't shift them one millimeter either way. Maybe *they* understood, that morning in January, that past morning, running down the drain, they who played without thinking twice, they who pretended to catch each other without ever catching each other, and watched each other running, spinning around the trunk of a solitary poplar, they returned to the center of the field, in the large scrap of sunlight that had opened up by tearing a hole in the clouds—they understood more than me, they who didn't think about it, because in that moment they were playing, more than me who . . .

Each man, I see written on the sheet attached to the refrigerator.

(Translated by Thomas Simpson)

TWO STORIES

DARIO VOLTOLINI

The Saddest Thing

There are a lot of sad things in the factory. Just to bring up the word factory brings on a bit of sadness. The reason is that nothing gets manufactured there any more, leastwise not in the current meaning of "manufacture." There's no particular thing that gets to you—it's an emotion that comes over you when you're inside, when you walk through its aisles and passageways. Someone who comes from outside maybe isn't aware of it, because one plant looks like another, and all the big windows, apparently the same, don't give you a sense of how different they are. Anyhow, to go into the ex-workshops and see them turned into a shipping warehouse, that gets to you. The floors, once drenched in the stuff of production—lubricating oils, cleaning fluids, grease—are now all dried up. Somewhere, some thing is getting produced, there's no doubt about it. But not here, now.

The liberal-minded manager also makes you sad. You see that he's someone who knows how things ought to be organized, you see that he's skilled and well-trained for the job, you see that he changes assignments and gets shifted around all too often in the company's organization chart—not because he's liberal-minded, but just because he's a manager. The managers are just too numerous—so many that for every employee there are two of them—and they get shuffled around and dealt out like so many hands of poker.

And the heads of personnel? Well, you can forget about them. You never hear the cleaning ladies complaining, but those guys you hear griping all the time. They think they're performing some kind of heavy-duty, heroic labor, depending on who you talk to. Nevertheless, one far-out, but well-founded, hypothesis might raise the question as to whether what they do can really be called work. How can we tell them, how can we make them understand that they should get off their high horse? How sad.

A green underground passageway. Groups of people move through it. At the end there's a flight of stairs and the old smells of the lunchroom, of boiled rice. The cafeteria. The cafeteria, the meetings after 5 in the afternoon, the hushed voices of the secretaries with their eyes ever on the alert, as if, at any moment, the school principal might come into the room. Sad things. Sometimes a green lizard, a bat, or a turtledove makes a wrong turn and comes into the factory. Then there's a little uproar, solidarity with the animal. People try to snare it, set a trap for it in order to catch it and put it back outside, into the open. The animal acts like it's gone berserk. Its sense of terror makes it skirt around crazily, senselessly. When, at last, the hunt is ended and the animal is freed, everyone goes back to their job. And I know that their thoughts turn to the animal, to its desperate behavior—something *we* can't give in to, something *we* keep under control with our more rational and composed faculties. But you can see the solidarity with the animal—it falls like a veil over the eyes of the person who sits back down in his chair, the person who opens a drawer. A veil of sadness.

It's sad to see the union rep who drags his feet, walking hunched over with the loudspeaker in his hand and with the look of someone who really can't take it anymore. And even sadder to see the other union rep who announces the meetings to small groups and, withered like an apostle, encourages us to talk about our problems on the job—it's like the gloominess of the catacombs, like the return home from the fields in the evening with a stiff back. And everything is out of place.

But the saddest thing was something I saw on the way out. There are these little contraptions into which the employee inserts a card with a magnetic band—an electronic way of stamping check-ins and check-outs. Well, one day I saw the saddest thing just taped to one of these time-clocks. It was a sheet of paper, and the writing on it said: *"Thanks for making us feel less lonely in these sad and painful times."* I wrote the phrase down in my Casio 32K Digital Diary SF-4300, because I just couldn't resist.

(Translated by Lawrence Garner)

Precedent 2

You see the elevated, the plant, the overpass, the railway, in that place on the city's outskirts habitually called gray. A cat squashed on a chunk of asphalt, the red of its intestinal tangle yanked out flung photographed in blood, pressed flat on the asphalt a cat with no head. The carcass is still there the next day but the intestines faded, the skin dry and stuck to the ground by the tires' impact. The cadaver won't be taken away: it will get absorbed. So the elevated is composed of cats and dogs. When the number of carcasses on the tracks will exceed the number of cubic meters of reinforced concrete, the overpass the railway the outskirts will become a mix reinforced with steel rods tar bituminized ex-felines. The railway the steel ribbons color of brown pebbles of commuters' shit on suburban trains that don't follow instructions for use of the railcars' facilities. Above the overpass hovers a mist of urine of ammonia of rust of non-potable water from the railcars. The station on the outskirts the shops on the outskirts the streetcars, the stops under the little tiled overhangs: a cat at the switch sliced in two half marks track closed with the red strip of liver intestine squirting out from the cat photographed from the streetcar. The trolley wires the power lines the streetlights the signs lend color to the sky. The elevated the overpass the zebra-striped urban carpets of Siamese cats of Afghan hounds caught in the net. The plant heaves its smokestack ejaculates inoculates mysteries chemicals mark lungs all around the smokestack the asphalt from the wires of the aerial net. The din of dogs' bones with the din of human beings on the dynamo of nickel-plated scrap. Squashed exploded intoxicated blood dripping through porphyries red trickle around porphyries absorbed by the earth down down trees of flattened cats grow underground with imploded eyes dripping water and glass are absorbed in the earth give birth to plants of cats' eyes you see at night: the stoplights are cat plants that become uprooted snapped off by compacts, vans, semis men nailed to the asphalt by other automobiles pressed to the ground squashed like metal worker hands in the plant's presses like the overpass' suicide with the train that rolls him up like a smoke-stack cigarette with lungs full of blood of cats skinned by streetcars attached to the aerial net to the brown apartment buildings of shit of the inhabitants that fall from the windows glass decapitating the clients of the shops on the outskirts that buy clothes they put on when they are decapitated by glass that falls on the rails of the streetcar that passes and tinges with bilious green of stomach ulcers the little tiled overhangs. The truck driver is crushed to bits while the truck mows down automobiles shopkeepers and their clients the old woman who sells flowers the slap the mother readies for her son instead of her husband he too mowed down by the ambulance with a sick man in back the family the nurses the I.V. the gasoline that sets the priest on fire who ran to savor the scene is hurled against the streetlamp that splits him in two and spills the eye of a soul slowly slithering through the grate of a rusty drain.

(Translated by Paul Vangelisti)

from UNEXPECTED HAPPINESS

ANDREA GIBELLINI

If One Day

If on a May day that to you seems pleasant
from a bench along the seashore you raise your gaze
noticing a vague horizon of menacing clouds
birds speeding like a black light through the air
passing over you and the calm mirror
where with oars ready rowers plow distant shores,
of a love by then ended.

When the Car

When the car drives up
to the edge of a sunset
I hope for a welcoming house
a soft pillow, washed dishes,
a cheerful long-tailed dog
and a love sturdy like a rock
beneath a tumbling waterfall.

Hope has always been my downfall
my eyes used to lower at every sunset
a foot on the pedal and there'd be no one there,
no one would call my name.

When Your City Is Far Away

When your city is far away
and if one morning you wake up and get a glimpse
of the dawn's silent fire,

and if you raise your eyes and at this crossroads
you greet
the white underbelly of the airplanes

the boom that comes from afar
from unknown hemispheres,
like that wind that shakes

the tall grasses of the fields
reddened by the sun,
knowing that right in the city

still beats on an unknown street
the unique happiness of a young love.

Letter to Italy

I don't want to tell you the venom and the love that I feel.
I lived prey to a language not my own,
I who by family tradition don't even have

a dialect, playing almost naive among swings,
in houses built on trees with unsafe branches,
and long benches made of dark-gray wood.

The territory was a refuge often uninhabited:
on the quiet afternoons we pretended to sleep
awaiting the arrival of spring.

And now that we've come through to adulthood
that is proper (given our maturity!) but hardly comfortable,
many are leaving or talk of your inexistence.

Leaving? I ask myself—is as senseless as staying,
but in leaving the words would no longer have feeling

leaving the land that distractedly cradled me.

My City

My city is not a city

it lives between the river and the fields
it is suspended near the hills
and if you dig there you can discover
fish come from the past
sculpted in the limestone;
the blue of the sky is like the sea only in a quiet
dream, under the white of the stones
and the few flowering bushes.

The branches of trees that are no longer trees

bend to touch the river
beat against boulders, break
the cold waters troubled by the silence—
distant the Secchia flows in the dark—
but it is the vision of a young river,
gone away.

Those Who Remember

Those who remember can never forget
the scream of the demented
in the street,
the tired rivulets from drainpipes
that streak Piazza Garibaldi with water,
the hills fanned in the sun—
refuge, out of all worlds,
of young loves
where the wet street encircles the brushes.

It was morning, then suddenly evening
arrived in the cold, dazed,
dissolved in a distant secret,
we returned home by car.

The motionless odor
of the ceramics' breath
the still whitish sky in the deepening blue
and the rain like fog
with no longer any boundaries
between the tight folds of the earth.

Scherzo

The crystalline sun has cooled the air.
And nothing sharpens the air more than our hearing.
Now all is clear more than truth.

Only a shadow dropped down by the evening
can break the enchantment, the lofty quiet,
the contradiction of an era, the pains of childbirth.
But a weak wind ruffles my singing.

And you who listen to these my poor words
—fallen ivy branch, way of tears, black smoke—
like a crowd distracted by a distant melody,
now that aboard buses you travel long avenues
for only an instant I beg you to stop:
the obligations of need be stilled
like a veil—the wind has risen beyond the trees—
descended over a young bride's face.

And let the Ocean conserve like a splendid
medusa the few truths we have conquered.

All Good Things Are Far Away

All good things are far away even summer
which is here in its full suffocating
light.
In the shade of a malformed tree
few squalid fronds give shelter
grass pricks, bothers,
flies and mosquitoes annoy—
all good things seem far away.

A long and livid
canal covered in white cement
awaits the wide calm green
waters of the Mincio.
The rods are placed in a circle to dig out
in the slime the shadow of a pike.
Sunset doesn't come,
it passes as by magic, one almost doesn't see it
if not for the few scattered colors
that vibrate on the little artificial river—
but by now it's night, it's only night.
Few stars in the sky
and no news,
none,
the hoped-for pike.

All good things are far away.

(Translated by Antonino Mazza)

A HUNDRED LITTLE TOTTIS

SANDRO VERONESI

My little boy, encouraged by a friend, told us that he wanted to enroll in the soccer school run by the Roma club. Of course, he got his wish. Never let it be said that my son wanted to play a sport and I stood in his way. My wife and I worked out a schedule with the parents of his little friend to take turns going, twice a week, to the Testaccio soccer field—the *glorious* Testaccio soccer field. We paid the enrollment fees, we bought the boots, and we kept the boys' names afloat, week after week, in the mysterious waters of the waiting list for the equipment that was supposed to come with the fee—heavy jackets with the Roma badge, Roma tracksuits, shirts, and shorts, and Roma sweatshirts, but they seemed to be available only in huge sizes; the children's sizes were always *on back order*. Meanwhile, however, we failed entirely—both we and the parents of my little boy's friend—to purchase the official Roma shirts with a player's name and number written on the back, and the name of the sponsor on the chest. No, that we failed to do. And, let me point out, the boys never asked us to do it. As a result, my son and his little friend are the only two boys going to the soccer school run by the Roma team, on the glorious Testaccio field, who are not wearing the Roma strip: neither the strip that is theirs by right, which is still on back order, nor the extra strip, the one produced by the marketing division, to exploit the team's image, because sports teams nowadays are corporations, and they have to produce profits, and so on and so forth. They are the only two boys, in this cluster of children, who are not wearing a single item of clothing with the yellow-and-red Roma club colors.

They're just small boys, in the youngest age group, so they are shunted off to a distant corner of the field with others their age and immediately unleashed in pursuit of a soccer ball. In fact, even before they begin learning the basics, these little boys must necessarily go chasing madly after a soccer ball, the way we did on the fields of our youth, so that they can pass through the old healthy process of natural selection. It's just that, since there are no longer any fields for them to play in, if we want to get even a little piece of a field for them, we are obliged to enroll them in a soccer school. And they hit the ground running, they try their best, they sweat and they run and they tumble in the dirt, under the bored gaze of an instructor who can't say anything yet, can't teach them anything yet, and who, in fact, does nothing. I begin to see that there's not much to watch. Nothing but a cloud of dust in the distance, a swarm of frenzied flies, all moving in unison behind the soccer ball. This is still barely the dawn of soccer.

But it is pretty interesting to watch the boys in the more advanced courses, because they have been selected, equipped, and trained. The instructors make them do training exercises for half an hour with the ball or with cones, okay, now sprint! now shoot! come on! hustle! before they get to play a match. So after awhile I find myself losing track of the chaotic swarm, in the distance, where my son is busily trotting to and fro. Instead, I start to watch other people's sons, especially because they are training and playing in a section of the field that is much closer to the bleachers where all of us parents sit watching. Some of the kids are just on the other side of the netting, right there in front of us, and I can watch them closely.

There is one thing you can't help but notice: they all have shirts marked with the number 10, with the name Totti emblazoned on the back. All of them, I notice, except for two. There is a little blond boy, with long straight hair and a lovely face, who hunches over whenever he sprints. His parents, lulled by the articles that ran during the summer in the *Corriere dello Sport*, made the horrible mistake of buying him a shirt with the number 7 and the name of Bartelt. There is also a massively built young boy, as solidly planted and burly as a fire hydrant. From here, he almost seems to have a *receding hairline*, and inevitably he is wearing a shirt bearing the number 4 and the name Di Biagio. So, on the glorious Testaccio soccer field, on a luminous afternoon in the magnificent October weather found only in Rome, here is the scene that presents itself to our eyes: one hundred little Tottis, one little Di Biagio, one little Bartelt, plus my son and his friend—clearly a pair of interlopers, in the distance, scrambling back and forth in their nondescript shirts.

Then there are the parents, or the care-givers: they offer a fairly interesting show of their own. There is no mistaking the babysitters, cell phones glued to the sides of their heads, oblivious to everyone and everything. There are clusters of mothers chatting away, likewise largely indifferent to the play, though they at least have succeeded in laying their hands on the elusive soccer accessories—how on earth they managed is beyond me—and they happily show off their spoils. Then there are the solitary fathers, like me, who sit in silence, wrapped in heavy jackets. And there are whole families, one might say, with faces straight out of the pages of Pasolini, wearing sweatshirts and sweatpants, smoking MS cigarettes, faces you might encounter in a prison yard, with stingy smiles and sandpapery voices, clutching desperately at the natural talents of their boy, in the old, familiar hope that he is going to lift them out of poverty.

Directly in front of me, there are four boys at play, always the same quartet: four little Tottis, each totally unlike the other three, playing in teams of two. Each time I see them play, it's a duel that lasts till the end of training, with goalposts made of cones. In theory, they are all pretty talented, but one of them, a chubby boy, basically plays alone, and never passes the ball to anyone else. He plays attack, defense, and goalkeeper all at the same time, and the other boys almost never get to touch the ball. It is nerve-wracking. There are two standard plays that are repeated before my eyes ad infinitum. In standard play number 1 (attack), the chubby Totti gets the ball, and begins to move forward, dribbling, toward the defending Tottis, taking on first one, then the other, then both together. In the meanwhile his Totti teammate, completely open and unmarked, calls for the ball, but the chubby Totti orders him to take his place in the goal. After that, it doesn't much matter what happens: he may score a goal or lose the ball, wandering off into the intricacies of a final, pointless, yet exhilarating dribble, but it makes no real difference. In standard play number 2 (defense), the chubby Totti orders his teammate to mark the attacking Totti without the ball, then he moves up to mark the one with the ball. When his man, quite correctly, passes the ball to his own teammate to try a one-two play, he promptly abandons his man and runs to the goal, so that he can show off by decisively blocking the ball when one of the two attacking players appears alone before him—or, on those rare occasions when he lets in a goal, so he can accuse his teammate of failing to defend aggressively enough. That is how he plays, basically alone, and the instructor smiles at his antics. The other three Tottis are increasingly frustrated, and don't know what to do about it.

This chubby little Totti who does everything on his own, however, bears a little study: with his thighs that rub together, the lard that overflows at the bottom of his T-shirt, his full-fledged pork loins, it is very clear that he has no real future as a soccer player, despite all the gifts that he works so hard to display. In fact, he is one of those graceful, coordinated fatties, like John Candy, the ones that grow up to be good dancers, and when he has a ball underfoot he is a steady spectacle of dribbling and hip feints that remind you of Gascoigne. But he is genuinely fat, a dead loss in athletic terms. The profound irritation that he provokes when he is on the field is slightly undercut by one's sense of pity at the thought of the dead end to which his hormones have ineluctably destined him. So I feel a certain empathy for the instructor, who ignores the complaints of the three other Tottis and never demands that he adopt a somewhat less autistic mode of behavior. The instructor must be thinking that these little explosions of style are the chubby Totti's last opportunities to take a degree of pleasure from playing soccer, and so he chooses not to ruin these moments by urging him to be a team player, to show some generosity and self-sacrifice and all the other qualities that a soccer school ought to instill in its pupils. Because soccer, even more than being a team sport, is a sport, and a fat boy like him can never hope to play that sport on a serious basis. As soon as full-field games begin, he will be relegated to fifty square feet of turf where he can only watch helplessly as teammates and opponents flash by him at three times his speed. And when that time comes there will be no need at all to explain to his father why the chubby Totti was not selected for the C-level Beginners' Championship of the coming year. He himself will understand, sooner or later, and he will channel his skills into Subbuteo table soccer or his Play Station, and his passion directly into extreme soccer fan clubs like *Curva Sud*. Still, it is truly irritating, and I find myself rooting for the two Tottis playing against him, or hoping that his Totti teammate might just once manage to extricate the ball from chubby Totti's feet and score a goal, or even (most unlikely of all) that the instructor would lose his age-old Roman sense of pity and yell at him, in a harsh, no-nonsense voice, to pass that fucking ball to another player, God damn it to hell.

Then, suddenly, I notice something. Whenever he is playing goalie, while his Totti teammate runs feverishly around the field, all alone, to ward off the two attacking Tottis who charge at him repeatedly, the chubby Totti narrows the goal, delivering sharp little kicks to one of the cones that serve as goalposts. The more the three other players take advantage of his absence to actually move the ball around, the more he narrows the goalposts, until there is an opening more or less as wide as him. That is why, even if an attacking Totti does manage to attempt a shot, he almost always manages to block it. Then, when he puts the ball back into play (which amounts, in his case, to passing it to himself, as if from goalie to defender), he just gives a sly little kick to the cone to re-widen the goalposts, and then runs off as if nothing had happened.

I stand up and I walk over to the netting, and I carefully observe the instructor, an overgrown boy with the bowed legs of a halfback, shaved head, unquestionably a Roma supporter—and therefore culturally preprogrammed to accuse other people of breaking the rules, even without justification. Now, I think to myself, when he notices that the fat boy is cheating, he will jump on him with both feet, not only with the proper degree of indignation for his unsportsmanlike conduct, but also with the long-term frustration that beats in the heart of any Roma supporter (Turone's disallowed winning goal, Aldair's throw-in, the loser's mind-set), making the chubby Totti the scapegoat for twenty years of disappointments. That boy is *robbing*, I think to myself, and when the instructor notices it, he will denounce him as a Juventus fan, and he'll toss him off the field.

Instead, to my enormous surprise, the instructor has already noticed and he is simply letting him do it. It's only when the fat boy goes too far, moving the two cones together so that there is not even an inch of goal space (and it is obvious that he is doing it on purpose), only then does the instructor signal to him with a thrust of his chin to put the cone back where it belongs. But—to my astonishment—he does it with a smile, indulgently, and even, it almost seems, with a hint of admiration for that sly little operator who manages to make fools of the three boys at the same time (the three other Tottis, in fact, never notice a thing). The fat boy complies but immediately afterward—unbelievable! *immediately afterward*, without even the decency to wait ten seconds, he is nudging the cone with one foot, narrowing the opening between the goalposts to half its size. And the instructor doesn't say a thing, he pretends he hasn't noticed.

"Hey," I yell, "open up that goal!"

I know, I know, it's none of my business, I shouldn't meddle, but this situation is just intolerable. And when something is intolerable, it can't be tolerated.

"Whadja say?" asks the instructor.

"That little boy," and I point to him, "is narrowing the goalposts!" The three other Tottis stop playing, and the fat boy takes advantage of the opportunity to score a goal, and then dances his victory dance, shamelessly. Well, I think to myself, at least this time there will be some outrage: the two attacking Tottis will complain, there'll be some rough shoving, at the very least, or maybe an outright brawl, and the instructor will be forced to do something.

But nothing happens. They ignore my objection, they ignore me entirely, the goal is accepted as good, and play continues. At a loss, I turn to search the faces of the spectators for support, at least the father of one of the two opposing Tottis, or even a mother, or one of their fucking baby-sitters. Zero. No one pays the slightest attention to me. Standard play number 2 unfolds as outlined, the chubby Totti runs to the goalposts, which he narrows to the dimension of a mousehole with a kick on either side, the attacking Totti shoots, he kicks the ball out of the way and then returns to the attack with standard play number 1, without even bothering to widen the goalposts before hustling off.

"Look!" I yell. "He's done it again! He's narrowed the goalposts!"

This time the instructor comes over to where I am standing behind the netting, signaling to the boys to stop playing. The fat boy stops only after shooting a goal, but without celebration.

"You see how narrow the goalposts are, mister?" I say to him. "That boy has been narrowing the goal."

The instructor looks over at the narrow goal, but he has already seen it, he already knows. Then he looks back at me.

"Who are you, jack?" he says. He calls me jack. I call him mister and he calls me jack.

"What do you mean, who am I?" I answer. "What do you care who I am? I'm a guy who watched one of your students systematically break the rules, while his instructor systematically let him do it—an instructor who ought to be teaching him just a bare minimum of sportsmanship. That's who I am."

The instructor looks at me, his eyes unsmiling and indifferent, and says nothing. The four Tottis have gathered around him, irritated, annoyed, and look at me askance, all four of them, without giving a second's thought to what I just said.

"Leave us woik, wouldja," the instructor says to me, making a great show of patience. In his eyes I can see that he knows me, he's seen so many guys like me, fathers like me, their hands clutching the netting to argue with the manager's decisions, argumentative buffoons, unable even to see how they are identifying with their sons. He knows how to deal with them, he knows how to keep from being sucked into an argument with someone like them, like me. He looks at me with pity and returns to the field without another word, followed by the four Tottis. And the fat one, before rushing back to take the ball for himself, stops for a moment to hiss at me, masterfully, "*Whyncha mind yer own fockin' bizness*?" He must be ten, maybe eleven.

How could this be? I wonder to myself. How do things like this happen? How do people set about transforming children into cold athletic machines that care nothing about the rules? How do they manage to transform me into a ball-busting father who interrupts their training session just to defend (and all five of them must have thought this was what was going on) his own son? How can I be wrong on this point?

I cast a glance to the far end of the field, where I see that my son, garishly visible in his yellow and dark-blue shirt, is feeling the first effects of natural selection, and has already been relegated to guarding the goal; in the opposite goal, wearing a white and dark-blue shirt, I can make out his little friend. Between them, in a patch of field about the size of a carpet, I see a furious scrum of Tottis, kicking and shoving one another in turn. And all around, dense and suddenly visible, as if a special chemical solution of some sort had been sprayed into the air, I see, louring over this glorious little soccer field, all of the dusty, age-old, proverbial, ferocious, unconscious, and even, conceivably, innocent—if you compare it with some of the other forms of evil you can find in the world—but nonetheless crass and intolerable dishonesty of the Romans. That total suspension of morality that led Giacomo Casanova to compare the people of Rome to the men employed at the government tobacco works, who are allowed to take gratis as much tobacco as they want; that dim-witted cunning out of a folk song, where the tavernkeeper waters the wine but the customers are all happy because they therefore don't have to pay him; that *stereotype*, yes, the cliché of the Roman character, which I have done my part to fight, from time to time, but which occasionally, inevitably rears its ugly head, undeniable, in the very institutions of this city (the city traffic police, the Roma soccer club, Alberto Sordi) to remind us that, sadly, beneath certain stereotypes, even the most objectionable, there is a deep-rooted truth. And it is as if these hundred little Tottis, here, on the glorious field where Fulvio Bernardini perfected his *system*, were finishing the little speech that their agreeable young comrade had delivered to me in rough, initial form: *hey yo' buddy, now don't take this the wrong way, y'unnastan'*, they seem to be saying, *but whyncha mind yer own fockin' bizness, yo, no offense intended, but ya know we're all Romans, and ya know da way we ack, and 'at's how we've been doon' it f'r as long's da Pope's been da boss heah, and even before dat, when dey were feedin' Christians to da lions, and Rome was just dis small town dat was in ruins, fulla lousy grapevines and orchits, and dere wasn't even such a t'ing as Itt-ly, and just to make ends meet ya hadda be sly, and not worry too much about da details, ya hadda filch and pilfah, and den say confession inna choich and eat da wafer, but da big guys, da princes and da priests, dey was chowing down on roastit lamb wit' foahks and knives made outta solit gold? Oh, we've seen 'em, reshpectable individjools who yack and yack about laws and commamments, and morality and sincerity, we've seen 'em every day of da miserable week, doin'a woist t'ings imagin-a-bull inna front hallways, like da domestics who see deir boss comin' home at night wit' some goil, while da wife is away gettin' mud-baths, and won't be home all week. An' it's just cuz, ya know, it's dis wunnaful air, it's da light glancin' off dat dome of St. Peter's, when da sun is sinking slow in da west, an' it casts a golden light on 'em sleepy seven hills . . .*

From that afternoon on, it suddenly became impossible for me to hold up my end of the agreement to take the boys to the soccer field, when it came my turn, and our understanding with the other parents began to fall apart. After skipping two, three weeks in a row, my son began to realize that it was actually more fun to have those two afternoons free to play with Lego and MicroMachines. As for sports, he was already taking swimming lessons with his little brother, and I take them to the pool much more frequently than I used to, and I stand on the balcony and watch them swim, along with a hundred other little tadpoles their age, tall, short, skinny, fat, some with no talent at all, others quite gifted, and all of them magnificently incapable of dreaming up tricks.

(Translated by Antony Shugaar)

SIX POEMS

VALENTINO ZEICHEN

Spaghetti with Clam Sauce

Within the tangle of spaghetti
the clams migrate
taking the shape
of precious pendants;
in opening their valves
hope catches a glimpse
of a lost silhouette, but
the inside of the mollusk
has closer likeness
to your tender sex.

Female Students

Two black female students
of the Lycée Chateaubriand
are walking along the Flaminian Way;
one of the two appears to be cutting
with her modeled chest the wire
of an imaginary finish line
or rather, to cast a bridge
between our two civilizations.
Her spit traces the beginning
of an elegant parabola in the air,
it flies over half the road: it should
splatter on the sidewalk opposite.
I admire the beautiful throw
from that fiery mouth
and dodge
the white bullet
by a hair.

• • •

Where did the wings of the chicken go?
and the slim thighs?
The Philippine girl turns the pages of a *Mickey Mouse*
and evades the question;
her pubic hollow appears
to be tuning an instrument
emitting a fitful tune
that doesn't help the memory.
She skims through the comics magazine and
the seven dwarfs march past in succession;

in the count there is a gap: Sleepy.
Nostalgic for Snow White
the deserter slips his head
in a plastic bag
and suffocates in spasms,
among poisonous mushrooms that
emanate feminine odor.
Where could the wings have gone? Flown away.

Aurelian Column

Stranger,
many centuries before
an ancestor of yours
enrolled in the
East India Company,
his predecessors
were soldiers of Rome
in the Britannica Legion,
one of the bravest.
You are waiting
at the base of the column
for the elevator to climb up
to your ancestors
carved there at the top,
on the final stones
of the Aurelian Column.

In Piazza del Popolo

In Piazza del Popolo
I lean toward the basin
next to the barracks,
while refreshing my face
in the fountain's mouth
between my hands and
running water
are the facial features
of the one who's buried
in that sarcophagus.

Broken Wall

Along the Muro Torto[1]
towards where nowadays
Villa Borghese extends
there was a common burial pit,
a cemetery for the nameless.
From votive offerings of food
and oil lamps the prostitutes ate
offering themselves pale and weak
as dark recompense.
There, as children
we played soccer
on overgrown playing fields
seconding those feeble
spirits underfoot that
incited our feet
with their circus cheers.

---

[1] The walls between Porta del Popolo and Porta Pinciana are called Muro Torto or Murus Ruptus (Broken Wall), because at one point they seem to collapse. Even in Roman times, this stretch was never fortified or rebuilt, in the belief that St. Peter himself would protect the city at that point (translator's note).

To Dig Or Not to Dig

All air oxidizes
the pride of discoveries.
Stranger, when you see
excavations under way
turn your gaze
direct it elsewhere.
The sight of new ruins
falsifies the tourist map
and raises not by a single rung
the inaccessible ladder
of returned remains.
In our absence
we'll entrust the subsoil
to cosmic mail
to be delivered
to unknown descendants,
in future memory of us,
in accordance with Western Tradition.

(Translated by Antonino Mazza)

PROFANITIES

ANTONIO PASCALE

Some guys have got to spend the day collecting kickbacks at construction sites. The shakedown guys are either young or guys who haven't killed anyone yet—or else maybe they're older guys who, even though they've killed their fair share of buddies and bad guys, haven't managed to move up the ladder.

The rookies are usually teenagers and sometimes they don't have a car yet—so, when they go to the construction sites, they have to get themselves there on a scooter. The scooter should look a little beat-up, if for no other reason than it's a bad idea to take a good one to the construction sites. First of all, the roads on the sites are torn up and filled with potholes, so the mufflers go right away; and there are also all those mounds of earth which make it easy to bust one thing or another on the bike. And then if you take into account that it's necessary to go to the construction sites all the time, you've got your explanation for used scooters. As a rule the young rookie will steal some beat-up scooter, for example a Vespa 50cc special (one of those you see without taillight or kickstand, leaning up against a wall in some dark corner); and then he'll rig it up as a 125cc. Or else he'll pick out some other kind in terrible shape.

What may happen then is that the victim of the theft gets all upset, throws up his hands, and trudges off wearily to the *carabinieri.* He files a report, stressing the fact he had an old, beat-up scooter precisely because he didn't want to have it stolen or to excite anyone's envy—which is certainly not in short supply. The police officer writing up the report also responds wearily: That's what they do, that's what they do.

And so when the victim of the theft goes back home, he swears to himself that sooner or later he'll leave this country. But then he gives up thinking that way and begins to look at the cost of new scooters. Finally, he goes one day to a secondhand dealer, looks around, decides which one he wants to buy, and writes out a check. He truthfully complains about what a hardship this unexpected expense is—he's still unable to get over the loss. But he knows there's no way around it: he needs the scooter and he'll just have to buy one.

Before leaving, the victim of the theft looks the secondhand dealer in the eye and asks him for a really strong chain, the kind that even a bomb couldn't break. And the secondhand dealer shows him a whole run of heavy-duty hardware. But then maybe it happens that the secondhand dealer, looking his customer in the eye, begins to feel sorry for him—almost as if he recognized a shared anxiety.

So the secondhand dealer throws up his hands and explains that if they want to steal the scooter, in the end they'll always manage to do it—it's better, therefore, not to put too much hope in the chain. Sometimes, the secondhand dealer gives the chain away to the victim of the theft.

In the meantime, the young rookie will have put on a warm-up suit and with the beat-up scooter he takes off for the construction site. That's where he'll shake people down for money.

It's got to be said that those who go down to the construction sites to pick up the kickbacks almost always wear, for reasons of simplicity and practicality, warm-up suits with flashy logos—and they're often confused with the unemployed and the down-and-out, who also wear warm-up suits with flashy logos. The unemployed and down-and-out wear them for the same reasons the rookies wear them, though for the former it's to save on the laundry and clothing costs. And their logos are phony.

In any case, the guys who go down to the construction sites are like priests and cops: they always go in twos. The duo consists either of a veteran and a novice or else two first-time guys. If there's a veteran in the duo, he'll certainly be someone well-known because he's already made a name for himself. His reputation for acts of cruelty means he'll have an easier time getting what's owed. If, on the other hand, the duo is made up of two beginners, they'll have to learn how to do things the hard way. And this is especially true because no one is going to get frightened seeing a couple of kids come on a beat-up scooter that's bumping along over the potholes, the two "motor-centaurs" hardly able to hang on.

So it's up to the two of them to earn the respect of others. Generally they're short on ceremony and get themselves respected right away. There are other times, though, when they don't manage to get a single thing—no matter if they lower their gaze as if they're taking aim to land a head butt on the nasal septum of the guy they're talking to, no matter the cigarette that's always lit, no matter the phony hoarseness to their voice, and no matter their language, which starts out polite and right away becomes obscene. When they don't get results, it's necessary to enter into extended negotiations.

Because whenever the relationship with the targeted businessman is not based on a shared understanding, it's a good idea to make it so. It doesn't make any sense to start out by killing the person you're trying to get money out of.

In fact, since the organization follows the logic of a business enterprise and draws up a detailed cost-benefit balance sheet at the end of each month, you can't immediately resort to explosives or bullets, because there's a cost associated with them that's got to be measured precisely against revenues. This is why it's necessary to come to an agreement which is not totally demoralizing to the businessman. And this is why the two guys have to go back so often to the construction site, and why they wait awhile before resorting to any strong-arm stuff.

There's no doubt that the use of strong-arm measures is proportional to the level of resistance proffered by the person who is being shaken down. If, for example, you have a businessman who simply refuses to come up with anything (and this might actually happen), then the two guys would have their work cut out for them to generate some income without a significant expenditure of energy.

But there's also the businessman who leaves his home very early in the morning, around 4 am, and goes home only when the sun goes down (which, in the summer, might be 9 pm). The two guys have to stay on him to keep the threat going non-stop, and they're forced to follow him around from four in the morning until nine in the evening. In order to make the businessman feel oppressed from early morning on, they've got to stick to him from that early hour on. And they too will feel oppressed. They'll have to give up seeing their friends for a good part of the day and put off other plans.

Not to mention those who have another job and take on the duties and obligations of a hood in order to supplement their income—these guys find themselves in serious difficulty when confronted with cases like the above.

That's why when they're in a *bar* early in the morning and they're knocking back a brandy or an espresso, at times they may already feel at least as oppressed as the businessman. When the barman asks how things are going, they reply: "Okay, thanks," and then proceed to spew profanities at Jesus Christ or the Virgin Mary.

In any case, under normal circumstances, the two guys follow the businessman around and harass him from block to block—first with words, then with their fists.

It may happen from time to time, then, that the businessman is so sure he can get away without paying up that the two guys have to resort to those strong-arm measures: sudden cuffs to the head, punctured tires, threats to the family—or just the opposite: free advice to the relatives of the businessman. They go up to his children or his wife and they kindly ask them to put in a sensible word with that dick-head of a husband, because otherwise someone is liable to get hurt. But if the businessman, despite the advice of his family members, still doesn't give up, then the guys will have no choice but to take him (however reluctantly) to the boss himself.

The boss himself lives the life of a recluse, enclosed behind exceedingly high walls. Although as a young man he may have been able to get out and enjoy life, now as an adult he has to live with his family all around him, amidst his children's toys and pets, passing the time with some boring and harmless hobby—all this because his life is in constant danger on account of the elevated post he occupies in the structure of command. And so when the guy they're trying to shake down is brought in, the boss is only too eager to swing into action: he takes it all out on the businessman, slaps him around, screams in his face, and orders him to pay up. If the businessman doesn't give in, and instead proclaims, "I *earn* my money," the boss and the boys really take offense and shout in a chorus that they too earn their money, they don't just waste their time doing nothing.

Finally the boss gives a signal to come down hard on him and to kill him.

Now, all the young guys who go down to the construction sites are dutifully given detailed instruction from the earliest age on how to kill someone. They've taken shooting practice at improvised targets, such as road signs or other targets with a human silhouette mounted on dried river beds or on state property near the tollroads, where they can fire away to their heart's content.

They also know that, besides taking good aim, they should never try to shoot someone in the face or chest unless they have a machine gun. The latter weapon is best left in the hands of well-trained professionals. So they should instead always try to shoot the victim when his back is turned, if at all possible in the neck. This is the preferred method because the victim is certain to be armed and, since he's aware of the danger he's in, will try to defend himself as best he can. It's best, therefore, to avoid any needless confrontation and shoot the victim dead without spraying bullets all over the place.

On the other hand, if they have to kill a businessman who's reluctant to pay up, they do it by shoving death in his face, with the hope that, in extremis, he'll shit in his pants and pay up.

Some businessmen, however, as soon as they see the boys arrive at the construction site, don't want to waste any time: they tell the boys that they want to talk directly with the guy in charge. The businessman speaks very brusquely and assertively, like he's short on patience. The hoods get the message and take him to the local head honcho. The businessman opens up to the head honcho, expressing his heart-felt gratitude for his having received him. He then goes on to say that he knows who he's dealing with, and that was the reason he wanted to speak directly to him and not through intermediaries. Soon the local honcho softens up and the two of them, the businessman and the local honcho, work out an agreement on percentages. A collaborative relationship is launched, guaranteeing that the businessman's bid will win all future contracts and that the local honcho will garner commensurate praise and compensation. Thus, life goes on with no spilling of blood.

It should be pointed out that the death of a businessman is always a defeat for the two guys: they failed to get their way and, most importantly, failed to bring in a dividend to justify their expenses.

It often happens that the guys in the duo start to hate one another. And one guy may blame the other guy for something his buddy is not even aware of. The two guys, who used to be buddies, may cease to be friends—though each does everything he can to keep the other guy in the dark. Indeed, it may happen that one of the two has already decided that the other guy has got to die. But he must absolutely avoid arousing the suspicion of the other guy—otherwise, he'd risk losing his own life. Generally, one of the two makes the first move, spreading the rumor that there's reason to believe his buddy may be planning to betray the family. And so an investigation is undertaken.

Since none of the investigators, however, wants to take sides against those under suspicion (because they too might, at some point, be suspected of treason without them knowing about it), they don't deny or confirm the hypothesis until the head honcho gives the order to kill.

And so one morning, like any other morning, the buddy comes by to pick up the other guy. They say hello to one another, ask how it's going, sometimes they reply, "fine, thanks," utter a string of profanities, and then finally, when the other guy happens to have his back turned, the buddy shoots him in the neck. Then the guy who is still alive goes and gets another kid, who, from that point on, is his number two.

Sometimes it happens, on the other hand, that one of the two buddies has got to kill the other without knowing why. They're true friends, he trusts him more than his own mother. But he has to carry out the order, and even though he may have tears in his eyes, he does it.

Some of the guys who commit a murder may become, that same day, victims of horrible nightmares as the nighttime comes on. Some of them don't even try to sleep, and go out to some joint along the *via Domiziano* towards Pozzuoli and hang out there until the early morning. They go into the place with a girl or two and a few friends, and they start ordering a lot of drinks. They knock back quite a few rounds of liquor, and the more they knock back the more they lose control. They make fun of the waiter, who has to keep his mouth shut and not react; they start to paw the girls, who just keep quiet and let them do it; and they may even give a cuff on the head to one of their acquaintances, who might feel like killing them but realizes it's better to just laugh it off instead. They keep this up, in addition to the eating and drinking and throwing stuff on the floor, until they go off to the bathroom. And it may happen that before they can get to the toilet they vomit all over themselves—or else, if they manage to hold off (that is, with the vomit), perhaps they piss in their pants, get their hands all wet with pee, and everything gets filthy dirty. Then, later, when they see themselves in the mirror and try to pull themselves together, they realize that no matter how hard they try, their hair remains all messed up, their pants won't dry, their hands reek, their breath stinks. That's the moment they feel sad.

Before they leave the joint they turn nice again and leave huge tips to the waiters or whisper something sweet to the girl—and may even say thanks to her, without even knowing why they should be thanking her. They go back home around dawn, careful not to take any of the main roads, because that's the time the *carabinieri* set up roadblocks to spot-check IDs. They only travel on muddy back roads with plenty of potholes, some of them filled with water, and others not. And that's the time, while they're bouncing up and down on a back road, just as the air is becoming light again and the sky is lit orange, that's the time when they confide in a friend or the girl. They tell them they're unhappy because they're nothing but lousy rats, that sooner or later someone, maybe God himself, will punish them for being such assholes.

But the friend who's driving is still drunk and maybe doesn't understand him, or pretends not to understand him, and just nods—and the girl is half asleep and maybe hasn't even heard him, or pretends not to hear him, and just nods off enough to make it clear that she's not inclined to pursue a conversation. It's only later, much later, after they've gotten over that night out, and they wake up before noon and get back in the car to take care of some errands—it's only then that they realize they've been talking too much and they think back over their night out. Then they really begin to focus on themselves. They go back over the words they said and the responses or evasive reactions they got.

They've always known that sooner or later someone would kill them, but now they feel that that "sooner or later" is over—they know that their time has come. Something is in the works they don't know about.

Others, on the other hand, are convinced they hear voices. When it happens, they seriously believe that the voices aren't just any old voices but the voice of God, who speaks to them directly. Some seek out a priest and open up their heart to him.

In any case, as a result of these voices they start to lose sleep and in the morning can't keep their eyes open. Perhaps their fatigue leads them to act strangely, thereby confirming suspicions of their betrayal.

But precisely because the guy is still under the spell of his voices, he may not realize that the buddy he's had for years is about to line him up from behind.

Now, among the few buddies who manage to survive, there may be some who will finally be promoted to a higher rank and become a district head honcho—having demonstrated courage and an unblemished record of homicides.

Parenthetically, it needs to be said that, even though the local boss himself may no longer have to go down to the construction sites to collect the kickbacks, he is still supposed to perform a broad range and multiple series of leadership roles which are by no means simple and almost never routine in nature.

For example: he must travel constantly by car, back and forth, over the same old roads in order to get a feel for the territory; but, when necessary, he must also always be ready to consider an unexpected detour—for example, a road that leads to an unfinished overpass, the kind of place where they train horses and race custom-built racing cars.

You need the perspicacity to remember a turnoff unknown to most that can save the life of a few, or where to get on a road that starts out as asphalt and ends up all dug up, or to keep in mind an alley covered with mud all year round that conceals you from the gaze of others, or to always have a clear idea of the location of abandoned houses you can use as a hideout, or to know the bars along the route where you can take a break, or to be capable of venturing into places no one would think of going because of the excessive filth, mud, and cement. One has to be ready to give up a place the day after one has found it, and know how to ensure that useless places stay useless for everybody else while keeping them productive places for oneself.

You should never forget, for example, that pillar which was supposed to hold up a connecting ramp but now holds up only air: it may lie in a desolate area, in the middle of the countryside with high weeds all around, where the corn or wheat has not grown properly, feebly blossomed or yellowed ahead of time, passed over by the farmer, but serviceable as a reference point for a place to hide the goods. And one should know just where to find the unmanned railroad crossing that will put you on little-used shortcuts. And when you're on a shortcut, just forget about the potholes, the sudden dips in the roads, and don't bother focusing on the shoulder of the road to get a sense of what's ahead since you won't be able to see anything on account of the weeds, the bramble bushes, the reeds, the illegally dumped garbage with stuff like electrical appliances, hot-water heaters, mattress coils, armchairs and sofas, all tangled together and rusted out.

Never slow down for farm machinery coming your way or in your way, nor should you pay attention to cars that are pursuing or tailing you—when you're going fast, you want to bear down on the road and not just travel along it. Let circumstances dictate when you should be conspicuous or inconspicuous on the road. Never do anything that gives others the sense you're in trouble before you yourself feel it—therefore: don't flash your lights, don't honk your horn, don't observe the rules of the road,[1] don't slow down needlessly at stop-

[1] In Naples, to drive "normally" is to disregard the rules of the road. (translator's note).

signs,[1] don't look at the car in front of you but beyond it, out towards the end of the road on the other side of the curve. In short, you should drive as if you are going along a straightaway with no fear of losing control, not looking at all at the speedometer, not holding the steering wheel but being the steering wheel.

And then you have to remember to categorize properly the various construction sites and plots of land: some are the object of real estate speculation, others are likely to be expropriated by public authorities, and used to put up light towers or for digging natural gas pipelines, or where rail lines might be laid down, or sewers or drainage systems for runoff waters. One has to analyze in advance the land use of each parcel, its commercial value, study the price list for public works as if it were the Holy Gospel, be familiar with the property tax assessment, the formulas adopted for raising the investment capital, the estimate of anticipated profits. You must be well-informed and well-read if you want to occupy first place at the post ahead of the others; you have to know how to wait without getting nervous about when the companies are going to arrive, the third-party accounts, the sub-contractors. And above all, be able to get the maximum of information with the minimum of effort.

In order to be able to do all of the above, you have to create a network of acquaintances, draw up a map of the places where people like to gossip—perhaps because the food is good or because there's a lot of drinking. In short, set up a friend at every nerve center, a friend or a relative who's reliable, who will gather information in your absence, who can intuit things but not interpret them, who will give you timely reports but not on everything. You have to pay him well without going overboard, talk to him about everything but never tell him anything that's true—or if you have to say things that are true, keep the crux of the matter from him. You have to use him to get the facts

[1] Stop signs do not mean "stop" to the average driver in Naples. (translator's note).

and not to meet people—or if you need him to contact some obscure politician, he should do it shrewdly and obliquely, not zeroing directly in on the politician but moving gradually up the ladder one contact at a time, starting with the lowliest messenger boy up to his most trusted secretary.

If you come up with the right guy and the contact pans out, you should take pains to drop the friend from the loop (even before taking the matter in hand personally), maybe sidetracking the friend to something else. In that way, you guarantee that the friend's function as a beachhead has come to an end: the friend returns back to his little nerve center and the wheel starts to turn again *da capo.*

When everything is ready for the first contact, you should get involved personally and organize everything yourself. You write down, in order, the topics to be discussed. And this means you should be well-versed in them; hence: read up on the laws and ordinances, using expertise and cunning to make your way into public offices in order to obtain information from public officials—and whether they're compliant friends or not, always treat them with the greatest respect, doffing your cap and calling them "sir" even if they're just a piece of shit, or just a land-surveyor, or a do-nothing bureaucrat, or mere doormen, or the kids who do the cleaning. Always have your wallet ready to offer them something—to all of them, irrespective. Be willing to listen to the complaints of bureaucrats as well as personal matters, their own concerns and the concerns of others.

One should be prepared to give advice when necessary, but it should be in good taste, Catholic, moral, and level-headed. Make use of the facts given you to ascertain the bureaucrat's power or the insignificance of his office, whether he's a bigshot or just a big zero. In short, become one of the family, part of the office, known to everyone. Maintain a distant, absent-minded look about you, as if the matter didn't concern you.

Then, once you've got the information, and you're sure about the law and how to get around it, go ahead and organize your meetings with politicians and department heads, with flunkies who have connections with the relevant political forces, members of the city council, the mayor and vice-mayor (as well as their secretaries). Then move on to the investors, the businessmen, or the friends of friends. And in the course of the colloquies, never get bogged down in details which might frighten and intimidate—leave all the particulars and specific procedures up in the air. But let them soak in, so that they feel faintly troubling. Keep everything vague, because by keeping things vague you're not asking them to take on responsibility for anything that might make them anxious and block the illicit alliance—at the same time, though, you're cementing complicity.

Take pains to organize meetings in public places, if possible, knowing full well that a place out in the open looks less suspicious. On such occasions, you'll need to unleash, just outside the meeting place, a bunch of punks and criminals, young and of no account to anyone, so that in the event of their death no one would miss them. The hoods should also be completely in the dark, not even conscious of themselves—maybe drug addicts or guys about to become druggies—so that they wouldn't be able to testify to anything. They should, however, still possess sufficient strength, be sufficiently stupid, violent, wild, and aggressive, that in the event the police show up because of a tip or happen to be passing through on a routine patrol, the police would get tied up checking the criminal records of the hoods, maybe even arresting them.

In the meantime, you should take off for the road again, small roads, back roads, private roads, pathways not indicated on any map —and only return home after it's dark.

Now, it may happen that the local head honcho has to go running out of his house one morning to attend to one of his many commitments, and he may notice that there's an eerie silence all around him.

It's almost as if someone had plugged up his ears, so that he hears the world from the inside of a seashell.

To rediscover a more familiar sensation he lights up a cigarette—so he can feel the same old smoke in his throat and hear the usual sound of the cigarette lighter. He doesn't notice in that moment that one of his boys—one who's now ready to take his place as head honcho—is pointing a revolver at the back of his neck.

Then, some time later, after people have huddled around the dead person, as they usually do, it may happen that the fellow whose scooter was stolen awhile ago passes by. He looks at the dead person and recognizes him: it's one of his old classmates.

And then, even though he's barely finished uttering a string of profanities, he crosses himself, turns around and goes as far away as he can.

(Translated by Lawrence Garner)

from SMALL SONGBOOK OF FROST *AND* TENDRILS

Flavio Santi

I have been ruminating over how diabolical the family really is.
—Tommaso Landolfi

Small Songbook of Frost

I hate my father
I hate it when he goes up
the steps forgetting
the door is open
like the scalpel
in the cut and
then he goes down that way and
polishes the spoiler
of the latest car
like the great snail
betrays with its slime
I hate this dialysis and Fernet
father
that makes a hell
out of the belly:
father, shit.

*

If I close my legs
in a cloister shape they look like my mother's
garden, a patch of sparse
hair—crude parchment.
A fruitless orange grove.
It seems the most I can say—
about myself anyway—is this: stretch out
on my belly and do things.
With the clumsy
fatigue of a farmer
in a fruitless orange grove or
the ledger made of infected
sheepskin. And how much
sweetness there is to all this!
With what excuse does one rush to assume
that a baby will never bear
the weight of a grown penis
and a dark soul?
For many years
one pretends not to notice
how that underwear smells
of bleach and more
as *he* nears. Or that
the easiest way
to see love
is to pass the shadowed door,
to seize the fleshy threat
of the father on the mother.
It's as if one never thinks
that behind the end of the last
infinite page, Minnie
perennially offers her operculum,
her underworld to handsome Mickey.

Vacation

I'm stunned by the distance
between my family and me:
by now my brother in overalls or
with rolled sleeves
with vampire teeth
to disparage.
He, with tiled muscles, could easily
flatten me at will. He'd lead his friends
that I thought of as wimps.
He loved his girlfriends
that I considered vultures.
Never loved:
hearing him, my head
began to throb.
Hearing him with his friends, now
that they are butchers,
plumbers, hardly any—imagine—finished school,
usually flunked at least a year
while I, yes, sure, oh . . .

Mechanic, hated,
brother that doesn't
ever close the door
behind him, like
his hateful jackass friends
you don't know what you're missing,
you don't know who you're missing,
illustrious bourgeois
full of bullshit, you live or die
like stones—it's just the same . . .
One says then:

"For the meantime, we'll start
here, then if things go well
I'll transfer" (my brother).

Where to start
means with a business,
the shop. As for transfer,
it's understood to a town
other than his own.
But I also see my father once again
sleeping with his feet
sticking out from the sheet
since there was only one room
in which to sleep and hate.
And my mother's brooding over
her ovaries like precious jewels.
Nearing the bathroom
there she was, *my* mother always a bit lower:
behind a silver oxide hedge
gripping her wrists, her laces
undone, the red fruit drips.
This on vacation, the little swallows hear
and more excited chirps.

Return from Vacation

Everything's the same at home,
except for the appearance of the electric
razor for my brother's early beard.
Here they are: events
lighter than a dog paw's steps,
lighter than the kettle's egg
boiling in the kitchen over there . . .

*

Mother, if you can keep out
the world of thunderbolts,
mother of needs and corners,
apocryphal mother of the gospels, of the stoups
and of bidets . . . My dear mother,
who bore me with profound hope:
your son, look, has a splintered heart,
and milk in his testicles and such a swamp;
meanwhile—like everyone—
he shits from his ass.

*

"Do you have enough paper?"
asks the father cursing and rummaging
at the bathroom door.
Toilet paper he means:
Such tenderness for my bowels, I think.
I loved you through a crippled mist,
my deep mist.

Although more than one communist's heart
had already exploded for communism

(G.G.)

But the oldest rose I hand
to my father:
his death moves me
like the death of the liveliest
of beings.
It is between his teeth, few and stained,
that I'd see his animated tales
fill in with saliva.
And he was the one who loved to say
that "la pulitica" means nothing to us.
And he was the one who heard
the crumbs arm themselves with misery
and fall from the table.
He really belonged to an ancient
procession, by now false as
Greek casts.
And he had been at Valle Giulia[1]
and that was *pulitica.*
Now that the city closes in–
iodoform and anise—
and hangs over the family tomb,
that everything has become
all this and today has become
our now,
he seems

[1] Valle Giulia, a place in Rome where students and police battled in 1968 (editor's note).

more like a ruined horse.
The pulitica is also this:
complaining of cold,
finding a chain
to tie oneself to
to disappear behind a rib
or a dove . . .
Or just to say,
"We've looked for it for years—
that emotion as
fundamental
as taking first Communion. We have
looked for it, not found, at times
hoped for, always improved
in our own personal gallows.
We also cursed,
advised badly, at times
even despised each other."

Tendrils

As if heard from an intercom,
the cloudbursts don't frighten
and the water drains
into metallic railings,
where it mixes
with the words—inside
the intercom—coming
from below
sounds of torn cardboard.
Like this
television comes
to Naples in 1955 in December:
the newspaper reports it,
San Giuseppe and the oxen.

My freckles still hadn't exploded.
It still wasn't the Italy of '77
that Italy one faced
from the antenna of the TV transmitter.
There was no diesel smell, but just
a charming baby . . . a flower . . .
Between a *formaggino*[1] and a clot of blood,
especially if the cheese has an Egyptian-like
name (Ramek!) I couldn't tell the difference
and still can't, to be quite honest.
For me, outside's as good as in.
I don't distinguish, like everything else,

[1] *Formaggini* are little creamy cheeses for kids that typically come in a triangular shape (editor's note).

because I'm disgusted
enough by both. Shooting
and smiling comes out the same
just like little tin trucks
or tracks of marbles:
in the end, whoever wants to wins.
It's the bed I made:
fronds, pajamas, a face
like a solitary cabin.
I got used to it
and when mother called
"Giusva!"[2] to me, I answered
with a tongue spraying saliva,
opening fire.

"But how was Italy back then?"
"Pasolini was about to die; Mina was singing *Sei grande grande grande*; magnets were loaded with negative
storms; the Christian Democrats were preparing
to compromise themselves; pants ended in bell bottoms;
and we were all as used
to one another
as a dog to its master.
People kept on croaking on you
on a chessboard of chance."
"I get it . . ."

---

[2] These poetic fragments are subtitled "From the Confessions of the Actor and Terrorist Giusva Fioravanti." Giusva Fioravanti was a terrorist linked to the neofascist group NAR, accused of having carried out the Bologna train station massacre in 1980, which killed 85 people. At four years of age, Giusva Fioravanti had performed in the first TV ads and later became famous as a soap opera actor before his arrest (editor's note).

Oh bliss of the lit television
keeping one company
both in gleeful hours and in sickness.
My father died there before it.
His stomach's like a drum.
I inherited his reticence,
I realized it today
how he deflated in his deathbed
into the void of an eggshell,
his chest a basket.
You were allergic to shots.
Father who traveled with me,
and crossed an idea:
one can also die of a virtuous silence.

I would like to be one of those
fine August revolutionaries,
shouldering his heart, always ready
to laugh at God,
or at his predecessor
as well as his eventual opponent.
The voice under the hoarse tongue:
fewer thorns in the mouth and more berries.
Skilled at discovering
mole holes, at
talking nonsense
before bags of rice
and at praying.
I'd really like to be like that,
a tense convinced revolutionary.
By now my hope
is a delirium.

I'll never have the face
of the German *Jugend*:
fiercely freckled,
hay-shaded blond. The eye
curling straight back
to the Führer, perfect
as a silver keel.
And at night I'll never have
the texture of moon,
the reel of silk
to shine and make for me
the borders of *history*. And never
will I crawl beneath its new sheets.
I will always mistake
home for a tomb.

(Translated by Ann Snodgrass)

THE LESSON

Arnaldo Colasanti

These are my students: cats and chimps in a small classroom at the Professional High School at the Castelli Romani. Lucio is a mastiff. You would guess he was nineteen, but he's four years younger. He's clean-shaven, with a bleached-blond goatee, over his T-shirt is a heavy shirt that hangs down to his mid-thigh. His shoulders—a solid slab of muscle—seem like a hunter's bow tensed to its limit. Lucio isn't particularly fast on his feet, either: he seems to have difficulty walking, despite his tight-fitting skullcap and his enormous break-dancer's shoes. He isn't able to sit still for long, on his small, cracked classroom chair. His strength is entirely potential, an eleatic vigor, a bulky, primordial roughness and size—moving or motionless.

This morning, just as class was beginning, he said: "Excuse me, Teach, I need to talk to you about something." We left the classroom together and went to lean against the rusted radiator across from the coffee-vending machine. He asked me: "Listen, could you give me the street address of that slut that teaches Math? Or, maybe just tell me which car she drives? I'm fed up with her crap, and I want to set her little wig on fire." The odd thing is that there was no hatred, no resentment in his voice. He was perfectly calm: even resigned, perhaps. It was just that he couldn't see how to avoid this new labor that the world demanded of him. At first, I didn't understand. When he told me (after I had delivered my short sermon to dissuade him from action) that at the very least he felt duty-bound to punch her in the nose ("otherwise, I'll feel bad, and then it just gets worse," he confessed), I suddenly understood that "Goofy the Junky," aka Lucio, one of my students in Second Year/Class H: Advertising Graphics, is good-hearted and less of a savage than most of his fellow students. I said nothing. I raised both eyebrows, as if to say, "Well, this time you'd better drop it." He gave me a manly hug, suffocating me, the way friends do in the neighborhood. He knew that he couldn't do this to me, of all people.

There they go, back and forth, like every morning. It is always astonishing to see how incapable these kids are of spending time together unless they engage in this byplay of shouting and shoving. It is even more astonishing to discover this subterranean law: each and every one of them, and this is not negotiable, wants to have an exclusive relationship with me, in some manner or form. During the day, there must be a moment of undivided attention. That's the way they are. At some point during the day, they need to speak to me, privately, and never in front of the others. Either outside of the classroom entirely or else, occasionally, and with a degree of anxiety, along the vague border of the teacher's lectern, shrouded by the noise of the class. When I was younger and just starting my teaching career, I believed that my athletic, vitalistic management of the class was a test, a genuine intellectual challenge. I actually thought that it was an exercise of charisma with respect to children whom I had set out to captivate in this manner, through a form of culture fed to them indirectly, through play, closeness, mutual empathy—by means of the quick retorts that showed I was ahead of them, ready for them. Every morning, I had to conquer the classroom, capture their attention, and show them that I deserved their respect.

Today, I feel different. Tired, lonely. I've walked around the world, and now I just want to stop walking. I would like to be able to look at them, the way the other teachers do, without grief, with a sense of acceptance that they are going to leave this school and go out into the world, one after another, forgetting about me, and forgetting about everything I ever believed in: poetry, study, intellect. Or maybe not. I really can't say what remains of the past fifteen years of teaching. I do know that Lucio, remote, intractable, remains before me eternally: that, day after day, his fifteen-year-old eyes watch me, scrutinize me, continuing to ask me everything, concealing nothing from me, playing it straight, with the unripe, overwhelming gravity of youth.

Passion is a labyrinth, it is a soul: life smolders secretly at every moment. I might have gotten more out of life, I might have had an easier time in my personal relationships, and even my teaching might have been less complicated, if I had only been able to break away for a little while from this obsession—an uncompromising work ethic, my aspiration for a shared civilization, my desire to see in reality how culture shapes the mind, how a word can teach someone to understand, to attain happiness, the substance of life. But I am wrong, even now, to think about things this way. In fact, I still see you, I recognize you the way I always have. Already, in my mind, I am running through each of your names, each of your faces, never faltering: twenty-nine adolescents locked up in a rundown little schoolroom; girls and boys, all dressed identically, with a certain sameness, a heartbreaking uncertainty, and yet still intact, not yet worn out. Sometimes I think that a teacher is nothing more than a student who is left back, year after year. A ridiculous man: a child who walked into a classroom one day and then, somehow, couldn't find his way out, wandering this way and that through the halls, beneath the neon lighting, climbing endless staircases to countless floors, walking past the shiny, scratched metal of the locker rows. The child was a child; then he began to dream, and from that moment on he became older, more fragile—more self-aware.

"He was called Malpelo because he had red hair, and he had red hair because he was a mischievous rascal who promised to turn out a real knave."[1] "Hey, knucklehead!" Lucio cries out immediately, tripping up poor Daniele, who constantly raises both hands and protests vehemently because he wants to keep reading, despite his voice, which is cavernous, stopped-up, unctuous. "Hey, Mop 'n' Glow, what'd you do, put floor pads in your adenoids?" calls out Chiara, in surprise, one day (tiny blond braids, five or six sky-blue plastic hairclips in her hair, about thirty little rings on each hand, the rings that come with Easter eggs). The room explodes. Followed by laughter and the sound of chairs being jerked across the floor, while pens are whirled up into the air and then clatter to the ground. I hurry to the lectern, and I demand quiet. I glare hypnotically into the audience.

Really, though, I know perfectly well what's happening. All this is a little aftershock, the crack of a structure settling, almost a regurgitation of mother's milk, before the story works its magic, definitively, on one and all. Even Lucio, for that matter, is calm: he folds his shoulders over onto the desk, stretching out his arms with bovine complacency, ready to listen with docility to "Chat Line," as the designated reader is known, or, in certain cases, "Vick's VapoRub." The kids are finally ready. They curl up. They aren't quite asleep, but they fall into a state of perfect distraction, rapture, remoteness, and yet intensely alive; the way it is possible to be only when you are fifteen, as they peer into a dream world, amidst the words of a story written many many years ago. Rosso was "an ugly-looking creature, with a surly, quarrelsome and excitable temperament to match . . . He thrived on being kicked about, and allowed them to load him up more heavily than the grey mule, without ever daring to complain." The problem that afflicts those who teach is not so much the downgrading of the teacher's status, the deterioration of the schools, or the grueling routine. It is something different, a tragedy that is particular to the soul. Is there anyone alive, I wonder, who can stand the vision of life

[1] All citations from Giovanni Verga, *Cavalleria Rusticana and Other Stories,* translated by G.H. McWilliam (London: Penguin), 1999.

when life itself, at the very peak of its potential, seems to entail humiliation, defeat, and the weltering propagation of pure failure? And youth itself, when all is said and done, isn't it actually a secret bubble, the summit of solitude and perfection? Youth, in reality, is a coin that has been taken out of circulation: something incorruptible and finite, which finally becomes crystalline and unusable—a heartbreaking eternal voice that lies deep within the mysteries of each of our personal selves. We adults, held captive by school like Tancred, amidst the dazzling shadows of children, can understand in sketchy fragments the occasional miracle, or perhaps sense, with the gaze of the blind, the remarkable meaning of things—but no more. We must lower ourselves, overturn our minds, become humble, even humiliated. We must make them laugh and bring them to us in whatever way we can. Perhaps we are hovering figures: like those angels with bellies rendered transparent by the gleam of the light and with a stucco foot in midair, neither frescoes, nor true visions, in the corners of Baroque churches. We must fall into their fugitive bodies, and resigned, retreating, recall that at that moment, what is at work is the urgency of a formidable deed, a painful but authentic necessity. And so a teacher is a non-existent being. A teacher is also someone who, to them, embodies loyalty, a subtle confused threshold—the ridiculous, never definitively consummated tragedy of intimacy. "Outside the cave, the sky was teeming with stars, while down there his lantern was pouring out smoke and swinging from side to side. The big red pillar, ripped open by the blows of his spade, twisted and bent itself into an arc as if it had a stomach ache, and groaned on its own account. Malpelo cleared everything from the floor of the cave, making sure the pickaxe, the empty lunch bag and the flask of wine were in a safe place." The years of school are not used up for anybody. They are years that you possess, which is why you have to hide them, why they have to be lost. The kids who are yelling today, growing so fast you can see it, are actually standing perfectly still, and can have no more ripening to do. They will leave school when they have been stripped of everything, denuded of their own intangible youth. I have seen so many things in all these years; I thank destiny for having left me here, looking out this window. The kids that I have known have done nothing more than to leave intact their youth in the soft cocoon of these schoolrooms, walled in every day by the yelling, by the buzzing of voices—names, eyes, smiles: a million Francescas, Alessandros, Valentinas—as if all life, and what matters even more than life, had been sucked away, stolen forever, hidden in a drawer, in a quarry where everything that is unknown to us is kept, those things we can never hope to reach. School becomes a house full of ghosts.

"Stay back! Watch out! Watch out for stones or thick sand falling from above.

"Malpelo, who had turned away to stow the tools in the wicker bag, heard a dull, thunderous roar as of sand shifting en masse all at once, and the light went out." A teacher remains alone. A teacher must withstand seeing a light burning while no one is at home, the void that spreads and engulfs.

The sun behind my back has become stronger. The fumes of the smog, pierced by the folds of bright light, evaporates like a cream, like a wall of transparency. The creaking of the chairs, the scraping of a key on a desk, the flashing gleam of the books and then, the whispering of someone who is acting up when everything is supposed to be, finally, calm. Here, these colors, these voices seem to spin before me for an instant in a gust of wind, like an opening door that whirls the air and ruffles the pages, the pen caps, the crumbling walls, the sweaty lightness of my hair.

What have I done in all these years? What have I thought, dreamed in this school, moving along the various floors, climbing up and down the staircases, while the numbers of the classrooms mingle confusedly, dying and springing back to life like the seasons? I truly don't know why my life has gone the way it has. The students may have loved me, and maybe a few of them have learned to be less afraid—a demon or two may have faded from existence. But they have certainly been given very little, perhaps nothing at all. None of them has ever heard the real lesson that I have been dreaming about for years and that I run through my mind every second of the day, when I glimpse in my thoughts the long nights of Sparta, the ochre sky of Athens—and Troy "with its broad streets," Andromache, Hector before his slaughter, Ajax and Anticlus, Euryalus, Nisus, their lives, their deaths, the promise of friendship in a kiss, the lava-like beauty of Silvia and Nerina. I have failed. Perhaps many of us are failing. We are incapable of conveying that literature, in order to exist, must encompass communication, an open spirit, a radical commitment to meaning. School is coming to an end, perhaps it has already ended. It has been murdered by a new terror: kids, for the first time (in the Lord only knows how many generations), are afraid that they will no longer be able to attain the security and the legitimacy their parents achieved. They sense that study is no longer the main road—and it might even be a total dead end.

The sun is setting on school, it has been attacked by a root blight. Culture itself, first and foremost, has lost its ability to instruct, educate, generate passions and dreams (who still thinks, I wonder, that literature is still a way of being faithful to a feeling against which to test the present tense?). In all these years, I never delivered that lesson. And I am ashamed of that. I ran, I ran endlessly. Perhaps I became wrapped up in their insecurities, trying to dissipate them with a finger, with the endless labor of the gaze. And I have stayed here. "In the crowd of people all talking at once, nobody was taking any notice of a child's voice, yelling like a lunatic."

(Translated by Antony Shugaar)

from CEPHALONIA, 1943–2001

LUIGI BALLERINI

Hans D

I'm not one of those who stays up nights to claim that the face of a Jack Palance proves there were good guys even among the Nazis as even now there are, sumptuously frescoed with a Lugar in hand and suspenders. I maintain, of course, that to add "Proud to Be" to "Who Gives a Damn" (so foreigners know who we are) it isn't necessary to evoke the advantages of a coherent foresight: enough to be convinced of having once and for all overcome the temptation to appear as yourself. Who would dare speak of *Zeitgeist* for the peach blossoms a little old lady sells at the cross-roads "while it rains and pours through the fitful gusts of harsh wind?" Even if a son of mine had not eaten of my unleavened bread, it won't be this philology of who's left afloat keeping him far from the dangers of an apotheosis: the goddamnedest desire to make a difference is learned by watching those who with repeated nonchalance repent mistakes made illustrating the unstoppable rhythm of their own emancipation: queen of hearts is different from premature queen, from the high price that will not endure, that cannot endure, different, naturally, from the contempt I love, from which I must carefully demure

Ettore B

in the sun we can breathe, this is a fact, and it is facts that
give things meaning, pushing to say them before anyone
gets the idea to make a list, to put their anguish to sleep and
translate into closer, more adhesive horizons the challenge that
issues from them, that shells and grinds the out-of-the-bag law,
the truce of their vanishing. We can say: "We are and we will be
successful animals, those Pekinese with saccharine eyes"
and never die; or else, *"You disappoint me, Mr. Bond,"*
and end up dead with our own (shameless) luck at our backs:
in a field half-gray and half-black there are those poppies
and Mamelukes and mambas and manzanitas; there are also
industrious ducks who rent it in partnership with turkeys, who
however are not there, because to get there you have to go
across a ditch. Is it irreverent? Isn't it leftist? Or is it holy, holy,
thrice holy, the time when under the whistling (blowing) wind
and the thundering storm (raining down leaves), we too will
keep quiet about the last of us, seeing inscribed in the idea of
pattern the disappearance of the idea of holiday? I have never
been someone who enjoys another's illness (but irritating myself
irritates me plenty), and in the face of a massacre of infantry
that quietly moves forward, I say it's the winner who is lost
who keeps rubbing his hands to let out the smell of death

(Translated by Paul Vangelisti)

SECOND ONLY TO VERSAILLES

FRANCESCO PICCOLO

If people ask us where we're from, we tell them we're from Caserta. Then they tell us: You've got the Royal Palace at Caserta.[1] We already knew they were going to say that, but we don't deny it. Yes, we say, we've got the Royal Palace. Then all of us say more or less the same things about the Royal Palace: second only to Versailles—Italy's Versailles. If it were located in France (or in Germany—there's always someone who takes Germany as their model), it would be more famous than Versailles. We know it's stupid to say these things, but we can't come up with anything else. That's all there is to it.

We were raised with this rivalry. We can't stand the people of Versailles—though they never did anything to us. And if we go to Versailles, we walk through the rooms and the gardens in a tormented, competitive state of mind—filled with pride or dejection, depending on the victory or defeat in each comparison.

Then again, it's not as if we regularly go to the Royal Palace of Caserta. We are proud of it, but, we've seen it so many times, for us it's just there. When we were little kids they used to take us to throw bread crumbs to the fish, but then they got tired of taking us because we were always wondering how much longer this whole business of throwing bread to the fish would go on.

---

[1] The *Reggia* of Caserta was built from 1752 to 1774 for Charles III, then king of the Kingdom of Naples and a member of the Bourbon Royal family (translator's note).

We felt like doing other things.

Nowadays, we go to the Palace when relatives or friends come from out of town, and we tell them, as we go from room to room, "Second only to Versailles," as we've learned to say for many generations. They are delighted and say, "But what are you complaining about if you've got something as beautiful as this?"

At that point we might get the urge to tell the anecdote related by Vittorio Imbriani in his *L'impietratrice*. It seems Cesare Borgia went to visit the Carthusian Monastery of Naples, "perhaps the most delightful place in all of Europe." When the prior took him out to the terrace of the Belvedere, "whence you can survey all the city and the lovely surrounding hillsides and our charming little crater," Borgia "couldn't stop singing its praises, saying that the place was the replica of Paradise on earth and that the good monks should have no other desire than to dwell in its hermitage. The prior, amiable fellow that he was, took Borgia to see other things, and then took him back to the same terrace. Borgia, who had initially not stinted in singing its praises, said, 'It's a beautiful place—let's go see some other things.' They went into the sacristy, where they observed the very best in the way of silversmithing, embroidery, painting, sculpture—and then he was led back via another path to the terrace. But he didn't want to visit it, saying, 'Father, we've seen it two times. *Basta!'* And then the prior said with a smile, 'If Your Lordship is annoyed so quickly, think about us, who have no other view than this one, which puts before our eyes the one and the same city, the very same hillsides, and the same sea.'"

The fact is that if we went out on the balcony of the Royal Palace—which we don't— we wouldn't even see the city. The city is off to the left, all of it developed off to one side, so that the Royal Palace is not really in the center of town. It's not as if you go by it every day, it's not as if we ever say that we'll meet in front of the Royal Palace. No, it's simply there. From the city we can see one side of it, but when it looms near that means we're on the outskirts of town, and we turn around and head back. If we did go out on the balcony—which we don't— we would see landscaped meadows, the train station, and a major road beyond the station which runs long and straight towards Naples. The tourists can get off the train or bus, go and see the Royal Palace, and then depart without our ever seeing them.

Here it seems that life, real life, passes us by, as though real life were somewhere else. And that's the way it seems to everyone who lives outside of the big cities (who knows if the people who live in Versailles feel that way about it—it wouldn't bother us one bit if they did).

We always hang out together. And we usually just kill time, and not much more. From the time when we were little they always told us that it was better to be together in a group, and they taught us to be suspicious of anyone who wasn't in the group, who was always off studying or doing anything at all useful. We knew that it was better at sixteen to take out Dad's car without permission and go cruising around at three in the afternoon, to go one-wheeling along down the whole length of main street on our mopeds, to spend our afternoons in the street, drinking coffee at a *bar*; we knew it was better to always be ready for a fight, that it was better to smoke Marlboros and drink alcohol, just because we knew this was the way to be looked up to, to be "in." This was the way to get girls to fall hopelessly in love with us without their ever understanding why. The girls would say to the other guys that, of course, it would make more sense to be in love with them, because they were sensible and smart; but the girls always ended up deciding to keep the sensible and smart guys just as friends.

It was true, they found us captivating for some perverse reason ("What can I do," the girls would say, "it's not my fault"), and so in the end we were the ones picked—we were the best.

And so we fell in love, and the girls fell in love with us. But things dragged on and on; we would see each other every day. We could put things off as long as we wanted, especially since we were all there together, as if in a cage. And so we stayed in love for years and years with girls we didn't even know, and the same was true for the girls. We thought we were in love, and the girls thought so too—but we weren't really sure, and so we waited, and they waited. And we could do that because it was as if we were already engaged.

Later, when we were adults and we saw that the guys who'd studied and stayed out of the group had become doctors or city officials, we didn't really regret being the way we'd been. We'd laugh and say we'd never go to them for an appointment or cast a vote for them. After all, how could we ever think that they'd be able to do anything right if they didn't even know how to go one-wheeling on a moped, if they'd never had a girl, or if they got cuffed on the head every time they left school, were always studying, and at eighteen were already wearing glasses and still had acne pimples.

The rest of us, though, have seen each other every day since we were little kids. We feel as if we should do something, but we don't really do much of anything. It's a ritual that we know, and that gets played out every Saturday night. We also know that what we hope for will never happen, not even on a Saturday night—but we're sure next Saturday will be different.

When Saturday comes around, we start making threatening phone calls to each other in the early afternoon, and the message is always: "Tonight we have to have some fun, it's Saturday. We'll get together at the usual place and then we'll decide."

So, we meet and try to decide.

"How about going there?"

"It's too far."

"Well, let's go over there then."

"So close? If that's all we came out to do . . ."

"How about going for a pizza?"

"On a Saturday? It's a mob scene."

"But I know a place where no one ever goes."

"Sounds sad."

"Discotheque?"

"It's sweaty."

"A jazz club?"

"On a Saturday? It's a mob scene."

"How about coming over to my place for a really great plate of spaghetti?"

"On Saturday, we're gonna just stay at home?"

Finally we agree on a place which manages to get a majority of votes, but by this time it's midnight and so we have to move fast. It's not difficult, all we have to do is make a decision on the cars. We have too many of them, someone will have to leave his behind and go in someone else's car. But the problem is that Marco will have to pick up his girlfriend pretty soon (though it's hard to figure out how soon, since it's almost a quarter past twelve). So he can go with Stefania, but first he has to go find a gas station because he's down to his last drop of gas. Nothing difficult, it'll take a little time, but now we're getting it together. *Okay, let's see. You leave your car here. Oops, no, you have to drop it at your place because you don't have a car alarm. Okay, you go and Francesco will come by and pick you up. No, Francesco can't have five people in his car because the sticker's expired and the car belongs to his aunt. So, let's have the others get out and another couple go with them: Gianni and Carla. No, not those two, Francesco's girlfriend and Carla aren't on speaking terms-okay, so they'll just keep quiet. Are you really serious? Worse comes to worst it'll be like in the puzzle of the wolf, the goat, and the head of cabbage. In other words, someone takes Francesco and Carla, then he brings Carla back and drops her here, then he takes Francesco's girlfriend . . . alright, you guys figure it out. Otherwise, just stuff five in the car and if you get a ticket we'll split the cost, if they arrest you, we'll split that too. How many are left now, how many? Guys, you've dropped off too many cars, let's go get another one. Who do I go with?*

How about you, Francesco?

We've already got five.

So have 'em get out of the car for a minute!

Hey, what time is it?

One-thirty?

Okay, I'm not going—I gotta go keep my girlfriend company.

I got a game tomorrow morning.

Okay, forget the whole thing, by the time we get there, find parking, get into the place, get our order in, eat, pay, leave, come back . . .

It doesn't matter, we'll have fun next Saturday.

Once again, real life has eluded us. And so, at a certain point, we start thinking that we should leave this place. This is a recurrent theme: both for those of us who actually do leave and for those of us who will never leave but are always saying that one of these days we're going to leave. Those who really leave, when they come back and meet up with those who wanted to leave and didn't, hear: "You're so lucky—you left."

Many of us did go away. Off to the big cities, obviously, because otherwise it was pointless to leave, but we still return from time to time. When we go away, we say that life elsewhere is completely different. But then, as soon as possible, we come back. It's like we can't really escape. For those of us who have gone away for good, the Royal Palace takes on special meaning. When we see a side of it from the train window—the opposite side you see from the city—it means we've arrived.

When we get to the station, sometimes we take the bus. And it's a funny thing that we experience—maybe it's just a false sensation, or the reason we feel it isn't what we think it is—but this is what happens to us: When we get off, our hands don't feel all sticky and grimy the way they do when we're living in the city. Reason tells us to wash them as soon as we get home, the way we do compulsively in the big city, but we don't. Maybe our hands don't normally feel sticky and grimy in Caserta because the people around us aren't strangers. It's a stupid thought, but that's how we feel when we come back home.

Maybe it's because there's no one else on the bus, but sometimes we feel ashamed when we come back. The bus cuts across the only pedestrian mall in town, and it's a narrow street lined with stores. The driver keeps honking the horn, and the people have to throw themselves up against the wall to let it go by. Everybody looks inside, and there's just one of us and the driver on board, and we're causing all this ruckus, with the mothers pulling their children aside and the horn honking and all the rest of it. And there's this dense black smoke billowing from the bus, and since it's having trouble getting through, it takes a long time, and the sooty thick smoke stinks up the whole street. So, while this bus is having a hard time getting through, time goes by, and pretty soon another bus arrives and then another one. The drivers honk their horns, and the buses spew out clouds of black smoke, and you become more and more aware it's just one of us, riding the bus. Saturday afternoons we go for a stroll on that street before getting ready for Saturday night. There are a lot of us and every few steps we have to press up against the wall and wait and breathe in that black smoke. When that bus has finally gotten through, we hardly have a chance to begin our stroll again when another one comes along and we have to stand against the wall again. And you ought to try some time leaning up against the wall, and you ought to see how many people are out for a stroll and have to move out of the way so the buses can get by. And then you ought to count the number of buses which come by, and it seems as if we have heavier traffic than in the big cities. And then you ought to count the total number of people on those buses for the whole evening: seven, maybe eight, if they're lucky. Still it's great, because there's just us and the driver, and you can talk with him. Actually, you feel you have to talk to him because he's always alone; and sometimes, if we hit it off, he asks us where we want to go and he lets us off not at the bus stop but right at the corner of the street where our house is, just like a taxi. And then he says, "See ya," because he hopes that we liked him and that next time we'll ride with him again.

The narrow street is called via Mazzini, and when they decided to make a pedestrian mall—a stretch that runs 200 meters at the most—panic broke out. The storeowners screamed bloody murder, that it would ruin them. And even the city officials who wanted the mall admitted that it would be difficult. Every time that we want to do something in Caserta, it's always "something very difficult."

This is not a matter of party politics. It makes no difference whatsoever whether the left-of-center coalition is Christian-Democratic or the right-of-center coalition is Christian-Democratic. It makes no difference because even those of us who are Marxist-Leninists are Christian Democrats; and those of us who are Neo-Fascists, are also Christian Democrats. It's not just the former Christian Democrats who are Christian Democrats, but also the elderly, young people, workers, business owners, ecologists, protesters, city employees, the rich, the poor, the people who play sports and the shut-ins. Everybody. It has nothing to do with politics. It's our genetic make-up. Outsiders just don't understand it—not that it matters to us.

From a theoretical standpoint, we're not badly off. No. We think that everything should be changed, that nothing here is right, that Caserta should become one of those model cities of the North (it's got just the right size, the ground is level, and it has a temperate climate), and we keep saying that we could all ride around on bikes. This business of the bikes is one of the things we say to each other more than anything else: it's a kind of obsession, us and the bicycle, that we could all ride around on bikes. It's something we especially like to say when we get together in the *piazza* or at a *bar*. Actually, we say that city hall should make bikes available to all of us—as they do in other cities (though no one can give an example). The "good citizen" (that's what we call the guy who's supposed to pick up his bicycle in front of the town hall—the good citizen, as if we were sure it wouldn't be one of us who'd be doing it) each morning would leave his house, pick up his beautiful bicycle, go off, do whatever he had to do and then bring it back, so that someone else could use the bike, and then later, yet another person. Then Caserta would be one great pedestrian mall, a city with a genuine European feel to it (like other European cities that no one can name).

If we say this, everyone nods approvingly, and if others say it to us, we nod approvingly. If, however, one of us who works for the city in the Department of Transportation later thinks: Aha, if everyone is saying this, let's go ahead and do it. Well, the whole thing changes. Everybody, and by everybody I mean the poor, the rich, the people who play sports, the young people (who after all are those of us who say they'd like to change the world), all of us, and I mean all of us, say, "You've got to be crazy to think that we could do something like this in Caserta. After two hours the bicycles'll be snatched, they'll repaint 'em and say that they bought them themselves. You really think someone's not going to take his car in the morning and instead get on a bicycle, pedal, and get all sweaty. You know how they are, the *Casertani.*" "And when it rains, then what do you do?" "Alright, when it rains, we can suspend the ban on driving cars." "Oh, you've got an answer for everything—well, what if it starts raining all of a sudden and then stops all of a sudden? Who's gonna give the order then? And besides, how are you going to communicate it? You know what'll happen? Some people will take their bikes and get stuck in a long line of cars, while others will take their cars and end up in a pedestrian mall and get fined." We all say these kinds of things, and then we say that you can't trust the guy who's in charge of the Department of Transportation; he's one of those guys who, when he was little, didn't know how to go one-wheeling on his moped, who wore thick glasses, got cuffed on the head and didn't have a girlfriend. So, we forget about it, put the whole thing off until later when we begin to say that in other cities (we can't remember which ones), we saw people on bikes. We ought to do the same.

When, at last, we have to go back to the big city, we go to the train station and wait, watching the other trains pass by.

And that's when we realize that it's the train stations that make all the difference. Watching all those trains go by makes you feel as if life doesn't make a stop here: it passes through and goes on. It's all a matter of perspective. In Caserta, as in all the provincial train stations, the trains often pass by and don't stop. And if they stop, they really don't stay long—only for a minute, sideways, showing their flank to the station and to onlookers, always ready to move on. It's as if they're saying, "If you want to get off or get on, you're free to do so, but make it fast 'cause we have to go."

In the big cities, on the other hand, trains don't pass through, they arrive. And the stations welcome them as they head in. They stay put for a while. Then, later, they leave, and the head becomes the tail, and the tail moves off into the distance. When you go into the station it seems as if life is coming right at you, or is going out towards the world, but with you as the point of departure. You never have to rush to make up your mind. If you want to get on, fine, and if you don't want to get on, no matter. No. It all ends and begins right there. But later you run home and wash your hands because they seem all sticky and grimy. Go figure.

(Translated by Lawrence Garner)

THE CROCODILE OVER THE ALTAR

GUIDO CONTI

Two kids were walking along the sandbank of the great river, sticks in their hands. Horseflies and gnats buzzed around them. The noonday sun was blinding. The air was still and suffocating. They had crossed a strip of green water filled with floating black leaves, withered branches, and dead fish. They'd flipped the fish over with their sticks, shooing away the flies sitting on top of them, and had seen the bones and blanched eyes of the fish cooking in the pools of filthy water.

It had been weeks since it rained on the Po valley. The Po had receded so much it showed its sandy banks and rocks. No one could remember seeing the river so low. It had dropped so low that at some points you could even wade across, the water coming up to your throat. But people were still afraid of the river's mud and whirlpools, which could even pull a horse under. And the two boys knew where to walk, staying clear of the muck, the black pools of water, and the places that looked calm on the surface—because those were the places that were really frightening. The current is swirling underneath, deceptively, and the whirlpool could grab you, clutching your legs and dragging you down to hell.

Two years before, there had been a flood which had swept away the houses on the other side of the embankment; and now the drought had lowered the Po, revealing its never-before-seen skeletons and strips of sand. The bellies of the boats were drying out on the embankment next to the fishing shacks, resting in near-silence while flies and mosquitoes buzzed about. Large fishing nets were hanging limply in space.

The two boys were walking through the scrub and undergrowth, when they first noticed the enormous uprooted tree trunk which was stuck in the sand on the other side of the clearing. There wasn't a cloud in the sky and the hot sun was beating down, blindingly. The water was stagnant.

"It looks like the skeleton of a monster!" said Andrea, the smaller one.

Eugenio mopped his brow, and cupped his hand over his eyes, shielding them from the sun. They approached the old tree that had been carried downstream, by the river from who knows where.

"The river carried it down here when it flooded," Eugenio said, as he jumped up on top of the wood. The trunk was huge, and it was as if Eugenio had straddled the back of a dinosaur. Its gigantic limbs were covered with green muck and torn plastic bags that had come in with the tide.

"If only your grandpa could see it, he'd go nuts," Andrea said laughingly, as he hit its side with a stick. It was so big that not even three people could wrap their arms around it.

Farm workers were moving along the river on foot or on their bicycles, the sand burning their feet and their shoes, the smell of fetid weeds and foul water in the air. They were searching for tree trunks, highly valued wood which weighs a ton and is centuries-old. They competed with one another to find the biggest one, because when the river dropped, it pulled everything down with it. It chewed up the land and left gaping craters.

Eugenio's grandfather was still hoping, after two years of searching, to find his one big walnut tree in the midst of the muck and the acacias. Everyone made fun of him, even Andrea. But now that the Po had dropped, everybody was looking for something in the river's sandbars.

The two boys were also out looking for treasures, because the river is like a castaway safe when it becomes shallow—you can find just about anything in it. The sun was pounding down on them, and the foul air smelled of death and rot. Andrea and Eugenio poked their sticks into the grass and mud, their bodies half naked, and looked for things in the sand and under the rocks. They were sweating, their bodies black as soot, wearing caps turned around backwards.

"You really oughta tell your grandpa about this trunk!"

"Ya, sure, and who's gonna drag it home?"

It was Eugenio, the older of the two, who had decided on the expedition down into the river's bed. Just under the wharf they found a ramshackle old wardrobe, half buried in the sand. There were dead fish in it and one of its doors had been smashed through. Then they came across a washing machine, a bunch of truck tires, a sink, but no real treasures. Near the bank they found a dog's dried, rotting carcass, a feast for flies gorging on death—the kind of flies that have the dark sheen of fuel oil, all of them swarming and buzzing over the dead dog.

It was hot and the two boys were sweating. Squinting under the sun, they roamed around without their undershirts on, trudging about in rubber boots. Sometimes they sank up to their knees, and when they pulled their legs out of the muck, the soft mud would stick to their boots, and the boots would be sucked back down, as if into the mouth of a trout. The black, sticky mud had the stench of shit and rot.

"The smell here is disgusting. They bury the dead here, at the bottom of the river," said Andrea, the younger boy.

"It's dangerous here. You could sink in, let's go over there," said Eugenio. "Do ya know that my father once found a rifle in the river?"

"I don't believe you," replied Andrea.

"I swear! And then he found a whole suit of armor."

"I don't believe you," shouted Andrea angrily.

Eugenio made fun of Andrea as they walked under the sun, to get even for the way Andrea had laughed about his grandfather.

It wasn't long until Andrea spied a strange, smooth rock. It was right next to a large wickerwork cage filled with other rocks—that's where Andrea discovered a WWII German helmet. It was dirty and so filled with dried mud that it appeared, at first, to be a rock. Curious, Andrea poked at it with his stick, and it made a strange sound that caught his attention.

"What is it?" said Eugenio.

Andrea didn't answer, as he bent over the piece of iron and tried to dig it free. He dug with the tip of his stick, and finally, in a burst of amazement and joy, he cried out: "It's a helmet."

The other boy was eaten up with envy.

"Lemme see!"

"It's German!"

"Oh yeah? How do you know?"

"Some guy must have lost it when they were pulling back."

"It belongs to some drowned guy. It's got a curse on it. If you dig a little more, you'll find a dead guy."

"You're just jealous, that's all," said Andrea. "I want to see what it is!"

"What?"

Andrea had a hard time lifting the helmet up from the dry mud. He turned it over as if it were the shell of a dead turtle filled with earth, and then, with great effort, he carried it over to a pool of water. It was afternoon, hot, and pesky flies and gnats were swirling around in the air—their buzzing audible from many meters away. There were frogs and toads croaking and puffing themselves up. In the silence, voices died away and the cicadas hummed in unison.

Andrea washed the mud away until he was holding a piece of iron half eaten away by the water and rust.

Eugenio laughed. "I told ya, it's just a pot!" he said, hoping the other boy would leave it behind.

"Your head's a pot! This is a helmet!" And with great solemnity he put it on his head, even though it was still dripping, and then with the stick in hand he triumphantly stood at attention. The helmet wobbled on his small head, like a tin can might wobble on top of a pole.

Eugenio hit the helmet hard. It sounded like the muted clanking of a broken bell.

"Hey, whadda ya doin', you jerk? That hurt!"

"But didn't you say it was a helmet?" said Eugenio with a mischievous smile. Andrea hit him on the leg with his stick, and the older boy screamed at him to stop. They started to fight; they grabbed one another and tried to punch each other—both of them rolling to the ground. The helmet rolled away, and soon they stopped fighting. The heat had tired them out. They didn't say another word. They stood, looking at each other angrily—all dirty with that smelly mud.

Eugenio gritted his teeth jealously. He went off by himself, looking in the sand and mud, trying to find something, too. But all he saw were pieces of plastic, carried down by the river's current, hanging from the limbs of trees, along with old tins and detergent boxes discolored by the sun and water. He violently struck the old trunks with his stick. He broke off the dried branches of the acacias and the cracking twigs sounded like snapping firecrackers.

Andrea was sweating and smiling. He put the helmet back on his head—he'd have sooner swallowed a live garden snake than take it off. It didn't matter that the helmet made his head feel hot. He walked around happily, parading his over-sized, rusted-out helmet.

The sun was at high noon. The stillness of the river was disturbing. There was a strange silence in the air—it was much too quiet. Eugenio suddenly stopped hitting his stick against the trees and turned around to look for his friend. He saw Andrea just standing in one spot, bent over, poking around in the mud with his stick. The silence bothered him and made him squint. Even the sparrows could not be heard, and the whole plain seemed motionless, outside of time.

"Andrea," shouted Eugenio anxiously, for no specific reason. And then to break that silence he shouted again, "Andrea."

Andrea did not turn around. He was too busy digging. The voice was swallowed up in the torrid air. It was as if the shout had been lost, absorbed into the light. Eugenio put his arm up to his forehead to shield his eyes from the violent light. He shouted again, more loudly. Andrea straightened and turned around. The water was still, and there was just a slight ripple that rose up from the green mirror.

"Come and have a look," shouted Andrea.

Eugenio struggled to walk across hot sand clumsy in his big boots. "What's over there?" he said, just to hear his own voice.

"Come and have a look! Come and have a look!"

"What is it?" said Eugenio, as he got close to his friend.

Andrea stood and laughed. "Nothing!"

"You're an idiot!" he said to him, spitting on him, and he felt like giving him a good beating with his stick.

Andrea doubled over with laughter. "Hey, I was just kidding." He was sweating like crazy because of that helmet-shaped piece of iron sitting on top of his head.

"You're a stupid jerk."

The other boy shrugged his shoulders, the piece of metal wobbling on his head like a big bell. "Let's go over there!" he said, as he pointed towards the bend in the river.

"No, let's get out of here!"

"You're just a scaredy cat!"

"Whadda ya talkin' about? You're the one who's the little chicken!"

"Okay, then let's go over there!" And he stretched out his arm.

Up ahead there was a big bend in the river, green like an oil slick—motionless, even if the current was treacherously deceptive beneath the surface. To get to the river's current it was necessary to go by a pool of water filled with black shadows at its bottom: large schools of catfish were imprisoned there.

Andrea started walking. The sun annoyed him, like an eyelash caught in the eye. Eugenio, the older one, didn't move, uncertain about what to do.

"Aren't you coming?" Andrea shouted out of the light. "Chicken," he shouted.

"No, you're the one who's chicken," and he started walking, fear in his heart. When they got to the water, they looked around to see if there were any snakes. There were tracks on the mud, left by strange birds, and also a long trail, as if someone had hauled away a heavy bag, dragging it over the sand for many meters.

"Who do ya think made these marks?"

Eugenio shrugged his shoulders, and didn't answer.

"Let's get out of here!"

"What for?" said Andrea, as he started to throw pieces of dried mud into the water.

"Because I say so, let's go!"

The smaller boy laughed and kept throwing pieces of mud into the river.

Then, suddenly, both of them fell silent, as though they were waiting for something. Before them the river opened up, the current flowing just beneath the surface.

"But don't you feel it too?" Eugenio said.

"What?"

"The silence."

The other boy didn't reply, and they stood there listening, looking out into the emptiness around them.

"I don't hear anything," the smaller boy said.

"That's just it. This silence, don't you think it's weird? I don't like it. It's scary. Let's go."

"Why?"

"Let's get out of here."

Andrea saw the water in front of him moving, as if it had been stirred up by the wind, as if a swish of silk had touched its surface. Then it started to churn, the water became greener at first and then white and cloudy with mud. All of a sudden, as if it were a log of wood bobbing back to the surface after it had been pushed down, a crocodile rose out of the water, its mouth wide open, and it latched onto one of little Andrea's arms. Andrea did not cry out, but sank into the water, dragged down by the crocodile—his blood mixing with the water and mud. The crocodile tried to drag Andrea down, but instead he tore the boy's arm from his body. Andrea, soaking, tried to get up. He saw blood gushing from the stump of his arm. He got up, stunned and reeling, and Eugenio ran into the water, and, without even thinking, grabbed his friend. Staggering like a drunk, Eugenio pulled Andrea up. The crocodile immediately attacked again, opened its mouth and churned the water in all directions—as if it had gone crazy over the loss of its prey and the scent of blood. Then it sank its teeth into Andrea's leg and dragged him down to the bottom despite all of Eugenio's efforts to save his friend.

Eugenio watched as Andrea disappeared. Then Andrea's arm disappeared. It simply vanished into the blood-tinged, frothy water.

Eugenio was paralyzed with fear; and then, without any sense of what he was doing, he started running, panting as he ran, his feet sinking into the sand. He fell down and tried again to run away, getting up with difficulty because the mud caked on his boots weighed him down. He looked back at the blinding light, terrified that he might see the jaws of that crocodile coming out of the water. He kept on running without thinking about what he was doing, without crying out, his eyes wide with fear. That's the way he ran, like someone crazed, all the way to his home on the other side of the embankment. When he got there, sweaty, his eyes bulging out of their sockets, blood streaming down his legs which had been scraped by the scrub and undergrowth, he couldn't say a word. He just gasped.

His parents looked at the terrified expression on Eugenio's face and asked him what had happened, why he had run like that. They wanted to know what it was that had frightened him so. Eugenio couldn't speak. He was shivering as if he were freezing cold. The image of the bloody arm, the exposed bone just hanging there, kept him from speaking.

Eugenio could not speak for days, and for two nights he did not sleep, trembling, stunned by fear. He caught a fever and when the lights were turned off, he would scream. He stayed in bed for a week.

There was no sight of Andrea, and everyone thought some accident had taken place along the river. They asked Eugenio what had happened to Andrea, but Eugenio didn't speak. He wasn't himself, as if he were paralyzed—until one day, after a sleepless night, he said that he wanted something to drink, that he was thirsty.

"Where's your friend? Did he drown?" the *carabinieri* asked him. "What happened? Where were you?"

The police and the *carabinieri* had looked for Andrea on the sandbanks of the river, but they had only found the tracks of the two boys near a big bend where the green water shone like petroleum. They believed Andrea had drowned. The tracks suddenly ended. They didn't find any traces of blood, and they began to look for him further down the river, in the stretch where the current slow.

After a few days of searching, they found Andrea's arm, a kilometer or two further on, snagged in the nets of a large fish trap.

"There are too many giant catfish in the river," two fishermen were saying—they had seen just about everything imaginable in the Po. They were leaning up against a fence, at sunset, as the *carabinieri* pulled in the net with what was left of Andrea.

"But ya know they even eat dogs, those SOBs. If you run into one that weighs 200 pounds, what are ya gonna do? It'll eat you up, that's what it'll do," the other fisherman said with a smile.

They buried Andrea's arm in the cemetery. All the rest of him had been swept away by the Po.

The *carabinieri* believed that Andrea had drowned and that his body had been eaten by the giant catfish. His parents and the townspeople were overwhelmed by grief and despair. It had been almost ten days since anyone had asked Eugenio about Andrea. Then one afternoon, as Eugenio was sitting on his chair, he said into space, "It was a crocodile."

"What?" said his mother. She ran to hug him, and while she gently stroked his forehead, she cried out with joy.

"It was a crocodile." Trembling, he raised his eyes to look at his mother.

"The child has a fever," she said to her husband, touching Eugenio's forehead.

"No!" he cried out desperately, "Andrea was eaten by a crocodile!"

"But how could a crocodile live in the Po? How did it ever get there?" she asked.

"It was a crocodile," he insisted. "He had his feet in the water and the crocodile attacked him. It tore off his arm and then it dragged him down to the bottom. I tried to save him but the crocodile pulled him away."

His mother smiled, but with a look of terror: "A crocodile?" She looked again at her husband.

Eugenio kept on trembling and burst into tears.

The *carabinieri* looked for the crocodile's tracks in the mud and found them near the bend in the river, much further down near another sandbar. Up till then they hadn't paid any attention to those strange footprints in the mud.

And so, the hunt for the crocodile in the Po began. They sent *carabinieri* and village men armed with rifles into the river basin, along the sandbars and the banks. They looked for its tracks in the mud; but the tracks began to disappear because the river, all of sudden, started to rise again on account of the early rainfall in the Apennines—even though the Po valley stayed hot, without rain for months.

"A crocodile? That's one I've never heard!" remarked an old man on a bicycle who had stopped at the wharf near Roccabianca.

"Whadda ya talkin' about? There's one hanging in the Church of Santa Maria delle Grazie in Mantua. People say that it was found in the Po during the middle ages. It's chained to the ceiling."

"You've been drinking too much wine," a friend said to him smilingly, as they sat in the shade of the boathouse of the local club.

"Maybe it came down with the flood."

"But you tell me how a crocodile would be able to live in the Po? It's much too cold in the winter!"

"God knows how many years it's been living there and we never saw it! We like to blame the catfish, but dogs have been disappearing in the river for ages. They always yelped before drowning in the river, but who's to say it wasn't the crocodile?"

"But how can you say it was always the crocodile?"

"Now people even raise them in their homes. I'll bet someone just threw it in the Po to be rid of the thing without having to kill it . . . ."

"The whole thing doesn't make sense to me!"

"But that one in Mantua's a real crocodile. They stuffed it, attached it to a chain, and then hung it from the ceiling of the church's central nave."

"Where'd you ever come up with that one?"

"Go to Mantua and see for yourself . . ."

"Ya know somethin'? They oughta put my wife all stuffed in that church in Mantua. Maybe that way I could finally relax a little, knowin' I won't ever run into her again."

The others laughed, releasing the tension everyone could feel in the air. They looked at the river, dark and moving slowly, but rising due to the rains in the mountains. And they thought about the crocodile, and about the fact that the Po was a strange river, where just about anything could live. All of them were well aware of this—fear and anxiety took hold of them. Many of the fishermen didn't even go out in their boats anymore.

"It's a curse, the river's curse. If it's true that there's a crocodile in it, it's the river's curse," said the fellow seated by the boathouse, very seriously. "We oughta call the priest, he'll know what to do."

They went to call on Don Peppino, an old, thin priest who had presided over many funerals of children and adults who had drowned in the river.

"Every year the river always wants its human tribute," he would say in his sermons. "Every year the river or the stream takes a man or a child for itself, because otherwise that river would die," he would say earnestly—because it wasn't just a popular superstition. And he didn't laugh at the rumors about the crocodile, nor at what Eugenio told him.

When he heard the whole story, Don Peppino prayed the entire day, closed inside the church. Then he asked to conduct the funeral for the child whom he'd watched grow up in the parish courtyard, and seen play soccer with his schoolmates for afternoons on end.

After his day of prayer, Don Peppino had gone down to the river, near the sandbanks, and he began to walk along the banks alone. He knew how to catch the crocodile. He looked for signs of it on the plants, on the ground, in the mud and the sand. Even if the river was rising because of the rain falling in the mountains, he searched for those signs in places only he knew about. He also knew what to look for there. He gathered up some weeds and pebbles, a piece of dried mud with the crocodile's footprints (or so it was said), put them in a jute bag, and took everything to the rectory. The old priest continued to hurry back and forth along the banks on his bicycle, his black garments flowing, his hat on his head, the jute bag on his back. Each evening he would say mass till midnight, and then ring the bells till one. And it got to the point that the farm workers and the townspeople began to think that Don Peppino had gone mad, keeping them up as late as he was. All this went on for three days.

"Hey, Don Peppino, if you keep this up, you're gonna cause more babies to be born!" the men in the local tavern jokingly shouted to him. "Nobody gets any sleep here anymore!"

"But what's the matter with that priest these days?"

"I'll tell ya what's the matter with him, he's probably just got a horny itch and can't get rid of it," they said between sounds of laughter.

But Don Peppino didn't care about the gossip. He pedaled from one end of town to the other, seriously, as if he were in a hurry to finish up with some task.

One afternoon, behind the rectory, he lit a fire which sent up a cloud of black smoke along the banks. He kept it going for another day, so that at a distance it looked as though the church had gone up in flames.

That Friday morning, the third day Don Peppino had gone to gather signs from the river and ring the church bells, he left on his bicycle very early. He arrived later at Mantua, along the banks of the sanctuary of Santa Maria delle Grazie, where the stuffed crocodile was hanging from the central nave. He had gone more than sixty kilometers on his bicycle. As he was pedaling along with the bag on his back, the priest would look at the sky and smile. But he was also worried, so he would pedal even harder, as if there were no time to lose.

When he arrived at the outskirts of Mantua, he turned off towards the sanctuary and saw, under the portico of the large square in front of the church, a monk who was walking back and forth with a rosary in his hand. Don Peppino stopped his bicycle. When he got off, he didn't even greet his friend, the monk, who had been waiting for him.

"So? When can you bring it?"

"Sunday. We'll bring it Sunday. Get the procession ready, because we're getting it ready for Sunday."

When he went into the church, Don Peppino made the sign of the cross, and then looked up at the crocodile, with its paws cut off and its mouth wired shout, chained to the ceiling. Then he went up to the altar and, when he had finished praying, he looked around. There were no images of the Virgin Mary, of Jesus and the saints. Instead, there were images of the travails of the afflicted. He looked at that church, and he saw it as a kind of great theater: all around were niches enclosing giant figurines *ex voto* in the moment of their torment. There was a man with a large stone tied around his neck as he came up out of a well, still alive, giving thanks for miraculous intervention from the Virgin Mary. Elsewhere, an executioner, who had been crushing heads with a hammer as if they were watermelons, was laughing at a condemned man who had survived the blow. In another niche, there was another who had survived a hanging, the rope around his neck and a small image of the Virgin Mary in his hand. Also striking was another man with his legs held tightly in a vise, saved from the ordeal and torture of putting fire to his feet. And then there were the wooden hands, eyes and breasts attached to the walls as if they were grand decorations. That enormous church was a theater of violence, human torment, and divine grace, and it found forceful expression in those wooden figurines—so old they seemed like mummies.

Don Peppino held on to his bag tightly, and when he had finished praying, he looked again at the crocodile hanging from the church's ceiling.

The monk handed a small bag over to the old priest, who returned late that night to his church.

Early the next morning, Don Peppino went back to the bank of the river and to that strip of sand where little Andrea had died. He threw a fishing line into the river, and after an hour or two of silence he pulled out an enormous carp. The old priest took the fish, slit it open, and sewed it back up, only after inserting a large fish hook and the small bag the monk had given to him. He tied the fish to a long line made of very strong nylon, dropped it into the water, and let the current carry it down river. Then he sat down and opened a black umbrella to protect himself from the sun, the sleeves of his black cassock rolled up on account of the heat, and a handkerchief knotted at both ends around his head. Under that blinding sun he was sweating, and as he mopped his forehead with his arm he looked at the motionless water.

The sun made the stifling air shimmer. There was complete silence. The flies buzzed around the old priest as he waited, sitting on a piece of wood, an umbrella over his head.

The ground was sweating, and a smell of rot came up from the cracks in the dried mud. Suddenly the tip of the pole began to dip slightly, and the priest went into action as if he had expected this moment, holding the rosary between his fingers. The prey was taking the bait and the pole began to sway back and forth. The priest got up and pulled on the pole with all his strength. The prey had swallowed the bait, bending the pole like a willow until it snapped. The priest felt a strong tug that pulled everything away. Then he made the sign of the cross, threw the last bit of the pole into the current, and put the rosary back into his pocket. He closed the umbrella, got on his bicycle, and, with his sleeves rolled up and the handkerchief around his head, went back to the church to pray.

On Sunday a great procession was organized. A van came from Mantua and it stopped in the rectory's courtyard. Don Peppino had opened the doors of the church, which has been decorated with red roses, lilies and large orchids. Yellow and red streamers waved in the sky, tied from one poplar to another all along the broad street leading to the church. Everyone in town carried a flower in their hand, and other flowers were strewn in bouquets over the ground which was to be the starting point for the triumphal procession. The bells had started ringing at around nine in the morning, and many people had gathered in the church to pray and recite the rosary, while a few men worked on the wooden platform which was to bear the statue of the Virgin Mary in the procession. The sky was dark, and at last, there was the threat of rain, but it did not rain—a few drops fell, but it didn't rain.

Towards ten o'clock, after the mass was over, eight men lifted up the wooden platform bearing the statue of the Virgin Mary. The doors of the church were opened again and people prepared to join the procession. The entire town was there to celebrate. When the Virgin Mary was taken from the church to the gravel road, everyone threw flowers on the ground before the sacred statue. The men took turns carrying the wooden platform, and those not carrying it prayed along with the women, wearing handkerchiefs on their heads. The children marveled at the colorful petals flying in the wind.

Once the procession had begun, Don Peppino signaled with his hand and another platform was carried out from the church. Held up on a pole, as if it had been freshly speared, was the old chained crocodile of Santa Maria delle Grazie. It was losing bits and pieces of its hide. Still it had to be carried along the banks of the river to the townspeople's final destination. Don Peppino, with a cross in one hand and his jute bag in another, led the way, followed by men and women who all prayed and sang.

The sky became more threatening. The poplars bent in the strong wind and the wind ruffled the singing people's hair. Along the banks, where the march was heading, big gusts of dust were kicking about and people had to close their eyes. Don Peppino stopped when he reached the port's wharf. He called an altar boy over to help him hold up the monstrance. Then he stepped away, walking about ten meters towards the river. He made a few circles in the air with his arms, opened his jute bag, and threw a kind of powder into the river. It began to gurgle, as if the bag had contained calcium carbide. A white froth formed, and the priest lingered there, as if waiting for something. The march had come to a halt, and the people tried to hold their ground against the force of the wind. It was thundering, and the sky was filled with dark, threatening clouds. A few drops began to fall, but the procession didn't move, happy to see the first rainfall after so many months of drought. On that stretch of the river, where there was a bend leaving a large sandbank exposed, the people could see a kind of tree trunk moving on the surface of the water amidst the whirlpools. There was a splash, the kind made by fish when they're mating, and a tail seemed to flap, and then there was nothing. It might have been a giant catfish or a tree trunk sucked down by an eddy. No one could see for sure, it was so far away, and the wind was kicking up the dust, making people close their eyes.

The priest waited a bit longer—then he made the sign of the cross and turned back. His hair was blown to one side by the wind, and as he walked he tried to straighten his paraments and black cassock. The stuffed crocodile was swaying on the scaffold, filling the air with the sound of clanging chains.

"Let's go back to the church," he said to the altar boy, taking the cross from his hands.

The whole town started to go back towards the church and they began again to sing and recite the rosary. The thunder grew louder. The wind bent the poplars, making the leaves turn silver, but it didn't rain. A few cold drops fell, but it didn't rain. Clouds of dust were kicking up, and they stung the skin like little needles, and the wind howled, carrying away the voices and the prayers. It still didn't rain until the procession had gone back into the church and the doors had been closed, protecting all of the people from the fury of the elements. It was thundering, but not raining, and people were struggling with the doors. Just as they heard the doors close, it began to pour on the Po valley, and the rain began to splatter the dust that rose.

They never captured the crocodile and the story of Andrea became legend. Still, the tracks had been there. Many claimed that Andrea's body had been eaten by the giant catfish, and that that flash in the middle of the water, at the time of the procession, had only been a tree trunk sucked down by the current. After all, giant catfish sometimes could be two meters long and weigh more than 200 pounds—and it's not unusual for duck hunters to lose their dogs, sucked down by the current. You have to be careful with the currents and eddies of the Po. They can pull you down—and it's as if someone had grabbed your legs and dragged you down to hell.

(Translated by Lawrence Garner)

from MADDALENA

ANTONELLA ANEDDA

March, Maddalena Island (during an earthquake on the Continent)

Sensing the roots stirring in the distance. The earth trembles to the north.
Perceiving an eastern sound. The houses slide in the mud.
"I hollered from the rooftop and waited
for the furniture and the other remnants to return to earth."

Calling out to loved ones and hearing only my own voice:
"The rain thrashes in the wind, whirls red against the sea."

8 p.m.

Staring at the tempest. The water that beats, the earth
that cuts off. Precisely because I am not eternal I want
each departed love to be everlasting, to be heavy
and not turn the stone of his pages,
to sink together with me in the water
(rocks in garments, dark hooves and black-
green of the grotto in the salt's crust).
To spin in this room
hitting the corners of the furniture and pressing on
as if he were alive with his arms and tongue over my body.

The sea spills over the pier.
The animals shiver in their enclosures on the island

. . . yet no cliff cracks, no door falls from its hinges.

The island swallows fire and wind,
still in its body of salt.

April, Maddalena Island. Remnants of Dreams

Clear, but dense as one imagines the weather conditions
of an Aurora Borealis
a silent fishing scene.
Water in the ice. The hook that sinks carefully.

(Puff of air on Bonifacio's Mouth, forward flight to the cliffs
upwards till the cold, the continents, your house, the wooden
heart of the armoire, the unknown dark bed by now.
Your face is the chestnut door's arc
mine the dawn that invades the window.)

A silhouette oscillates inside the dream.
It is the drunkard who in yesterday's wind on the dock
swung side to side singing with a closed mouth.

May, Maddalena Island. Remnants of Dreams

Against the arc of mountains
the curve of your chest
that used to bring calm to my space.
Your gentle commands in the dream, the voice that used to say:
"Turn, stretch out here on the beach
as if a bed were dug along the way."
Obeying and finding calm in that cavity
your body weighs, while my spine bends
and you scatter wild lilies on the sand.

July 22, Feast of Santa Maria Maddalena

8 p.m. A boat with its procession of cliffs, a prostitute
covered with flowing hair, a body
of plaster among the lanterns and the dead
sunk in the sea. They ripple the water, they ring the bells
with stones. A dry murmur is in the sand.
A buildup of anticipation in the granite.

7 a.m. The slim twigs resemble me
in thinness and dryness. Writing I draw myself.
My name is a whistle exceedingly long.
I am a vowel on the tombstones in the sun.

September 2001. Archipelago of the Maddalena, St. Stephen Island

This little island pierced underwater by American submarines where my great-grandfather planted vines and citrus trees
built stables and brought ten cows from the Continent.
Their trembling hooves on the boat, the wind on their backs,
beaten till then only by northern rains.
They are still there, their horns mixed with sand
the sunken skeletons snug against the cliffs
no longer fearing, no longer distinguishing the grazing land from the sea.

October, Maddalena Island. Looking Toward the Port

Still dark, raining—yet
on the mountains of clouds one discerns
the clearing that will become morning
that slim tongue
with which it will take away in the air
shadows of things and animals:
the nose of a lynx, an island, a sea bay
with its smoky-green light.

This only, in waiting for day,
I call "faith in the sky":
the empty space that fills with shapes
another earth that simply rises.

November, Maddalena Island. Looking Toward the Port

In the sky a ring of clouds comes together slowly.
With its cargo a boat crosses the harbor.

With this same precision we ought to—not write—
discern, turn our glance to this foam that brings together
and then tears apart: filth, clouds, water.

Stiffen your spine, contract your whole body.
Scrutinize the sky now clean and gray.
Perhaps from this void—with no act of conception—
will come the radiant poem of the month.

Archipelago (a Fall)

Red and gray, a broken crown of granite and a puff
of air rises in the center of each cliff.

I fell under a few clouds
one day in full spring
with a shrub bent under my body
and the entire promontory on my neck.
I had sand in my ears. The dog's paw
uncertain on my temple.
It was a slip similar to those we know from our dreams,
an instant in which motion seems to catch the enigma of space.

All the islands were flying
reproducing, with precision, the void between the rocks
filling themselves with wind at every pause
the stones shot off whistling
like sling-stones to the feet
and the breath was a trunk with leaves to be swallowed
with eyes shut, down to the roots.

First there was the house, gray, perfect in the sun
loose planks, old nails, a chair,
then that whistle mixed with voices
two kids and the dog's tongue
like a touch of infinity on the throat.
Perhaps it was this that showed fate
how a lifeline still burned in me
when the grazed hand stirred
to chase off a fly
that headed directly skyward.

"Wild geese that fly with the moon on their wings . . ."

I sure like this: watching birds in the morning
being glad for the airborne substance of that bird
for that brown wing that beats in the clouds.

With membrane subtlety the terror evaporates.
It flies towards the houses: it's not a memory, its cares gone away.
It leaves us. We are alive, with very warm hands.

(Translated by Antonino Mazza)

DAGGUANNO

VANESSA AMBROSECCHIO

I don't remember Dagguanno's first name, and I believe there is a reason why, a reason that may not justify my forgetfulness, but at least helps to explain it. On the other hand, I will certainly never be able to get his surname out of my head as long as I live, a surname that I had never heard before but which, ever since then, whenever I see it printed in a newspaper or glowing brightly on a sign, I cannot help but associate immediately with that young man.

I said young man but really he is a child: a student in seventh grade, 10 or 11 years old, chronologically speaking, but 8 years old at first glance, like so many other children who live in neighborhoods where vitamins and proteins are not ladled out on a daily basis. He is four feet seven inches of scrubbed raw nerves, a big head and big hands attached to short, spindly arms and neck. His face seems filled with an excess of eyes—a dingy sky-blue—and mouth: here and there, toothless, and it is not clear whether his adult teeth are coming in late or tooth-rot is setting in early—and often his mouth is colored by a cluster of herpes or a bloody scab or two.

With his curved legs and arms, Dagguanno doesn't exactly walk. Rather, he clutches at the air, paddling with his hands, rolling his locust-like eyes, watchful, always nursing a subdued snarl. He is all-too-well portrayed by his surname, reminiscent of a wild animal about to lunge. The first time I took roll call in his presence (he hadn't showed up at school for fifteen days, and I was a substitute teacher, beginning in mid-semester), when I read his surname, an animal cry burst out: "*Cca-à è*" ('Here he is'), with a heavy accent on the first vowel. Dagguanno uses very few words, always the same, but when he uses those words he always drags out the vowels to an amazing degree, yelling as he does so, and that is how he expresses himself. Also, he always speaks of himself in the third person, as if he were unfamiliar with himself. He sits sideways, his right leg perpendicular to the desk, his left leg parallel with it, and his outsized head propped against a fist.

He seems less a child than a wino who can barely contain an explosion of rage. "*Cca-à è*." He said it in a tone of voice that suggested that he had been brutally rousted from a well-deserved rest, and that he was protesting unfair abuse. Then he hunkered down again behind arm and fist, in his customary position. It is not a position of rest. Arm and fist may be still, but you can just see them vibrate. You are almost afraid to brush against him, and that is a reasonable fear, because if you brush against Dagguanno, an electric shock is the very least that will occur.

He welcomes every opportunity for a fight. I don't mean just with his classmates: that's obvious. I mean with adults. All you need to do is to ask him, along with everyone else, to pick up his grammar book. "*'Un l'havi. L'abbruciò,*" he immediately responds—"Ain't got it. He burnt it." He repeats his cry of protest with an increasingly and desperately unpleasant voice. At first, I would insist that he pick up the book, wasting time and doing nothing but whipping him into a fury. Then I noticed how my fellow teachers handled him, and I started to follow their cue. The whole time I was a substitute teacher, the only method that I was able to adopt with him was indifference. I usually ignored him and continued with my lessons. But Dagguanno is a paradoxical boy, and as soon as I turned my back, he would leap to his feet with a clattering of desks, triumphantly waving his book, "*Cca-à è! Cca-à è! L'havi! L'havi!*" ('Here it is! Here it is! Got it! Got it!') and laughing, laughing endlessly, with his enormous mouth full of gaps and teeth, pulling his scanty skin taut around his cheeks and eyes, furiously, like a magpie.

The laughter is short-lived: today, it is his turn to do the grammar exercise and Dagguanno categorically refuses to take part, pounding his hands on the desk to emphasize his point: "*'U-ùn lu sapi fa-àri!*" ('He doesn't know how'), and it's not enough to leave him alone and go on to the next student. "*L'abbrucia! L'abbrucia!*" ('He'll burn it! He'll burn it!') he warns me.

This fascination with fire is one of Dagguanno's recurring motifs. I wonder where and how he learned it, I wonder primarily because we know very little about his life. From the educational psychologist, we do know that he lives with his grandparents. Once, at a staff meeting, one of my colleagues, deeply upset, described how, when she asked him to take out a certain textbook, Dagguanno lunged down and began to pull all his books out of his backpack, throwing them to the floor, three at a time, screaming that he had burnt the book in question: "*'U vidisti? 'U vidisti? L'abbruciò!*" ('Did you see it? Did you see it? He burnt it!'), as if the mere fact that something or someone happened not to be there was tantamount, in his mind, to having gone up in smoke. "He should be searched every time he sets foot in the school building," my colleague insisted, harshly. What really frightens me, though, is when he asks calmly, his eyes a cluster of red capillaries: "*L'abbrucia?*" ('Burn it?'), handling a notebook with excited, trembling froggy fingers.

What is Dagguanno trying to tell us with this story of fire and burning? Surely, to him "burning" is a horrible, defiling expression, far more defamatory than any curse word, even curses directed against mothers or sisters. To say that he burnt a book is to say that he annihilated it down to the tiniest fiber, or to tell a classmate that he will burn him is to tell him, I want to disintegrate you right down to the marrow of your soul. For Dagguanno, fire is the inferno, even if he doesn't know it.

One thing that I have learned from Dagguanno is you need to think twice before touching children, be it only a pat, a tousling of hair. Once, when I was trying to convince him to work, I placed a hand on his shoulder to make my words more persuasive, and Dagguanno began screaming: "*Làssa! Làssa!*" ('Get off! Get off!') as if warding off a beast, with a sort of frenzied fear in his eyes.

I didn't try that again. The "starting point condition," in the personal ledgerbook of the teacher I am substituting for, states that Dagguanno is an "individual predisposed to aggressive outbursts." Clearly, resentment disguised as educational zeal, but I can understand. You certainly can't deny that Dagguanno is aggressive. It takes only a trifle with him to trigger complete mayhem: a classmate might ask to share his book, someone might take his eraser without asking, or a teacher might ask him to explain why he was absent from school. It seems that he is just waiting for provocation, that he is just waiting for the opportunity, holding his breath until the chance occurs, and yet he is never the first to start something. It is as if he is obeying a law of the jungle. I understood that when I saw him quarrel with a classmate, the head of the class.

His classmates could not be described as particularly sensitive to insults: certain cursewords and profanities are exchanged cheerfully, amid laughter. But certain other references to mothers and sisters—these entail swift and systematic revenge. It is not a matter of authentic indignation, of wounded pride. The offending party is given a beating even if there is no real desire to do so: it is an ethical duty. It is pointless, in these cases, to try to get in the middle, to trot out the old 'now, your classmate is going to say he's sorry': they can't see you, they won't listen, to you or to anyone else. They stare at each other, for a long time, without blinking, like cats about to battle for dominance in a territory. Then they start butting heads, forehead to forehead: you can hear bone smacking against bone. You would say that is how they test each other's strength. Around them, their classmates are cheering for one or the other, crowing insults directed at the opponent, encouraging their friend, but without the slightest thought of actually wading into the fray, attempting to separate them, in obedience to one of the basic laws of the jungle.

But nobody cheered for Dagguanno when he happened to hear offensive words spoken about his mother. His uncontrolled, unpredictable rages, evidence of fragility, do nothing to make him popular. I watched as he, swept away by insane rage, cracked his forehead repeatedly against his adversary's forehead. His eyes were reddish and, if possible, even wider than usual. His skinny body was trembling all over and a sob choked in his throat. For a moment, it almost seemed as if he were appealing to his opponent, a gleam of terror in his big eyes—I didn't want to think it, but it looked as if he might burst into tears, just like any other child. His body continued moving but without clear intent, his arms held high, his fists balled up. Don't cry, I thought to myself, because I couldn't bear to see him surrender. When his opponent decided the time had come to take the initiative, Dagguanno responded with breathtaking speed, as if to outpace him and astonish the onlookers, proving that he was the one who had made the first move, whereas if it had been left up to him, they would have just kept banging foreheads. They were immediately locked together, so that you couldn't pry them apart if you tried with all your might, and pretty soon they were rolling on the ground in animal fury, and you could hear teeth gnashing, heads banging against the wall, knees hitting the floor as desks went over in the mayhem. I couldn't even imagine my arms, my fingernails trying to scratch their chain mail. I was afraid they would kill one another, and I immediately ran to call for help.

One day he attacked the assistant teacher. Dario was assigned in that class to keep an eye on Giuseppe, a mentally retarded child who is well behaved and a hard worker. Dario is in his forties. He is strong, a former factory worker who became a phys-ed teacher and is now assigned as an annual student case worker—he has no official credentials, but he is devoted, sensible, and hard-working, and his real job is to grab the most troublesome class members and keep them in line while I try to teach epic poetry or prose narrative. Dario speaks their language, and the kids generally accept his ear-boxing and shoulder-jerking pretty willingly. From him, they are glad to accept it, and the scolding often ends with an unexpected burst of laughter and an exchange of great and jovial arm-thumping.

On this day, however, when Dagguanno began to act up, making rude noises because I asked him to read aloud (he actually did start to read, struggling to make out the words, syllable by syllable, mistaking one vowel for another, but after a couple of lines he burst into a rage, blood surged to his head, and he began to yell, slamming the book shut, opening it and slamming it shut again so hard that it bounced off the desk, and yelling that otherwise he'll burn it) Dario lost his patience.

There was no good reason. Dagguanno hadn't caused more disruption than usual, and he would have shut up if I had ignored him long enough. But Dario just allowed irritation to get the upper hand: maybe he was tired, maybe he had argued with his wife. Anyway, he did what he shouldn't have done. He grabbed the boy by one arm, dragged him to his feet from a sitting position, gave him a good shaking, and tossed him into his chair, with an "*O-ò?*" that was more provocative than waving a gun in his face. I barely had time to wish that I were blind and deaf so that I would not have to witness what would be happening in the next few seconds.

Sure enough, Dagguanno, exploded in a Catherine wheel of flailing kicks and punches that flummoxed Dario, more than offending him. At the same time, his eyes open wide in terror, he started to cry, but this time he was really crying, sobbing the way children do when they are beaten, with tears running down his snot-swollen face and a moaning sob that convulsively sucked back his lower lip. He sobs like a child being beaten, even though he is the one doing the beating. A crying child who is beating someone else: Dagguanno is a child of paradoxes. Once Dario recovered his presence of mind, he seized Dagguanno by the nape of his neck and sent him down the hall to see the principal.

For half an hour, we enjoyed peace and quiet, without Dagguanno, although Dario and I were upset, and we didn't exchange a glance until the class ended. But when the bell rang, the door flew open as if pushed by a gust of wind. "*Hah — hah — hah!*": there was Dagguanno, with his mooncalf's groan, bellowing with laughter, right in Dario's face, jumping, clomping, and stumbling noisily over desks, shouting: "*Nenti ci fici, 'a preside! Nenti ci fici! Non l'ha sospeso!*" ('The principal did nothing! He did nothing! He didn't suspend him!'), in the grip of an ecstasy that, while it fills his face with wrinkles, also disarms his innocence, as he laughs, indifferent to the fact that he is baring his anemic gums, in the corner of his eye still moist with tears, in his relentless, relentless yet futile quest for approval.

Dagguanno spoke the last phrase in Italian. He and his classmates all pronounce in perfect Italian any word that has to do with school, because they cannot find a corresponding term in the dialect that they speak at home. And how would you say "to suspend someone" in dialect? Or "to hold someone back a year"? Or "recess"? The kids pronounce these words correctly, almost without accents, because these words are part of a separate world, the world of school. Perhaps the children think of school as a prison or any other place where one's presence is obligatory, but mastering its language is clearly a sign of resignation. Is this good?

Dario accepted the blow, muttering "Good for you, good for you" between his teeth. At the moment, I wonder if Dagguanno could help the way he was, with his surname that smacks of ambush, a small fierce beast. A beast that snaps, plunges its fangs, in order to save itself. Perhaps that is why Dagguanno can't wait to be provoked:

because he wants to tell us his story. But we don't want to hear his stories. The other teachers just get angry with him. It's already hard enough to keep the kids inside a classroom for five or six hours a day. It's already an achievement to get them out of the school in one piece at the end of each day, and get ourselves out as well—without getting reported for neglect or arrested for harming a minor. The other teachers complain about the educational psychologist who urges them to be more human with the kids. Why don't you try spending five or six hours a day in this inferno of a classroom, instead of in your office with your drinking glass, your mineral water, and your conference chairs? Becoming vulnerable, lowering our guard, wasting some of our precious energy: we can't afford to do that. And they are right, it's true: we can't afford the risk. The only method of teaching, the only system that we can adopt with these kids, against these kids, is indifference. Otherwise, we would drown in a sea of pity, rage, conscience.

One day, there was a class dictation.

Actually, we had one every week. It was the only way I could keep them under control on a Friday, when I had them for three hours in a row, and one of those three hours without the assistance of Dario. Obviously, the dictation exercise took place in an atmosphere of objections and catcalls, and in twenty minutes they had all turned in their papers, but just to keep them twenty minutes with their butts glued to their chairs, in this inferno of a classroom, is always a precious achievement.

For Dagguanno, the dictation was a disaster. It's not hard to guess that he refused to try. "*No-ò! No-ò! Talè... Talè...*" ('No! No! Look... Look...') and to express his disdain, he rudely folded the sheet of paper lengthwise into columns and, gripping his pen in concentration for a minute or so, he wrote his name and class and handed it in. "*Te'!*" ('There!') he said to me, holding out the blank sheet of paper, with a scorn for me that was first and foremost a scorn for himself.

"At least, try drawing something," I insisted, even though I was aware that asking him for more than a minute's concentration is risky. "Predisposed to aggressive outbursts"—the phrase repeated itself in my head.

That time, I guess I overdid it. He leapt to his feet, kicking away his desk and chair, and attracting a shower of catcalls from the classmate sitting next to him, who was still writing. "*O-é? O-é?*" he yelled at me, doing his best to be menacing with that scratchy voice. So, as usual, I ignored him, and I encouraged his classmates to do the same. I continued to dictate the text, making a great show of unconcern. Dagguanno, in a frenzy, began to bellow indistinct animal sounds and to threaten to set everything on fire. He stepped around his desk, he gave it two hard kicks, then he turned and attacked the teacher's desk. He bent and tore the class record book, then he scratched his gnawed fingernails on the blackboard. With every move he made, he sought me out with smoldering eyes, waiting a second to see if I would scold him, then he would come up with something else. I continued reading, strolling from desk to desk, my back turned to him, and in the meanwhile I considered to myself that if the windows were tightly shut, at the very worst he might rush out the door, and the hall monitors were always ready for trouble. I never turned my back, I maintained my position.

Then suddenly I couldn't hear a sound. Slowly, very slowly, to keep from offering him a sense of victory and out of a fear that the worst had happened, I turned around. His skinny legs protruded from underneath the chalkboard, extending out straight. I walked over, and I peeked around behind. There, directly behind the black square of the chalkboard, sat Dagguanno, the elbow of one arm propped on the other arm, in his usual posture, his closed fist against his forehead, covering his face.

I looked at him, wordless. He barely moved his fist to one side, opened one eye, just one, and stared at me, unblinking. He had ordered himself to sit in the corner for punishment, and he was telling me as much. "Come out of there," but he wouldn't move. His pale eye remained wide open. He lowered the eyelid for a moment, when I told him to come out, but as if out of a momentary weakness, or weariness. Then the eyelid returned to its fully opened position. And I, in turn, looked straight at him, listening to that wordless confession, that relentless self-punishment, that shameless disgust with himself. We both stopped, hastily, when we understood that we were beginning to feel love for one another. I went back to my dictation, and he spent the hour in the shadow of the chalkboard.

Now that I teach in a school with well-behaved students, where I need not fear animal calls and insults, where I don't need to keep the phone number of the nearest police station in my pocket, I have forgotten Dagguanno's first name. In exchange, I won't be able to get his surname out of my head as long as I live.

* All references to actual events are coincidental.

(Translated by Antony Shugaar)

THE WOMAN

Nino De Vita

Luciano, who had
three years on me, one morning
said that in a secluded house,
at the gates of Maràusa, a gorgeous
woman gave sex
for five hundred lira.
"And how do you come to know that?"
I asked him.
"Francesco Paolo told us,
the son of the barrel maker, who's been there."
"We'll go Sunday,"
I told him.

And so, in our best clothes,
off we went on the scooter to that place.
We were going for curiosity; and as well for the pleasure
of being able to tell
the boys of our quarter
that we'd been there.
                                        But, along the way
Luciano confided
that he had in his pocket
the five hundred lira

and that the thought of that woman
was stirring up—as they say—his blood.

There was the front door, open,
and a Vespa leaning
on the wall.
We approached and drove past
a couple of times
along the street, looking
in.
                    Couldn't see
no one.

Then a man came out,
got on the Vespa and went.
So, driving by once more
we saw her: sitting,
with her legs stretched out on a chair,
smoking.
                         "Look,"
whispered Luciano. "Now I'll turn back
and we'll go in."
I started to shake. "Isn't it better
if we left and came
another time?" I told him.
He didn't listen and stopped
the scooter right
in front of the door.
The woman, whose eyes were smutty
with green and whose dress was showing
her thighs, gave us

a hard look.
"How much you want?"
asked Luciano,
from the seat of the scooter and with a foot
on the ground.
"How much you want what?!" the woman
rhymed back.
"Beauty, I'm of age,"
said Luciano. "He isn't,
but I am, beauty, I am a man."
The woman sized him up and down.
"What man," she said,
"if you've just now come out
of an eggshell?"
Luciano turned
all red

Slid his hand
in his pocket and pulled out
his identity card. And opening it—
"Wanna see, here, take a look,"
he told her. "I'm of age."
"To come in here you gotta be eighteen,
boy," the woman
said, annoyed.
"Yeah, eighteen," echoed back
Luciano, laughing.
"Somebody I know, who lives near me,
told me you let him
come in; and he's not even
fifteen, I'd say, by a long shot."
"Oh, yeah?" shouted the woman,

removing her slipper
and raising it in the air.
"See this?" she yelled. "I'm gonna use this,
if you don't leave, you and your friend,
to smack your little horns.
And don't you be seen around here again. Big piece of . . ."

We went away, slowly.
And on the way Luciano,
turning, said to me,
"Tomorrow I'll go back,
for sure, with somebody
older, Elio or Carlo, Aunt Agostina's son, and I'll
show you, little runt, if she won't
let me in."

(Translated by Antonino Mazza)

COFFEE

Vitaliano Trevisan

F., says E., who worked with F. hanging telephone lines up and down the poles for more than 20 years, wasn't completely normal—he was, as they say, "a little slow." He couldn't even speak correctly, he stuttered, couldn't twirl his "r's," slurred his "s's," and his "f's"—when he tried to pronounce a word with "f" in it, like "coffee" for example—didn't even sound at all like "f" but like some kind of sound midway between an "s" and an "f," a kind of "sf." But he was a great worker, never got tired, and was also a really nice guy. He smoked like a chimney, says E., one cig after another, and with the butt of his last one he'd light up the next one. It was unbelievable how much he smoked! Something you wouldn't believe, never saw anyone smoke so much. But his real passion in life wasn't tobacco, but coffee. Wherever we went, says E., F. wanted a coffee. If we stopped at a *bar* to get something, F. always downed a coffee. Summer, winter, whatever the day or season, it was always coffee. And if someone who saw us working outdoors invited us into their house for a glass of wine, he would always say no to the wine and ask for coffee instead. Actually, E. says, he didn't really ask for it straight out: "Mocha?" he would say, "m-m-mocha, ma'am?" Usually the lady would understand and went right off and made some, and the stronger it was, the happier F. was. The cig in one hand, the cup of coffee in the other: happy. He liked coffee so much, says E., that on more than one occasion he said he'd like to die drinking coffee, a cup of coffee in his hand, the aroma of coffee in his mouth and nostrils. "To d-d-die like that would be r-r-really g-great, it wouldn't really be like d-d-dying, n-no!" F. used to say, says E. And one evening his wife made him some coffee, strong the way he liked it, and then she went out into the garden. She came back a little later. She called to him. He was seated at the kitchen table, but he didn't answer. She called to him again and, seeing that he still didn't answer, went up to him and shook him. It was only then she realized that he had died right there on the spot: his right hand curled around the coffee cup, a cig that he'd been smoking still dangling between the fingers of his left hand. A good death, says E., just the kind of death that F. had always dreamed of.

We ordered two coffees. "Make 'em strong," we said to the barman, "as strong as you can make 'em."

(Translated by Lawrence Garner)

1992

Nicola Lagioia

I arrived in Rome in 1992 to study law. It would seem a very weak excuse for leaving home at someone else's expense, since there's been a law school in Bari for years: crowded, prestigious, poorly attended and poorly run, like all the law schools scattered around Italy. Autumn, for some thousands of new graduates, is the season of a pathetic migration. The girls arrive in Rome to study psychology. The boys go to Milan to enroll at Bocconi. And they all, more or less, indulge themselves in a little trip to Bologna for the admission test for Communication Sciences. I was not such a case. Mine was by no means a caprice. After what had happened during the summer, a change of air was the least one could do.

I moved in August, forcing my parents to pay two completely useless months of rent. If it was really going to happen, however, it was better not to lose time. We were all in agreement on this. My parents waved me goodbye almost with relief. Giulia, my girlfriend, even with a certain gratitude. And I, as I ascended the Adriatic in a Eurostar, I already felt better, as the uniformity of yellow and blue out the train window exercised its hypnotic effect, I already felt better, as I asked myself what was it that was so beautiful about the cars stopped at rail crossings (the waiting), the low stone walls (the lizards petrified in the sun), the fields of grain passing before me (the flat vastness of the fields puts things back in order; you're the one who's passing through, they remain where they are), when near Foggia the train veered suddenly toward Caserta I felt relieved, crossing through a vestibule of hell composed of illegal sprawl, furniture outlets and local television, why was it so consoling, I asked myself, this architectural delirium the traveler is forced to deal with for the mere fact of passing through (the wretched literacy imposed by television sales, corrupt contracting, and yokel mannerist design does not prevent, nearby, in the most hidden part of the Appenines, the survival of human beings completely incapable of reading and writing), what was it, I asked myself, as the train now ran up the Tyrrhenian coast (already feeling better), tracing an ideal line between what I was leaving and what awaited me, that was so beautiful and damned in the apparent sobriety, stasis, and hieratic monotony of Romanesque building (a perfect covering over movement and a completely oriental folly), in the apparent folly of the Baroque (a folly so apparent as to be the last and most devastating stage of folly). Good.

1992 is an important year. Marlene Dietrich dies. Francis Bacon dies. Barcelona wins the Champions Cup. *Petrolio* is published, the posthumous novel by Pier Paolo Pasolini. In the heart of Europe, after less than a half century, the concentration camps reappear. In Italy, a century and a half after the Five Days Uprising, the Clean Hands scandal explodes. A small step for our country, this last event, but a true tragedy for many of the under-20s of the era: enrollment in law school peaks clamorously. Everyone wanted to become a magistrate. Or more precisely, everyone wanted to become a Special Prosecutor, although no one was actually able to explain the difference between a judge magistrate and a prosecuting magistrate. Roberta and I hugged the walls in the Law School corridor, we hugged each other and watched, dumbfounded, this crowd of aspiring jurists. "Generation of shit," we remarked, referring to ourselves as well, except that this term "generation" had already crossed, in our vocabulary, first the threshold of vague perplexity, then of profound suspicion, until it finally came to define itself as a nauseating lie, regressing ultimately into a nonce word, an inarticulate cry, an ass's bray, an elephant's trumpet, a sound more disgusting than the most coprophagic of sounds, something you couldn't pronounce without feeling degraded. What did these children know, we asked ourselves, of the law school entrance exam (nothing), what love for justice had compelled them to fill out the application form (none), what advantages did they think they'd attain with a thesis in international law pointedly entitled *Juvenile Justice in a Sample of Eighteen Developing Countries* (infinite, but they were way off). How many of them, rather realistically discovering themselves devoid of vocation or talent, intended to utilize their status as students to put off important decisions about their lives? Many, certainly. But this honest acceptance of things blended into the absurd conviction that a miracle, a sudden stroke of luck, or worse, sudden inner growth, would arrive *in extremis* to save everyone's ass at the last minute, like in a John Ford movie. But instead, many found themselves, after less than two years, in Taranto, Cuneo, or Caserta, contemplating, dumbstruck, the urban landscape of the Italian provinces from the low tower of a military barracks. Others departed on Erasmus. Others had anxiety attacks. Others counted on royal jelly, ginseng, taurine, benzedrine, speed-reading techniques, photocopied handouts, notes, early rising, recommendations, postponed appeals, improvisation, on night courses, on the return of the mandatory passing grade law. Everyone drank coffee. Everyone wanted to become a Special Prosecutor. Everyone said they did not want to become a lawyer. Everyone, after an exam that went well, looked out over a fifth-floor terrace feeling an inexplicable sensation of general failure. And everyone, more or less everyone, sooner or later graduated. Without understanding very well what they were graduating for. Without ever having felt true joy, they had had to read thousands of pages on tax law, bills of exchange, international treaties, divorce, sentences of ecumenical councils, the exasperating slowness of civil procedure, rights of usufruct, the enfranchisement of slaves in Roman law, the exposure of infants, the election of the President of the Republic, declarations of war, condominium associations, presumed death, ecological disaster, attempted suicide. Without any joy they had imagined their own suicides. They had prepared study plans. They had undergone their first exams. They had received handshakes, congratulations, pats on the back, or, on the contrary, they had had to exhaust themselves in humiliating discourses on the imminent perfection of their own personal study methods and their own person in the course of absurd, disordered, and incomprehensible family interrogations, in which, without fail and ever less convincingly for all, genuine lexical horrors emerged, curse words such as "commitment," "sacrifice," "future," "waste of time." Without any joy, in fact, they had wasted time. They had recovered it. They had gathered together the crumbs of the world that surrounded them. Without ever becoming vicious. Without raising their heads. Without even wholly degrading themselves. Oh, certainly, the emotions remained. We had even been moved. We had felt the famous tug at the heartstrings, the strangled sob, the tears rising in the eyes. For example, after the Capaci Massacre, we were overcome with emotion (still, however, without having quite grasped the difference between a prosecuting magistrate and a judge magistrate), we were overcome with emotion at the news that Sarajevo was the last European capital to have remained stuck in 1945. After the first, second, and third viewings of *Ghost*, the movie sensation of 1990, we were overcome, and we were even overcome after seeing *Beauty and the Beast*, the latest peerless and ever-punctual Disney wank job, which opened at Christmas in every cinema in the world in 1992. We did feel emotions, therefore. We had wept neurotically after having failed, for the fourth time, the exam in Commercial Law, at receiving a minimum passing grade, at receiving a C, and even at receiving an A plus. But without joy. Without malice, even. We had simply cried, just like that, as a physiological release. And we hadn't laughed, we hadn't guffawed our guts out, we had not celebrated the folly of the universe in response to the news of the definitive rehabilitation of Galileo Galilei (in 1992!) (on October 31!). We had not fallen out of our chairs when we read the newspaper. We were not seized by convulsions. We had not rolled on the floor listening to old Wojtyla's reparatory speech, "The Catholic Church, in condemning Galileo for his confirmation of Copernicus' heliocentric theory, committed an error." (As far as I know, Roberta was the only one who demanded an explanation from Father Bacchelli, iron Jesuit and our Philosophy of Law professor. Who, recognizing the girl's spite and subtlety to be equalled only by his own, was pleased to raise his eyes from the ponderous volume of *Capital* splayed on his desk and to intone, in his falsetto, "My daughter. The Church is a millennial design. An eschatological dream. Three or four centuries of delay make little difference.") And forward, still forward. Without having the strength to flee far far away, we had been photographed dressed like fools at the conclusion of our degree exams. Faster than lightning and taking advantage of our confusion, our exhaustion, our suddenly being out of the game, Pasquale Pinelli, rajah of all school janitors, had set a heavy black toga onto our shoulders for the exultation of our relatives, who now photographed us pitilessly, handed fat tips to the janitor, applauded for no reason, gave us bunches of roses, covered us with caresses, and tore out checks, giving us in this way a jovial and charitable viaticum to the world of work, which, with its overcrowded qualifying exams, letters of recommendation, interviews at the limits of absurdity, rigorously unpaid internships, and whole days spent photocopying, would definitively destroy every one of us.

In the afternoon, after eating, as Rome filled up with transparent light, I caressed Roberta's back. Outside, airplanes crisscrossed the sky. The Tiber was dead. The windshields of the buses sparkled in the sun. The ministries overflowed with notarized forms and the newsvendors dubiously stacked up huge piles of the *Financial Times*. Everything gave the impression of a huge ball of gold and diamonds gently assaulted by an incurable disease. The cars advanced one meter per minute. The scooters collapsed under sudden gusts of wind. The Tiber still quivered with life under the Bridge of Angels and the cancer of the Colosseum flowed slow, precious, inexorable. I caressed Roberta's back. I lay there in silence and touched her. With my fingers, I ran over and annulled the entire sequence of the preceding hours. I had woken up at seven. I had made breakfast. Then I had unplugged the telephones. I had also unplugged the stereo and I set myself to studying uninterruptedly for hours, without distractions, without ever raising my eyes from the books, without thinking about anything but our iniquitous plan. I had closed the lawbooks. I had washed my face. I took the number 24. The tram crossed wide streets flanked by plane trees. I had gotten off at Piazza dell'Esquilino. I had made it to the train station. I had bought a pack of cigarettes. I looked around. October was the perfect month. The city mirrored itself in the new autumn weather. A feeling of glorious ending, threatened eternity, trees reaching up and the police on the asphalt with punctured eardrums. I had opened the pack of cigarettes. My life was finally perfect, I told myself. I had descended into the subway with the spent butt between my lips.

Roberta lived on the top floor of a building near Piazza Fiume, in a big apartment decorated in a taste she shared with no one else. In bed, she told me about how happy she had been in Galatina, the town where she'd lived until she was eighteen, and how all her problems had begun only after she'd left there. I'd listened to her for over an hour. Then we made love. Roberta was a great storyteller. I had wanted to slap her whenever her description of churches, dusty roads, altarpieces, Saracen castles and medieval villas suddenly slowed down, expanding like maturing fruit, to disclose finally the radiant figure of a youth I envisioned as perpetually dark, slim, lanky, and sixteen, set off against the background of a Salento summer. We had eaten. We had made love again. This time with more abandon (satiety never left us spent, on the contrary satiety rendered us ever more aggressive and impatient). We had briefly interrogated one another with questions for the exam we were studying for. The answers had come out perfect, rapid, adamantine. They were a masterpiece of synthesis that excluded, *a priori*, any further questions on the part of our imaginary examiner, to whom they left no space for any dissension that would not come off as uselessly picayune, superfluous, contentious, when not plainly idiotic. Then I had moved on to smoking like a madman. One, two, three, ten cigarettes. Roberta shifted in the bed. I had to practice. I was still a beginner. I would probably forever remain one. "How am I doing?" I asked Roberta. "Not there yet, not there yet," she had answered. "It always looks like you're smoking the first cigarette of your life." But after a half hour, after three quarters of an hour, when the smoke was finally etching a grimace of suffering onto my face, when the room was impregnated with an unhealthy odor and my voice descended to a ridiculous depth I never could have achieved on my own, when my head began to spin, when Roberta bugged out her eyes, when we had silently convinced ourselves we were worthless, that what we were doing was worthless, that our life was worthless, the people we hung out with were still more worthless than we were, in the dead point when anything could have happened (I imagined that Roberta would burst out crying or I imagined driving her to tears by insulting her brutally), in that moment something dissolved, took off, hit its proper groove. I blew out two or three perfect smoke rings. The cigarette fit softly into the left corner of my mouth. My arm moved back and forth elegantly, with technique. My hand paused in mid-air like a moment selected for an anthology. I took the last puff. I put out the cigarette in the ashtray. I whispered to her, "Turn over." A few months before, in Bjeljina in northeastern Bosnia, the so-called Arkan's Tigers had massacred more than 500 Muslims. I smoked another cigarette. In Italy, Sergio Moroni, a Socialist Party congressman involved in the Bribesville investigation, had killed himself several weeks earlier. In Palermo, Salvo Lima had been liquidated by the Mafia. Shortly, Francesco Di Lorenzo, Secretary of Health and Human Services, would be indicted. Bill Clinton was the new president of the United States and in *Basic Instinct*, the umpteenth billion-dollar shitpile of the year, Sharon Stone, mystery writer and bisexual nymphomaniac, would answer detective Nick Curran's question, "How's the new novel going?" with one of the most idiotic lines Hollywood screenwriters have ever managed to conceive. "It's writing itself," Sharon Stone had said, as young people in Italy enrolled in law school, wanted to become Special Prosecutors, wanted to become soccer players, wanted to form a rock band. In Bari, my former high-school friend Michele Teutonico, in an unrepeatable moment of inspiration, abandoned business school after less than a week of attendance. In Rome, Karol Wojtyla rehabilitated Galileo Galilei. On the other shore of Christianity, the Venerable Pavle, Patriarch of the Serbian Orthodox Church, had made a speech several days before the Bjeljina massacre which, some years later, still inspires fear and leaves open the question as to whether Christianity is an unstoppable delirium, a sublime chain of misunderstanding, a disaster founded on the best of intentions, a satanic dream, or so precisely worked out in its sudden revelation as to be the outline of a perfectly planned conspiracy. The Venerable Pavle had said, "What could the Serbs do to vindicate adequately the crimes they have been victim to in this century? They would have to bury people alive, cut their throats, dismember children before the very eyes of their parents. But the Serbs have never done such things, not even to savage beasts, much less human beings." Karol Wojtyla had said, "By sacking Byzantium in 1204, we committed an error." Roberta, stretched out on the bed, had taken me by the arm. She had said, "Now you turn over." It was truly inexplicable how from all that context (we were false beyond repair, the people we knew would never make it, the world had reduced itself to an unrepresentable mass of information and could no longer stand on its own two feet), it was crazy how from all that disintegration, from our mediocre emotions, from television, from radio, from Rome and from autumn, something real, glorious, and tangible could be born, an extraordinarily clear, clean sensation, a *still* image before our eyes, a thought capable of intoxicating us, of conferring a fundamental meaning on us, of returning continually to itself. In sum, a kind of miracle. Roberta and I found it in front of us without knowing either how or why. We grabbed it on the fly. We started fucking again. But it wasn't born from us, this miracle. It was not an act of Heaven. Neither, even, did it come from the past.

After having dinner, I asked Roberta whether I could use her phone. Outside, the traffic had almost completely dispersed. The offices were closed. The neighborhood filled up with a silence interrupted by a rare ambulance or the passing of a tram. In that moment, Rome was decidedly elsewhere, it retreated toward the center city (toward Piazza Navona, toward Campo dei Fiori, into the little restaurants, into hotel rooms), leaving us with the disagreeable sensation of being nowhere. I felt discouraged. I thought that at that hour all Italy was being seized by a great shudder of boredom, of tiredness, of unconditional surrender. I imagined a country made up only of piazzas, fountains, transistor radios, porticoes, fog-enshrouded outskirts and televisions left on at night. A country whose inhabitants had disappeared forever. Up to now, I thought, only the great painters have been able to realize this challenge. It struck me that the famous exemplar of *The Ideal City*, attributed to the school of Piero della Francesca, one of the peaks of our Renaissance, excludes, completely, rigorously and luminously, the presence of a single citizen. I realized that in the most beautiful scenes of city peripheries by Mario Sironi, there are dark skies, smokestacks, gasometers, train tracks, but no human beings. I remembered a fascinating and little-known painting by Guttuso. The picture is called *The Evening Appointment* and shows a decidedly Mediterranean garden (it could be a villa in Capri as easily as buildings facing the coast of Smyrna) ornamented by the passage of a tiger. Okay, I promised myself again, you can be happy for a long time, not only for a few seconds. In fact, you could be happy forever. Then I pictured Italy completely deserted, made of porticoes, gardens, basilicas, made of statues in the middle of piazzas, but also of streetlamps, hospitals, telephone booths, high-tension pylons. In this ideal country of mine, its people banished, the things would finally be left to dialogue among themselves in Olympian peace. Things, although indebted to man for their existence, would ask at last to be left alone. In no other country but Italy would this dialogue sound more musical, more inspired, more fecund, more dense with meaning. No other place but our peninsula could realize the intimate, secret goal for which things had been created. A point of arrival, this, well-hidden between the veins in marble, inside the fibers of the great stained-glass windows, and even inside the sad amalgams that compose cement and plastic. Not only, therefore, would the cathedrals, the mosaics, and the consular roads participate in this grand design, but also the factories, the highways, the monstrous turbines of the power plants, the apartment blocks left half built, the skeletons of bridges, and the incomplete railroad overpasses facing out over nothing. Because these things, seen all together, in their unstable, pathetic equilibrium, still managed to conserve some kind of meaning. Even the hospitals begun in 1975 and never finished. Even the project houses in Palermo, Bari, Torino, Naples. Even the chilling hinterlands of Milan. But it had to be done soon, I told myself, ever more prey to this species of delirium, as the evening descended longitudinally over all the cities on the second meridian, and Roberta, behind me, cleared the table in T-shirt and red underwear, apparently tranquil. We had to hurry, because a force still more terrible than real estate speculation, a background noise darker and more senseless than the speeches of the tribunes of every weight and color strewn through the piazzas, the newspapers, and the cathode tubes of our country over the past fifty years, an entirely impersonal horror this time, a monstrosity more wretched and dangerous because unburdened with any reason or even rational apparatus, something that Roberta and I sensed clearly in the air (we watched it slither like an army of larvae, we heard it scratching in the void like a gigantic sewer rat), but we still couldn't quite draw it out fully defined, this will emptied of any possible substance and therefore virtually invincible, that threatened to overwhelm the cities, the ports, and the highways, forever nullifying any correspondence between the things that retained a minimal dignity, sense, beauty. A colossal tragedy that we could avoid only by flight. And then I told myself, only then, as I watched the number 19 slowly cross Queen Margaret Avenue, as Roberta whispered at my back, "As many as you want. You can make all the telephone calls you want," only in such an impossible context would I ever be able to be completely happy.

In a country finally disinfected of our presence, every day, after the setting of the sun, when the light had almost completely gone out on the marble, the glass, the cement, the plastic, would Guttuso's appointment finally take place, in perfect imitation of a myth buried within the centuries.

I phoned my girlfriend, Giulia, in Bari. Roberta, who had been listening to me talk until that moment, simulated a sudden attack of discretion and disappeared, smiling, into the kitchen. I told Giulia, "Yes, it was sunny here today too." Then I told her, "Don't worry." I said, "Me too." I said, "Good night." I slept well. I slept extraordinarily well in 1992.

(Translated by Thomas Simpson)

WATER PURIFICATION

ENRICO PIERGALLINI

Where the thick water is stagnant like manure
to breathe is enough to faint
so this morning in the canal
she raised her humpback like a sack

Best not to trust the current
that digs unfathomable channels
grinds up those who fall into the mire
(a heap of bones resurfaced among the gravel)

They say in the hidden river bends
midwives worn out by babies' wailings
dump from garbage bins
cocoons of swaddling bands wrapped death tight

The river flows viscous along the bank
under the bridge you glimpse a water tank
a parked car hides among the rushes
with fogged-up windows from the sweaty heat

Renetta, you who here roil among the refuse
from the weight that pulled you down
and the brains-like thick placenta soup
still fermenting and fermenting like must!

Water Purification

Sooner or later, Renetta, it makes no difference
in a time that grinds us like discards
and has granted you a life so dire
that by now you barely fill a garbage bag

A three-wheeled van drones by oppressed by the trash
along an inland road of illicit traffic
where girls late into the night
sit open-legged on the milestones

Stitch up the vaginas if the child
generated to feed its parents
sharpens its gums on the nipples
grows up chewing on its own kind

They are laid in the seashore
mineral deposits turning to stones in the shallows
the newborn deprived of birth
buried inside clam shells

(Translated by Antonino Mazza)

THE TRAVELER

Carola Susani

This has changed: my pleasures have become small. For example, I like it when I get to the windows with my cleaning cart. I always stop there. I stand still, without doing anything, and watch the planes. Tonight, the planes turn green in the light. They have an old, lived-in look, they don't shine, they're opaque. Sometimes they bounce as they land. It's fun to watch. It's not true that my pleasures have grown smaller, they're the same as ever. My contemplative pleasures. I used to watch the milk spill onto the formica, then drip onto the floor, I watched how the drops separate. I didn't realize how good it made me feel. No, they haven't become small. They may have grown. I never would have dreamed of having an airport. In a little while, all the to-and-fro will come to an end, it'll stop for the night.

Because a time comes when the airport gets quiet. The airplanes sit on the runways, the bars and stores close. Nobody's around, just a few guards. And a few cleaning people like me. We watch the last few passengers disembark and go away with quick steps. They look for buses or taxis. They'll find a taxi or something. It's not a time of day I care for. Nothing is flying anymore, there's nothing to enjoy. I just want to finish my work and go.

I push the cart into the men's bathroom. The cleaning carts are well organized: a place for the broom, for the trash, for the bucket and mop. The carts are an autarchic structure. Granted, of course, you have to change the water. Which I don't like, I do it rarely.

So the cart is already inside and I hang back to watch one of the last airplanes take off, an extremely old DC9, I've never seen one here before. Then I go in too and I hear groaning. There's a man standing there. The upper part of his body is hunched over, he's white and sweaty. These are symptoms I kind of recognize. Finally he faints and falls down. I think, That's a good thing for him. Because I don't have any opiates in my pockets. True, I can't be sure at this point whether he's having angina or if it's a real MI, I mean a myocardial infarction. It could be that while he's passed out, the pain continues. It could be one of the worst kinds, that goes on for well over two hours and then kills you. Either way, all I have in my pockets are nitroglycerin tablets. I always carry them with me, ready for just such an eventuality. I take off my gloves and put one of them under his tongue.

Only now do I stop to look at him. He's a handsome man. Thrown there on the ground like that, he looks like a fallen angel. I can't tell his age, maybe forty. If it weren't for the heart attack, I might want to kick him: he has a light tan, his features are too regular, just a few crow's-feet around the eyes. But he's defenseless. He has short hair, he's wearing a Burberry, a fine pair of corduroys, a pair of shoes with rubber soles, a sweater that looks handmade, but isn't. In the airport light he and his clothes seem green like everything else.

Who knows why his man had a heart attack. He seems so sporty and healthy. Maybe it happened like with my husband, for no comprehensible reason. He had even stopped smoking. I came home and he looked strange, white and damp. Bleah, I go, you look awful. He says: It hurts here. I said: Your chest? Maybe it's a heart attack. Him: Come on. Me: Does your arm hurt? And him: Go on.

He was not stupid. His father had died of a heart attack. He had every reason to understand. Not me. He asked me for some Motrin.

Excuse me, I go, why that? And him: It's rheumatism.

You have to picture all this with my husband breathless, gasping. He killed himself with Motrin, who knows why? Stupidity and ignorance?

He was a political philosopher, which I am too, as a matter of fact. He had a board exam to become Associate Professor in two days. The Associate exam is the worst in the world. You have to present a lesson before the luminaries in your discipline. You have very little time to prepare it. If one of the barons doesn't happen to care for you, he takes pleasure in massacring you. It's purely arbitrary, there's no law. Each one has his own criteria to judge you: whether or not you've cited him, and how many times. Still, it's not a good reason to kill yourself. Especially because it was his exam to shine for, the one he was supposed to pass. All the old Behemoths were there, all ready to embrace him with open arms like one of their own. I can't bring myself to forgive his decrepit, spineless circulatory system. He arrived at the emergency room with a face out of *Scream* and was dead. Fifty percent of heart attacks arrive already stiff at the hospital. After that, mortality goes all the way down to 6 percent. The hard part is getting there on time.

My husband never lost consciousness. The man on the ground should thank God for having passed out. It's better to be weak. I know. True, I should call 911. But my cell phone is dead. I have to wait for the next paycheck to buy a new one. I couldn't do otherwise. I should look for a public phone, but I don't have a card. Fortunately, however, I always carry nitro with me. I still have this absurd wish to save the dying.

I bend over him. He's making light jerking movements. He has extremely long eyebrows. I get this idea: they look like centipedes, I'll cut them for him. But there's no chance, I hate bugs. I should look for the cell phone in his pockets. Sure, right, 911. This guy will be dead before the paramedics arrive with their sirens. This is urgent. After Francesco's departure I took a first aid course. I place my hands on his chest. The torso is hard and rubbery, like an old chicken. But it's warm. I do a cardiac massage. Since Francesco's burial, it's my first physical contact with someone of my own age. I never allow my parents to get close, nor would they think of such a thing. The prickly wool bothers my palms. Plus there's a nauseating odor. Testosterone, I think, I remember it, although Francesco didn't produce much of it. I wouldn't have allowed him in my bed.

After Francesco's death, I went a little crazy for a while. I stopped going to the university where I was an adjunct. The professors drew a sigh of relief; one less. I spent my time visiting cardiologists, claiming to have symptoms of unstable angina, sometime even a heart attack, and as soon as they turned around, I grabbed the medicines off their desks and slipped them into my purse. I had pretty hands, quick and dark, like a spider. Now they're puffy and red because of my work. I accumulated medicine. So I still have a house full of beta-blockers, calcium channel blockers, and aspirin. I brought them here with me. My sweet burden.

I stopped paying bills and rent. It hadn't gotten as far as eviction, but the landlords did not show themselves to be kind people. They sent two muscular little blond men of some foreign type I couldn't recognize to my house to threaten me: you have a month, then we burn your furniture. Oh, I would have let them, but my parents and mother-in-law would have been desperate.

Then I became normal again. It was time to put some order in my life.

I have a friend, or rather an acquaintance, who comes from the lumpen proletariat. Her mother is a maid in apartment buildings. But she, Marinella, is a girl of substance, intelligence, and she has established a cleaning business which has developed some good contracts. For example, this one in the airport. I said to her: Hire me. She laughed: Camilla, you wouldn't last a day, you'd end up in the hospital, your muscles give out and you get asthma. But me: Put me to the test. What do you know, I found out that I was strong. The first two days, I had terrible pain and wept and thought I was dying. Then my body understood. Now I'm nice and strong, like a woman should be, better than a contortionist.

I found a basement apartment in a house built without permits right up against the fence of the airport. I manage to pay rent and maintain myself. I'm an autarchic structure, like the cleaning cart. I like my house, because I can put a chair out on the grass, sit down, and look through the holes in the airport fence. It gives me a sense of peace to watch airplanes, it's much better than trainspotting. A privilege. You can't beat the flight paths, always different and variable. And there's something sweet in the rumble that accompanies you with an irregular rhythm throughout the day. It accompanies you wherever you are, not only at home, but also if you go grocery shopping or wander around Piazza della Pace. You can't beat it, sitting perfectly still while the whole world transits through your house.

When I came to live at Ciampino, I also resolved the problem of the mother-in-law and the family. I'm all they have. I put them in a rest home near here. The hospice eats up papa's whole pension and everything my mother-in-law gets from her late husband's pension. But it's money well spent. It relieves the burden. The parents and mother-in-law think I teach at the university. They're happy to have such a self-centered daughter. If they suspected I clean toilets at the airport, they'd die. They'd never speak to me again. Papa and mamma didn't raise me for this. So instead, every week when I ride my bike over to visit them, I wear the only decent suit I have left, and they insult me: Camilla, what did we ever do to you, do you only think of yourself? Or the other one: You're made of stone, it was you who killed my son.

I sold my parents' house to pay off debts. No one had made a claim against me, they were friends, people of taste. But I knew they were chewing their livers, thinking about me with both pity and anger, waiting perpetually, oscillating between worry and hope. So, since I knew their names and addresses one by one, I went and paid them off, finally establishing peace between us, and silence. I would have been glad to liquidate my mother-in-law's apartment too, but she put a tenant in there who sends the money directly to her, so I can't do anything about it.

When I left, I took all the medicines with me. I'm not sure why, perhaps in fond memory of Francesco.

The man moves just barely on the floor, like a snake. If I try to get an ambulance to take him away, I'll lose him.

I take a bag from the cart, I grab his body under his back and knees. He's heavy, but he doesn't slip from me, because by now I'm as strong as wood. But I can't set him down easy, he falls into a sitting position with a thump. He gasps. It gives me a jolt. But it wakes him. I'm glad because he's not dying. He's confused but seems to be better. So, I think, it's just arrhythmic angina.

- The egg – he goes in a breathless whisper and points to his baggage. Then he collapses again. I check to see that he's still breathing. I load the bags on behind and take the cart and push.

At this hour, the runway is empty. I push the cart. It weighs more than trash and more than water. I go to the door that opens directly onto the runway. I give it a push. As usual, it's open. The point is, to get home by the regular roads, you have to go around, outside the airport. Then take a car or a bus. It takes at minimum half an hour, and I and this man here are in a hurry. At this hour, there's no transport waiting for us outside the airport. There is only my bicycle. Loading a heart attack victim onto my handlebars is too much even for me.

Therefore, with him relaxed in the cart, I start running across the runway. The planes sit there like big, well-nourished predatory birds.

At this hour, they aren't dangerous. The lights on the control tower make me feel good, like my own private Christmas party. Nobody's thinking about us. They don't look our way, maybe they're talking among themselves or waiting for breakfast time. We don't take long to get to the fence. It's not cold out. It's that time of night when the heat is still sitting in the earth and oozing up little by little, like smoke, to give us comfort. The hole is small, I can barely fit myself through. I leave the cart with the man and his suitcases on it and I run into the house to get the wire clippers. I hurry back, as anxious as a mother who leaves her child in the car for a minute to run in and grab a coffee. But no one has taken him away from me. I clip away at the wire and open a gap. Ours is not a protected airport, the wire fence isn't electrified, you can do anything. I open my gate. I drag the cart to my house. I leave it outside. With a deep breath, I get a hold of his body and drag it down the steps that lead inside. Fortunately he doesn't resist, whether he's passed out or sleeping. I turn, I look at him, I discover his eyes are open and dilated. Maybe he's confused and still doesn't understand. It's hard but I manage to arrange him comfortably on my bed. I raise the nape of his neck, it's hot. It makes an impression on me, it's been so long since I felt warm skin. I put my pillow under him and let him back down. With the heat, I think, everything goes through him. I pull up the covers and then go get the suitcase that's still outside the door. Now he's keeping his eyes closed, he's doing it on purpose. Like when your mother comes to wake you up and you close your eyes.

I must begin treatment immediately, I take the beta-blockers, the calcium channel blockers, and the aspirin. I carefully study the instruction sheets. I choose the maximum tolerable dose and hope he's not allergic.

I pull his head up, I force him to drink it all. He opens his mouth like it was the most normal thing in the world to take medicine from a stranger. As though I were his long-lost mother. What could they charge me with? Certainly not of refusing assistance in an emergency. Perhaps of practicing medicine without a license. But it's a risk I have to run. Then I let his head go, and he falls back onto the pillow, but quickly makes a movement toward me with his chin and lips as though he didn't want me to let go. So, I think, he's hungry.

In the refrigerator, I have some chicken wings, carrots, zucchini, and onions. I should make him some broth, in case he comes to. I wash the vegetables slowly and take the skin off the chicken. I decide not to fry it. I pull out the small pot and fill it with water. I light the stove.

Then I sit on the floor near his bag and open it. There are a few light clothes. Perhaps he comes from a warm country and changed in the airplane toilet before deplaning here into our winter. Who knows how he did it? Airplane toilets are so small you can't even move your arms. Perhaps his plane ran into some bad disturbance, so he became afraid and fear triggered his attack. Perhaps it's really only angina. Then there's a package. I open it by splitting the cardboard box. It's well packed, there's something inside, something precious. Underneath a layer of polystyrene balls and straw woven like a bird's nest, there's a big egg. It seems like a fake egg, like a white chocolate Easter egg. But it's still a while until Easter. I don't know why, I think it might be a serpent's egg. I close up the box as best I can and set it in my bureau under the old sweaters.

Then I go to the man on my bed and look for the wallet in his jacket. It's in its place in the inside pocket. Inside there are dollars and five hundred euros. I leave them there. I only take the credit card and put it in my pocket. Now he's calm. His long eyebrows tremble, they rise, he opens his eyes. I smile at him. He opens his eyes wide.

- Feeling better?

- Why? – He speaks the same language as me.

- You had an attack, you know? Does it happen often?

His lips open up, he utters something incomprehensible.

- You just have to stay calm. You'll see, I'll get you on your feet in no time. Are you hungry?

He nods. He seems a good patient, perhaps he's only confused.

- Do you eat chicken?

He nods again. Then he moves his eyes like a bird in a cage:

- The egg? – All of a sudden he's anxious.

- What are you talking about? – I lie.

- In the bag . . .

- No. – I shake my head with decision.

- Did you open my suitcase?

I nod:

- Maybe they took it before I arrived. You know, you had an attack of angina, I believe. Or perhaps a heart attack.

- Are you a doctor?

- I have experience.

The loss of the egg must have been quite a blow for him. He didn't rebel, he collapsed onto the pillow as though in surrender. Now his eyes were open. He was looking at my ceiling. But it's true that I had administered a heavy tranquilizer. I felt a sudden cold between the base of my nose and my eyes like when a sneeze is coming on or when you're about to cry.

- I'll turn on the heat – I said – It's cold in here.

I leaned over to press the button.

I pulled him up and set the pillow nicely behind his shoulders. I went to get the chicken broth. The broth rose and fell in its bowl, deforming the yellow bubbles of oil. I almost wanted to eat it all myself and not leave any for him. He let me feed him, staring at me, opening up just wide enough to fit the spoon in. Close up he seems older, a beard is very hard on the skin. But it bestows on men that air of decrepitude. Sometimes I spoon-fed my father when he had the flu: they slobber, make noises swallowing, their lips get all wet. But maybe it's that way for all of us, it's just that you never spoon-fed people who are healthy, young, and strong. This man also lost a few drops onto his sweater. He studied me, almost as though he were afraid of me, a mix of fear and comfort.

- You were hungry, eh?

He didn't answer.

- Now you should rest. If you have any problems, just call. I'll give you something to help you sleep.

I settled down into the reclining chair that used to be Francesco's. I didn't sleep. I watched him. He moved a little. But he had his color back. The worst seemed over. To avoid the sleeping pill he pretended to be asleep. He curled up into a fetal position, he made himself as small as possible under my blanket. I had left his shoes on, I didn't have the courage to get close and untie his shoes. Around dawn he finally fell asleep. He slept with his belly up, like a calm baby. He made small movements and quivered.

As the light struggles to enter my house, down underground, I get dressed. I take my elegant suit of bottle-green wool out of my dresser. I put it on. Green doesn't go well with my skin, it clashes, it turns me into a tired little old lady. But I put it on deliberately. I turn and look at the sleeping creature. His regular breathing fills up my whole house, because it's little, just one room. His breathing raises his chest, it's loud and almost hurts my ears. I don't have anywhere to breathe. A feeling of claustrophobia seizes me. I have to rush outside. He seems fine, but I don't know whether he's out of danger, I can't allow him to overextend himself. I must have a ball of twine somewhere. I look in the drawers. I have to hurry, before he wakes up. Here it is. I take his arm. In sleep the man is docile, I manage to tie his wrist to the bed frame. His pulse is beating with a regular rhythm. You can see it puff up as the blood courses through. I quickly tie up the other arm too. Now I have to tie down his feet, so he doesn't get any ideas about kicking. I bend down over his calves. But the heavy shoes are blocking his circulation, I have to take them off. I unlace one after the other and toss them onto the floor. His toes move inside his long socks. I tie up his calves without binding them too tight. I don't know what came over me then. I take off his socks and look at his toes. They're white and clean. I put one hand against the sole. It's soft. But it's cold. I have the temptation to rub it, to warm it up. I have to go outside.

I go to the dresser. I slip the egg into my big purse, for safety.

As soon as I'm outside, I calm down, No, it's not calm. It is a subtle euphoria that comes over me as I walk through the dewy streets. The sky is half white and half black. It's going to rain. I love this place with no pretensions, where I can go out in slippers and a housecoat, as though it were the courtyard of my house. I like that it's a young city, where you can hardly find buildings over a century old. I like this faded gray-green color. Its gardens of persimmon trees. Only I can't think about the train station. I know it's there. Once, I took the train to come here from Rome, but afterward I would have wanted it to implode, I wanted the rails to melt, that the ground would absorb them, that no trace would remain. So I stay well away from the railroad, from its whistle. I live as though it didn't exist.

I enter the bar in Piazza Trento and Trieste. I smile. It's been so long since I went into a bar. My dress almost doesn't seem green. It must be because of the orange light in there. I order a cappuccino and a croissant. Cappuccino with a lot of foam and a sprinkle of powdered chocolate. I sip and nibble slowly at the pastry. Then I buy two big boxes of chocolates to justify paying with a credit card. I also ask for a phone card, I have to notify Marinella that I'm not coming in to work. I have a man at home, I tell her. She laughs, she's tolerant because I've never played a joke like that on her before.

With an effort, I leave the bar. Outside there's a diffuse humid fog that makes your bones shiver. It settles over the houses and your clothes, it doesn't rain but everything seems made of water. I stop in front of a shoe store window. Right there in the middle, between the loafers and the sharp-pointed shoes, there's something I want: a pair of red, shiny rubber boots. I go in, point them out to the saleslady, I put them on. I pay and abandon my old shoes in the store.

At the supermarket, everyone looks at my red boots because they reflect the light and shine it back at them. I fill my cart with pineapple, cabbage, pork, condensed milk, lasagna, and cookies.

I return home with the provisions. I open the door, I put them on the floor. From the bed, the man jerks at his bonds.

- Be careful, you'll hurt your wrists.

He falls back. He stares at my rain boots.

- Do you want to kill me? – he asks.

I'd like to laugh, but it doesn't come.

- Are you kidding? Maybe I'll slice you up? – I go – You seem to feel better already. Give me a moment, I'll find you a taxi.

I take the cell phone and call. I'm lucky, I get one almost right away.

- Ten minutes – I reassure him – Salerno 34.

I take a little knife, cut the twine. He massages his wrists, stares at me stunned. Careful to look away, I also free his feet.

- Wait – I say as he quickly puts his socks and shoes back on, as though after a one-night stand. I take the beta-blockers, the calcium channel blockers, and the aspirin and slip them into his bag.

- Take these, they might be useful. But I'm serious, see a doctor.

I load him into a taxi, smiling. Then I remember his credit card, pull it from my wallet, and hand it to him. He reaches for it through the car window.

- Don't worry – I say – I only bought a few essentials.

I like the taxi, it's yellow and bright, it illuminates the street, it goes well with my red boots. The taxi driver starts up and accelerates. They're sure to be going to Rome.

I go back in, I close the door. I don't feel like making anything to eat, I'm not hungry. After all, it's still early. I open the bag, I take out the egg. I didn't sleep a wink last night. But I earned a day off work and I take advantage of it. With my boots on, I slip beneath the covers, I keep the big egg near me. I drift off to sleep. When I awake, the egg is broken, a sort of lizard has been born from it. It's alive, an animal I've never seen before. I hear the airplanes pass overhead.

(Translated by Thomas Simpson)

ITALIAN REQUIEM *OR* "IS ITALY THE LAND OF THE DEAD?"

Edoardo Albinati

I

I watched the display of repressed sexual life
in the course of a party that celebrated nothing, young women
who had delivered a child were making their reentry in elegant attire
by dint of fitness centers and comparisons, they brought sugar
to my tongue. I learned the distinction
among red white and yellow onions but I can't remember it
they say I look like the gardener
worn out T-shirt full of tiny holes
and a hole in the middle of my hair. But I feel strong as a lion
and homosexuals still find me attractive.
That said, let us turn to the nation that everyone hates
save for rhetoricians and maybe I too am a rhetorician
because I exploit the gifts of my nature
as far back as primary school I wrote brilliant compositions
and got A's without opening a book,
in short, I cheated. The nation is in trouble
I don't need to back this up
"suis et ipsa Roma viribus ruit"[1] don't know what it means

[1] Horace, *Epodes*, 16.2. Leconte de Lisle translates: "et Rome elle-même croule sous ses propres efforts."

I copied it from *The Islands of the Blessed*
I saw those very islands a little beyond Ventotene
where there is the Roman port, smooth rock like
a plastic stamp, fields of lentils
and penitentiary from whose narrow windows Settembrini[1]
saw his wife depart, the white kerchief on her head
a tiny dot on the oscillating boat. Bad translation:
"And Rome is destroyed by its own men."
They sweat it out on pedals to trim down their bellies
and the sea is always bluer, painted
the day the summer heat finally breaks
and the grocers of the maritime republics start holding clearance sales
the stracchino cheese lingers on the shelves, the fennel withers,
the shopkeepers no longer trim slices from the hams hanging from the ceiling
at the same frenzied pace they did in the good days. People fear contagion
intimacy can agree or disagree with the powers that be
what the Marsi tribe, Porsenna, Spartacus, etc., did not succeed in destroying
is destroyed by those in power, ordinary men
who go swimming in Bermuda shorts
ride water-scooters
have wives and children who are overweight.
What I say will be oblique, personal, senseless
I will not hand out *Monday morning report cards*, nor will I harbor *Evil thoughts*
and neither will I point out *Who's up and who's down*[2]
with the tip of my cock, because I am happy
I have lost all hope and I love my country
the tribes that make it up tickle me pink

---

[1] The reference is to the prison on St. Stephen's Island near Ventotene Island. An event Luigi Settembrini narrates in his *Memoirs*.

[2] "Pagelle del lunedi," "Cattivi pensieri," "Chi sale chi scende," are the titles of popular weekly columns in newspapers and magazines in which prominent figures such as politicians or soccer players are issued weekly report cards by journalists.

with their arrows and their smoky pow-wows
used to buy their super cold De Longhi Penguin air conditioner[1]
the uproar relaxes me, Nabucco's chorus puts me to sleep
the boulevards of the Milanese suburbs stir up the poetry that's in me
because they are jagged like crocodile jaws.
Horace and Ovid in translation, Dante, Machiavelli
and Leopardi, Lorenzo Lotto, Pontormo, Bellini
and Vico and Belli and Jesus and Santa Claus and the emigrants
in the whistling poetry of poor Pascoli
an asthmatic gift of withered beauty
what's it matter that they're dead, so was Pinocchio
his long nose run through the earth
they know him even in America, they call him
my little Italian friend while they saw the wood.
Wise presidents knelt before the puppet
the Apuan forests boasted of having brought him to life.
I have nothing else to sell but this, like children
who play shopkeeper and want millions
for a marble with Ronaldo's portrait
me with a plastic sword in my right hand
placing whomever I like in the manger
in a procession that sets off towards the future:
on top of the hill there is a golden city, mounted like a jewel,
there I want to live, work, and be myself
without thinking of consequences, be a citizen
who has finally something in common with the others.
Trajan's Forum, are you listening?
Temple of the Vestals, will you glance at your girls' tunics?
But of course, it is clean, they are placidly singing. Everything's OK, Temple.

---

[1] A TV commercial of some years ago in which an old Indian chief, overcome by heat, points to innumerable smoke signals on the horizon and deciphers them to be saying, "Everyone—want—penguin—delonghi..."

I want to be buried under a column
that represents my exploits + those of my enemies
the young killer who now writes novels
got ahead by writing scathing reviews
he has a truly ugly face but I beg the sculptor to fix up his profile a little
come on now, don't make me cut a poor figure with such ugly enemies.
In this country what's not missing are good examples
good company: companies of mercenary soldiers
and good men who bury the needy
the best things came out of nowhere
new stories are rewritings
loudspeakers murmur prayers
underwater for extinct whales
Madonnas are buried upright
on purpose so to rouse future memories
their haloes are fake but not for this reason less venerable
and we never feel alone, ever, the radio
broadcasts people's complaints
who don't want to obey, the kings and the children
evidently don't want to obey
the men that make the laws don't want to obey the laws
only I still obey orders
like a ship's rat on the mooring line, taste of salt on its tongue, climbing
aboard again.
My fee for a poem is calculated by the gross weight.
The lovely rhyme, the lovely evening
that glows from east to the sea coast
and beckons you to dream, many still
dream of Il Duce as if he were Dante. No matter.
You are dead, Italy, before you were totally born
still enveloped in the placental sac
considered a good omen

it was I who killed you with your umbilical cord, I felt pity for you
while preparing for my matriculation exam on Sapegno[1]
and in his dream my roommate spoke of revolution.
Hey, Bruno, remember? What are you up to? Why do you send me
statuettes of the blessed X . . . founder of Opus Dei?
Everything is probable in the sense that everything can be proven.
Hey, Bruno, you still listen to Mozart?
Good thing the revolution didn't happen
I left for military service, the bugles
filled my heart with boredom
the airport's rabid dogs looked more military than we did
I read *Madame Bovary* and *Anna Karenina* instead of delivering
the dispatches to the command. I used to scrunch them up and burn them
with my lighter.
No one ever took notice.
My Italy you died an astonishing death
when they cancelled standard time
you fell into a depression with the speed
of a burst tire going downhill.
My backpack is huge, the books were not enough
to fill the afternoons on the deflated armchair
from which polystyrene pebbles dripped slowly
mixing up my personal destiny with the stories
of Arabian and Austrian playboys, of Argentinean soccer players
while out of the bushes came black bitches
they were toothless, hell doesn't exist
unless it is everywhere, it is red Siena clay, gravel heap of the Apennines
mound below which I awaited tumbling boulders
the sizzling legends of adolescence
have created a nation of brothers whom I loved.

[1] Sapegno: manual of the history of Italian literature.

II

A rabbit's nose is as sensitive as the fatherland
before people get out of bed the house chores
have all been done, so they can return to sleep at once
in their beds they find a toy house
where they perform their lives again. In the war
everyone wore a hat and a rifle
was not worth as much as a quality hat
while parking the scooter there was the ambush
with scarves and incessant shots
hey, Julius Caesar, how much did you get to see at your high school
I was born there, thanks to the kisses we exchanged
under your straight dictatorial nose, and now I will die
if I don't make love with someone
in the outside air stuffed with cold
impassive I watch the return of fashions
of the sailor's jacket, of the bell-bottom trousers.
Everyone was running and was busy selling flour and oil.
Dark eyes did not only make you fall in love
they were but the consequence of a series of other acts of love
so distant that not even the professor remembers them
Attila the Hun must have had something to do with it
Even the Arabs surely. They are ancient
even the girls with their black school smock
that once upon a time they had to wear
desperately studying like crazy, but it was no use
we like beautiful girls who wear boots
TV teaches us to listen and to discuss
inside the prism of songs and opinions
the spark that will turn on our heart is born
a game where you need exact answers
watching political programs and eating clementines

we used to change sides quite often
then we went to the polling station to vote. My ignorance shakes me up
the damned Bible slips through my hands. There is too much air
among these walls, on the couch, too much deferred vacation time
the olive trees are sick and silvery
we did not place the Christ Child in the manger
assembled and painted by Neapolitan artists
with their sexy touch, lips and cheeks too red
the prayer intensifies and the body heats up.
The truest Italians are Dolce & Gabbana
one beautiful one ugly. Really gifted kids.

III

To the birch trees that skirt the rivers
I don't know what to say, but that my love
is of little value. It gives no one employment
we'll discuss this again in the sawmill, in the disco
in those places where we yell a few words or none.
It's a new syntax. We have formed our ranks
we were ready to die[1]
death arrived and it loaded us up.
Jesus had made me despair with his sermons
devoid of emphasis, my heart used to be set on fire with nothing
ten lines, twenty . . . The spoiled spectators are shouting
for more action, even if we're already winning 3 to nil
it demands the total destruction of the enemy
San Siro[2] in flames, the Etna in perpetual eruption.
When I climbed it it was the two of us and the Germans

---

[1] From the Italian national anthem: "siam pronti alla morte."

[2] Soccer stadium in Milan.

the mouth opened a kilometer wide
to swallow up my girlfriend
who was wearing a pearl necklace
berries were growing so well in the ashes
it was an everlasting day and they still talk about it
the restaurants and the sour women of Zafferana
are still copying our prized names on their registry.
Well, that day too is dead
killed by a primordial burp
the Celts were stuck to the walls
we admired their jewel-studded swords, their unwritten history
while from a gondola came the sobs
of a woman tourist in tears
for having dropped something that the Canal will never give her back.
The Celts shook in disgust, they looked terrible
even the heels of their women's sandals gave fright
but Jesus calmed them with seven secret phrases
before he went to die on the hill. Everyone now sleeps
the earth has swallowed them and I'm preparing
the lesson that I'll give tomorrow
a linked forest of interconnected phrases
will cover the blackboard:
Celts Arabs Sicilians Normans
Ancient Greeks and Slavs
tawny Illyrian shepherds and Nubian giants
Berbers Ligurians Volscians and Sardinians and Assyrians
plus a couple of Aequian bandits of purest blood[1]
they will bow their heads to write on paper this sacred tongue.

---

[1] As with the Volsci and Sardi, the Aequi, also an ancient Indo-European people, who lived near Rome, were very talented in war. They fought for decades against the Romans, until their ultimate defeat and extermination in 303 B.C.

IV

The youth are the hope of Italy.
All right, now I said it, it's too late
to substantiate it, the phosphorous on the clock's hands is spent.
The dark is dark. The boys went out
to spit on the ads
their spit smells of garlic. "Voodoo Chile"
opened the afternoon radio show and I shut
my eyes as I drove home.
In winter the suburbs get further and further
the city is encircled by volcanoes
with houses in craters and gardens of cement
where axe and hoe are buried
in the garage the car shines
the dog gives a start hunted by nightmares
I'll take Giotto to give you your lessons
basketball breaks up the day
so you can learn to spend your time with other children
and babies cry left abandoned in their nursery school.
We never imagined the power of our country
it was compressed, it was wild and sinuous
from a crack it emptied out and it was whistling
the shepherds had little else to teach
besides that tonal scale, they used to watch the moon
round like goat cheese
it left a bitter taste on the new conquests
they had arrived by cart, eating the dust.
I watch television avidly
without questioning myself, I let the fires
destroy my favorite trees
I don't even know their name, when they still covered the mountains

I had a gecko named Bobby Charlton[1]
every night we used to look at each other, I from the bed and he from the wall
I would ask him: How many goals will you score tomorrow, Bobby?
Why are you so shy? The gecko watched over me
our hope was with the Italian team and their angel
with its little see-through body. Rather he was a god.
I made a gift of Bobby's tail to one of my friends.
I betrayed the expectations placed on me.
Everyone thought I would become famous.
In '90 they told me: *You are the hope of Italy.*
In prison the men regrow a fatherland
like lizards regrow their tails
and drag their fatherland along the corridors.
Through injections of African blood we will finally again become Italians
we will enjoy the warm rain, the black boys are the hope
they have dignity even in the way of looking at the ball, in studying it
I am proud of this death, it is my own.
Amen.

(Translated by Antonino Mazza)

---

[1] Bobby Charlton: soccer player. Manchester United (604 games, 199 goals) and English national team (106 games, 49 goals) with which he won the World Championship in 1966.

PERIPHERAL AT THE CORE

An Afterword Concerning Current Italian Writing

By Barry Callaghan

I am a storyteller.

As I sat down to read these stories and poems about Italy I thought, In a place called Italville, there will surely be a voice—even a kind of town voice—that will run through all the work—and that voice will tell me the story of how things are these days, "How folks are faring," as someone might say if we were watching an American movie called *Pleasantville*.

But of course, this isn't a movie from America, this is Italy, this is the old boot, and I thought—I know something about Italy and how that boot fits, I kind of know what to expect no matter how new or how contemporary these poems and stories are.

After all, Italy has its heart's core. And at the core is its language, the language of its literature, the honed language of its heart—and that language starts, I guess for most of us, with Dante and it runs like an aria on a loop—it runs as a song of soulful wonderment—layered and resonant—an accretion of morals upon an accretion of manners—all the echoes that one finds in our time in a writer like Eco, and though there are the contemporary stylistic ruptures of a Zanzotto or the suburban dislocations of a Pasolini, the voice of the heart's core is there, smooth as Barrico's *Silk*.

So, what a surprise I got as I read this book.

I wasn't hearing a voice.

I was hearing voices, striking young voices. Disparate voices.

And tonally these voices—though, I suppose, Pasolini is their precursor—seemed very close to my home, even familiar. Next door.

The next-door voices of Italville.

Voices peripheral at the core.

Strangely enough, the longer I stayed in Italville the more I found myself asking the question the pioneers in my country had asked when they'd first stood in our wilderness: "Where is here?"

I had this feeling, too, as I moved through these stories, that out of the corner of my eye I could see that Anita Ekberg had shown up again among us to take another midnight walk in the water except now she was sparrow-breasted and she was not in Trevi, she was in some non-descript suburb, standing in a disused wading pool for immigrant, latch-key children.

Many of whom were brown and black. And even if they had been born on the boot they didn't speak a honed language, they didn't talk Dante talk, or even Moravia talk, they spoke in broken-backed parochial tongues, a pigeon-Italian laced with Romanian (ancient Latin!), Albanian, Serbian, Somalian . . . This wasn't the story of lovers adrift in the elegant ennui of *La Dolce Vita*.

Pathos in Parioli.

No.

This wasn't the story of Marcello with his guileless cunning, his insouciant amorality, a self-absorbed mannish boy.

This wasn't Marcello watching his woman dance at 3 o'clock in the morning.

He was sitting alone in his car, the motor running, snorting coke.

Dante, I cried, where art thou?

(Working as a pharmacist in Bari, someone whispered, in Bari dispensing valium.)

And if he is in Bari, and if Casanova is rumored to be running a gas bar south of Naples, and if Boccaccio is writing jokes for Rai television, then who is holding the fort in the Vatican, at the Bridge of Sighs, in the Duomo? It seems that if anybody is living there (who could know? No one in these stories goes there), it is the tourists, toddling into the heartland of the boot with their sad little handbooks in hand.

But in the elsewhere of Italy, in the Italville where these often stark stories take place, plain—and most-of-the-time—pleasant folks are clearly suffering a massive dissociation of sensibility. And it is not just that they are fairly young and have come unstrung and are estranged from each other, talking to each other in a kind of prefab TV talk, trailer-park trash talk. They *are*—like any number of characters in stories by Joyce Carol Oates, Russell Banks, Updike, Richard Ford—their own environment. The qualities of their personalities are the qualities of their surroundings. Living in an impoverished landscape of plenty, they are full-up with themselves while spiritually poverty-stricken.

They hope only to harm no one while harming everyone.

As for any intellectuals, they have—to use Sartre's phrase—"the air of disabled soldiers."

So, as I read these stories I had to say to myself that I know the voices, I've heard them all through my adult life.

I know the tone.

It is the singular tone of a man who has hit the road.

And as he hit the road he heard his complaining children cry: "Mommy, you're a turd, you're a whore."

Never mind. He wants better things for himself. He wants to be a football coach or maybe a lawyer.

As for his friends: "Without any joy they had imagined their own suicides."

So he moves on up the road: "Forward, still forward. Without having the strength to flee far away."

Out of his window he sees an "architectural delirium . . . a vestibule of hell . . . an illegal sprawl of rotisserie shacks, used furniture shops, fast-food gas bars . . . and a lame dog, more breeds in its blood than teeth in its mouth, rummaging around in the garbage of an overturned dumpster."

As he passes roadside shrines he wonders "whether Christianity is an unstoppable delirium, a sublime chain of misunderstanding, a disaster founded on the best of intentions, a satanic dream, or . . . a perfectly planned conspiracy."

He knows about conspiracy, the wheeling of drug dealers, the dealing of politicians, the thugs and enforcers for construction site contractors . . . knee-cappers. Murderers. In his world there are many ways to die: there are streetsmart stony-eyed women working their way through men like yesterday's lunch. It's a world in which a lot of thought goes into being thoughtless.

"Of course, a lot of people would say a life like mine sucks. No anchors. Without any foundation. But it's fine with me. I could care less what other people think."

Shit happens in the hills of this man's illusions.

He has the vague recollection of a Great War. Apparently it had happened, he's seen it in the movies—"Wasn't Jack Palance a German general?"

He could care less. A black *butanna*, a hooker born beyond the Atlas mountains, beyond Lake Victoria, is working him over (she works the streets on the outskirts of Italville), and she says: "You give me papers you can fuck me, don't tell anyone that you've seen me, you can bugger me."

Thousands of these invisible blacks. Fucking their way into the heart's core.

They are his shadow, the shadow he cannot see.

But he hears their music, and he's tried to shake his hips, he's tried to dance to Bob Marley. Or, Latin music, he's tried "playing the guitar in bars and clubs, after catching some rays on the beach, dicking around with friends while a huge orange sun slips into the sea . . ."

Slippage.

Basta.

The poet he hears is D'Annunzio!

> *...the bones gnaw their bones,*
> *they never stop gnawing their bones.*

Basta, this stray-dog life, with all this freak shit, *basta* with sex without love, *basta* with drugs, *basta* with driving a sleek Audi just to end up by the side of the road eating frozen pizza and ice cream out of a carton.

He used to get pissed off at himself, "scream that he was fed up with living like a bum, shouting enough is enough . . ." Fed up, "he was going to go to Jamaica, but instead he ended up taking the dog for a walk in the park."

Even to himself, "he seems like an American actor."

He meets a casual friend. Can he trust him?

"Could I trust a thirty-five-year old cokehead who still lives with his mother?"

They talk about power. About politics.

They talk and agree that their lives have nothing to do with party politics because it makes no difference who's in power. They agree that they're not badly off because there's lots of money around. Money to buy a scooter, a Vespa, money for hookers, for regular phone sex, *talk talk talk* sex . . . the odd blowjob. Just lie back . . . stasis.

Except he's on the move on the road. Nothing else is standing still. Everything is moving, but it's not going anywhere.

And there's that menace he feels in the air.

A malignancy.

"There's a crocodile in the Po river," he is told.

A croc! How did a crocodile get into Italville? How did all these people who've never heard (let alone learned) the language of the heart's core—how did they get into Italville? How did they *become* Italville?

It seems that a retributive curse is alive in the Po.

A child has been snatched, eaten.

The town has found only his arm, brought up in a fisherman's net.

A remnant.

That's it. He feels like a remnant.

And life's a fucking crocodile.

(Maybe he will stand up and cry—à la our Atwood: "We are all immigrants to this place," not as a consolation, but as an admission of his terrible sense of aloneness.)

So mid-way in the journey of his life, worn out by going forward but going nowhere, he goes home. To his room.

Alone.

"I go back in, I close the door. I don't feel like making anything to eat, I'm not hungry. After all, it's still early. I open the bag, I take out the egg. I didn't sleep a wink last night. But I earned a day off work and I take advantage of it. With my boots on, I slip beneath the covers, I keep the big egg near me. I drift off to sleep. When I awake, the egg is broken, a sort of lizard has been born from it. It's alive, an animal I've never seen before. I hear the airplanes pass overhead."

That egg in the bed, that little lizard in the bed, has shown up in Italville but it has already been seen several times between the sheets in places like Pleasantville, Kansas, or Pleasantville, Ontario. That little lizard has long since crept into the hearts of all kinds of North American characters—our neighbors in Russell Banks' books, or Edward Albee's, or Raymond Carver's or Austin Clarke's, or Victor-Lévy Beaulieu's or Cormac McCarthy's, or Leon Rooke's characters—all of whom are secure only in their sense of estrangement from themselves—they are characters who *are* their "slurb" environment—characters who have become the staple of hundreds of Hollywood movies. Hello Pleasantville. Italville. Twin towns? Maybe, and maybe surprisingly so, but they are twins with one radical difference. There is a particularly "American peripheral voice not heard among the helter-skelter peripheral voices of Italville, and it is the spoken voice of a Kurt Vonnegut or the singing voice of a Woody Guthrie—that ever assertive, preternaturally confident American voice that insists not only on the goodwill of the singer but his belief that he can actually will fairness and justice upon the folks of Pleasantville. It is exactly this guileless American belief in their own good intentions—perhaps more alive in the ugly suburbs and the desolate trailer parks of America than anywhere else—that drives non-Americans crazy when they hear it. But it's always there, it's peripheral but it's at the core, a camp fire enthusiasm, a sing-along enthusiasm for themselves and for life that allows them to believe, even as they stand in that hallucinatory landscape of their own invention—a landscape very much like the landscape of Italville—that they can join hands and sing not only "This Land Is Our Land" but "We Shall Overcome."

I have heard the disparate voices of Italville. I know them, they are voices very close to me. They are the voices of my own suburbs. But since they are free from that guileless North American belief in good intentions, that guileless, if soulful, affirmation of the self amidst derangement and dislocation, these stories, extremely striking as they are, want for a certain kind of sardonic drama. Want for a certain kind of voice. Will that contrapuntal voice emerge, too? Who knows? Perhaps, as we speak, perhaps as Dante doles out sedatives in Bari, there is a young Vonnegut or a young Woody Guthrie working beside him. Think of it: suddenly a young Pasolini will stand up and sing "This Land Is Our Land," and mean it. With an unself-conscious enthusiasm. Even better, the young Pasolini will be played by a new Marcello. How sardonic, how surreal that will seem. But why not? Strange things have already happened in the prefab town of Italville.

Biographical Notes

Edoardo Albinati was born in Rome in 1956, and has taught in Rome's Rebibbia prison since 1994. He has published a book of stories, *Arabeschi della vita morale* (Longanesi, 1988) and various books of fiction: *Il polacco lavatore di vetri* (Longanesi, 1989, from which a film of the same name was made by Peter Del Monte), *Orti di Guerra* (Fazi, 1997), *Maggio selvaggio* (Mondadori, 2000), *19* (Mondadori, 2001), and books of poetry: *Elegie e proverbi* (Mondadori, 1989), *La comunione dei beni* (Giunti, 1995), *Sintassi italiana* (Guanda). He often works on theatrical adaptations with director Giorgio Barberio Corsetti. In 2003 he published *Il ritorno* (Mondadori), an account of four months in Afghanistan on behalf of the United Nations. *Svenimenti* was published by Einaudi in 2004 and won the Viareggio prize.

Vanessa Ambrosecchio was born in Palermo in 1970 where she lives and works. Einuadi published her first novel, *Cico c'è,* which was a finalist for the Strega Prize.

Niccolò Ammaniti was born in Rome in 1966. His debut novel was *Branchie* (Ediesse, 1994). In 1996 he published a collection of stories *Fango* (Mondadori), from which Marco Risi made the film *L'ultimo capodanno*. In 1999 he published the novel *Ti prendo e ti porto via* (Mondadori) and in 2001 *Io non ho paura* (Einaudi), published in English as *I am not Scared*. It was made into the film of the same name by Gabriele Salvatores.

Antonella Anedda, born in Rome in 1955, debuted in 1995 with a collection of poetry *Residenze invernali* (Crocetti), followed by a collection of essays and stories *Cosa sono gli anni* (Fazi, 1997), and by a volume of translations of poetry, *Nomi distanti* (Empiria, 1998).

In 2000 came *La luce delle cose. Immagini e parole nella notte* (Feltrinelli). In 2000 she won the Montale Prize with *Notti di pace occidentale* (Donzelli, 1999), and the same press published her most recent collection of verse, *Il catalogo della gioia* (2003).

SILVIA BALLESTRA was born in Porto San Giorgio (Ascoli Piceno) in 1969. She began in 1999 with *Compleanno dell'Iguana* (Transeuropa). From this and her subsequent book, *La Guerra degli Antò* (Baldini & Castoldi, 1992), came the film of the same name directed by Riccardo Milani. She is also the author of a collection of stories, *Gli orsi* (Feltrinelli, 1994), a conversation with the writer Joyce Lussu (1996), and the trilogy, *Nina*, composed of *La giovinezza della signorina N.N.* (Baldini & Castoldi, 1998), followed by *Nina* (2001) and *Il compagno di mezzanotte* (2002), both in Rizzoli's "Sintonie" series, in which she also has published the collection of stories *Ritornano gli orsi* (2003).

LUIGI BALLERINI was born in Milan in 1940. He lives in the U.S., between New York and Los Angeles, where he works as a professor in the Italian Department at UCLA. His poetry has been collected in the following volumes: *eccetera. E* (Guanda, 1972), *Che figurato muore* (Scheiwiller, 1986), *Che oror l'orient* (Lubrina, 1991), *Il terzo gode* (Marsilio, 1994), *Shakespearian rags. Stracci shakespeariani*, (Quasar, 1996, bilingual poems, Italian and English), *Uscita senza strada, ovvero come sbrinare una bandiera rossa* (Edizioni della Battaglia, 2000), *Uno monta la luna* (Mann,i 2001). He has written on the avant-gardes in *La piramide capovolta* (Marsilio, 1975). He has edited anthologies of Italian and American poetry.

GIOSUÈ CALACIURA (Palermo, 1960), journalist (he has written for *l'Ora* in Palermo), has written for theater and radio, and has run a restaurant. He has published the novels *Malacarne* (Baldini &

Castoldi, 1998) and *Sgobbo* (Baldini & Castoldi, 2002, finalist for the Campiello prize). One of his stories was included in the anthology of writers from the South, *I disertori* (Einaudi, 2001).

BARRY CALLAGHAN, the well-known novelist and poet, is included in every major Canadian anthology, and his fiction and poetry have been translated into seven languages. His works include *Di male in peggio* (Cosmo Iannone editore, 2001), *Niente è solo l'eco di sempre* (Cosmo Iannone editore, 2003), *The Hogg Poems and Drawings* (1989), *The Black Queen Stories* (1982), *The Way the Angel Spreads Her Wings* (1989), *When Things Get Worst* (1993), *A Kiss Is Still a Kiss* (1995), *Hogg, the Poems and Drawings* (1997), *Barrelhouse Kings: A Memoir* (1998), *Hogg: The Seven Last Words* (2001).

ARNALDO COLASANTI was born in Fiuggi in 1957. He is co-director of the literary magazine *Nuovi Argomenti* and editor of *Poesia*, as well as being the author of various studies on Italian and French literature. Among his most recent publications: *Novanta. Il conformismo della cultura italiana* (Fazi, 1996), the novel *Gatti e scimmie* (Rizzoli, 2001, Grinzane Cavour Prize), and the collection of essays *Rosebud. Una generazione di scrittori italiani* (Quiritta, 2003).

GUIDO CONTI was born in Parma in 1965, where he lives and works. After his first stories published in the magazine *ClanDestino*, he was discovered by Pier Vittorio Tondelli, who published him in *Under 25, volume III, Papergang* (Transeuropa, 1990). Subsequently there appeared the stories *Della pianura e del sangue* (Guaraldi, 1995) and the novel *Sotto la terra il cielo* (Guaraldi, 1996). He directs the literary magazine *Palazzo Sanvitale.* In 1998, Guanda published the book of stories *Il coccodrillo sull'altare* (Chiara Prize; Stresa Prize, Montà D'Alba Prize; Comisso Prize finalist), which was followed, in 1999, by the novel *Cieli di vetro*, a finalist for the Campiello Prize. In 2000, again from Guanda, appeared the novel *Il taglio della lingua,* and in 2002 he edited Cesare Zavattini's *Dite la vostra*, a collection of juvenile writing.

MAURO COVACICH (Trieste, 1965) lives in Pordenone and is the author of *Storia di pazzi e di normali* (Theoria, 1993), *Colpo di lama* (Neri Pozza, 1995), *Mal d'autobus* (Tropea, 1997) and the collection of stories *Anomalie* (Mondadori, 1998). He writes for the weekly *Diario della settimana*, and his journalistic pieces have been collected under the title *La poetica dell'Unabomber* (Theoria, 1999). In 2001 he published the novel *l'Amore contro* (Mondadori). From the same editor in 2003 appeared the novel *A perdifiato*. He writes for the *Corriere della Sera* and other newspapers.

MARIO DESIATI was born in 1977 in the Itria valley in Puglia. For two years he has lived in Rome, where he is the editorial secretary for the literary magazine *Nuovi Argomenti*. He has published poems in the anthology *I poeti di vent'anni* (Stampa, 2000) and the novel *Neppure quando è notte* (PeQuod, 2003). He writes for the Bari supplement of the daily *La Repubblica.*

NINO DE VITA was born in 1950 in Marsala, where he lives. He is the author of *Fosse Chiti* (Milano, 1984), *Cutusìu* (Mesogea, 2001), *Cùntura* (Mesogea, 2003) and of various chapbooks and collections of poetry in limited editions. He is recognized as one of the major dialect poets, winner of the Moravia Prize in 1996 and the Mondello Prize in 2003.

FRANCESCA GENTI was born in Turin in 1975. She has published the collection of poetry *Il vero amore non ha le nocciole* (MeridianoZero, 2004).

ANDREA GIBELLINI was born in 1965 in Sassuolo and lives in Bologna. He has published the collection of poetry *Le ossa di Bering* (NCE, 1993), *La felicità improvvisa* (Jaca Book, 2001; Montale Prize winner) and the essay *Ricercando Auden* (l'Obliquo, 2003). His poems and writings on poetry have appeared in *Nuovi Argomenti, Antologia Vieusseux, Oxford Poetry, Poetry Review.* He has translated Larkin, Mansfield, Kipling, and Bishop, and has edited an issue of the literary magazine *Panta* dedicated to foreign poetry. He founded and directed the center for contemporary poetry at the Università degli studi in Bologna.

NICOLA LAGIOIA (Bari, 1973) lives in Rome where he has worked as a ghost writer for more than one publishing house and written scripts and dialogue for radio and television. He has published a novel entitled *Tre sistemi per sbarazzarsi di Tolstoj* (Minimum fax, 2001). With Christian Raimo he edited the anthology of Italian fiction *La qualità dell'aria* (Minimum fax, 2004). Einaudi has recently published his novel *Occidente per principianti.*

MARCO MANTELLO (1972) lives in Rome. He has published poems and stories in the literary magazines *Nuovi Argomenti, Lo sciacallo, Storie* and *Accattone.*

VALERIA PARRELLA was born in 1974 in Naples where she lives. Her first book of fiction, the collection of stories *mosca più balena* (Minimum fax, 2003) won the Procida and Amelia Rosselli prizes.

ANTONIO PASCALE, born in Naples in 1966, formerly from Caserta, now lives and works in Rome. He has published *La città distratta* (Einaudi, 2001) and *La manutenzione dei sentimenti* (Einaudi, 2003). He writes for *Lo Straniero* and *Diario.*

LORENZO PAVOLINI, this volume's editor, was born in Rome in 1964. He is editor-in-chief of the quarterly *Nuovi Argomenti*, founded by Alberto Moravia in 1953, and which today is under the direction of Enzo Siciliano, Dacia Maraini, Raffaele La Capria, Furio Colombo and Arnoldo Colasanti. In 1997 he published the novel *Senza rivoluzione* (Giunti, winner of the Grinzane Cavour newcomer's prize). He publishes stories in literary reviews and magazines. He is the literary consultant for Radio3 Rai for which he is in charge of literary and dramatic projects. He works with the Fondazione Romaeuropa Festival.

AURELIO PICCA was born in Velletri, a town near Rome, in 1957. He first appeared in 1990 with the collection of poetry *Per punizione* (Rotundo), followed by, in 1992, the stories *La schiuma* (Gremese). In 1995 he published *I racconti dell'eternità* (Nuova compagnia editrice) and the novel *L'esame di maturità* (Giunti). The novel, *I mulatti* (Giunti), came out in 1996. In 1998, with the novel *Tuttestelle* (Rizzoli), he was a finalist for the Viareggio Prize, and won the Alberto Moravia and Superpremio Grinzane Cavour prizes. In 2001 he published *Bellissima* (Rizzoli), followed by, for the same publisher, *Sacrocuore* (2003). He contributes to the cultural pages of *Il Giornale*, and writes accounts and stories of Rome for *La Repubblica*. He has made two video documentaries and various productions for radio.

FRANCESCO PICCOLO was born in Caserta in 1964. In 1993 he was a finalist for the Calvino Prize with the unpublished novel *Diario di uno scrittore senza talento*. With the publishing house Minimum fax, he published *Scrivere è un tic. I metodi degli scrittori* (1994). In 1996 he published the collection of stories *Storie di primogeniti e figli unici* with Feltrinelli, winner of the Giuseppe Berto and Chiara prizes. Again with Feltrinelli, in 1998, he published the novel *E se c'ero, dormivo*, followed in 2000, by *Il tempo imperfetto* and in 2003 by *Allegro Occidentale*, finalist for the Strega Prize. He writes regularly for films, working with the directors Silvio Soldini, Paolo Virzì, Nanni Moretti, and Renato De Maria.

ENRICO PIERGALLINI (1975) lives in the Marche region of Italy. He has published two chapbooks: *Tra ròcioli disperso* (2000) and *Giacimenti* (2002).

FLAVIO SANTI (1973) lives between Pavia and Cudugnella (Udine). Besides what has appeared in magazines and anthologies, he has published the collections of poetry *Viticci* (Stamperia dell'Arancio, 1998), *Album* (En plein edizioni, 1998), *Rimis te sachete* (Marsilio 2001), *Aset* (2004). In 1999 he published the novel *Diario di bordo della rosa* (PeQuod).

CAROLA SUSANI was born in the Veneto in 1965. From 1969 on she lived in Sicily, then in 1984 moved to Rome where she still lives. She has published *Il libro di Teresa* (Giunti, 1995) and *La terra dei dinosauri* (Feltrinelli, 1998). Her stories and essays have appeared in numerous magazines and anthologies. She writes for *Nuovi Argomenti* and edits the children's supplement for the monthly *Accattone, cronache romane*. For Feltrinelli she has published the young adult novels *Il licantropo* (2002) and *Cola Pesce* (2004).

ELENA STANCANELLI was born in 1965 in Florence. Fourteen years ago she moved to Rome and attended the Academy of Dramatic Arts. She has worked in theater for Gruppo della Rocca for the Teatro di Roma. She has published the novels *Benzina* in 1998 with Einaudi (from which a film was adapted) and *Le attrici* for the same publisher in 2001. She writes stories for magazines and literary reviews.

Emanuele Trevi was born in Rome in 1964. He has published *Istruzioni per l'uso del lupo* (Castelvecchi, 1994), *Musica distante* (Mondadori, 1997), *I cani del nulla* (Einaudi, 2003), *Senza Verso. Un'estate a Roma* (Laterza, 2004). He writes for *Il Manifesto*.

Vitaliano Trevisan was born in 1960 in Sondrio and lives in Vicenza. He has published for Theoria *Un mondo meraviglioso* (1997), *Trio senza pianoforte/oscillazioni* (1998), *I quindicimila passi* (Einaudi, 2002), *Standards Vol. 1* (Sironi, 2002). In 2003 he wrote and acted in a film by Matteo Garrone, *Primo amore*. In 2004 he published the collection of stories *Shorts* (Einaudi). In 2005 his play *Il lavoro rende liberi* will be directed by Toni Servillo.

Sandro Veronesi was born in Florence in 1959. He served as editorial secretary for the magazine *Nuovi Argomenti*. He has published: *Per dove parte questo treno allegro* (Theoria, 1988), *Gli sfiorati* (Mondadori, 1990), *Occhio per occhio. La pena di morte in quattro storie* (Mondadori, 1992), *Venite venite B-52* (Feltrinelli, 1995); *La forza del passato* (Bompiani, 2000), for which he won the Viareggio and Campiello Prizes. In 2002 appeared *Superalbo–le storie complete* (Bompiani) which collects his accounts of the most bizarre and significant events of recent Italian public life—from which a film was adapted—*La forza del passato*.

Dario Voltolini was born in Turin in 1959, where he still lives. He has taught creative writing at the Holden School. He has written radio dramas and musical librettos. He has published: *Una intuizione metropolitana* (Bollati Boringhieri, 1990), *Rincorse* (Einaudi, 1994), *Forme d'onda* (Feltrinelli, 1996), *Neve* (Hopefulmonster, 1996), *Fantasia della giornata* (Morgana Edizioni, 1997), *Il grande fiume* (Fernandel, 1998), *Glunk* (Portofranco, 1998), *In gita a Torino* (Gribaudo, 1998), *10* (Feltrinelli, 2000), *Primaverile*

(Feltrinelli, 2001). With Antonio Moresco he edited the collaborative volume *Scrivere sul fronte occidentale* (Feltrinelli, 2002). In 2003 he published *I confini di Torino* (Quiritta).

VALENTINO ZEICHEN was born in Fiume in 1938 and has lived in Rome since 1950. His poems first appeared in 1974 with the volume *Area di rigore*, with an introduction by Elio Pagliarani. In 1979 his second book appeared, *Ricreazione* (Guanda), followed by *Pagine di gloria*, in 1983 (Guanda), and in the same year, with Lucarini, the novel *Tana per tutti*. In 1987 he published the book of verse *Museo interiore* (Guanda). His first book in Mondadori's "Specchio" series was *Gibilterra* in 1991, followed in 1997 by *Metafisica tascabile*. In 2000 he published a collection dedicated entirely to Rome, *Ogni cosa a ogni cosa ha detto addio* (Fazi). In 2004 Mondadori published his complete works *Poesie, 1963-2003.*

(Translated by Paul Vangelisti)